SALVATION AND DOOM

THE CATHARDI PROPHECY

C. BUCK JONES

WOLFSTAR PUBLISHING

Contents

THE PROPHECY

Hear me, children of Cathardi.

Beware the people who do not acknowledge me.

You do well to set yourselves apart, yet the time comes, and you will not see, for pride and arrogance have filled your heart.

You will say: we have built walls; we are the chosen; the creator will not let us fall.

But you worship the created and not the eternal.

Swift will be your destruction as the enemy pours in like water, you will call, but I will not hear.

Doom has come to Cathardi. Humble yourselves, listen to the prophet.

On that day, a herald will bring the warning. Seek the one. Seek the one, oh children of Cathardi, before doom comes to both worlds.

A stranger will save you if you heed the herald.

Seek the one, children of Cathardi.

Chapter 1

Josh woke to the clanging of the jump alarm. It only took him a few seconds to clear the disorientation caused by the jump. Then he quickly scanned the controls and silenced the alarm. Everything was in order. He reached over and shook Kim until she stirred, and then he did the same for Fauna, the ranking Cathardi for the exercise.

Once they recovered from the jump-induced blackout, Fauna checked on the rest of the crew over the ship's communication system. "All stations report normal operational status," she said.

"Have we located the beacon?" Josh looked over at Kim, checking the scanner for the distinctive signal of their target.

"I have the beacon located," Kim said. "It is quite close to our port."

"I am plotting your course," Fauna added. "We should be there in ten minutes using thrusters."

"Very well. Prepare to deploy the arm for object retrieval." Josh turned to Fauna. "I expected this to be harder."

"They did not design the exercise to be hard, just to test your piloting abilities. You have done very well and should have a good score on our return."

He nodded in acknowledgment. *She seems less rigid than most of the Cathardi I have been exposed to since the 'invasion'.* He distrusted them. His Father said that once they got what they wanted from Earth, they would desert it. But they offered Josh the opportunity to learn to pilot interstellar spacecraft. An opportunity to visit new planets and new people not confined to the political, racial, and religious tensions of Earth.

When the Cathardi first arrived, he was surprised by how closely they resembled humans on Earth. During the televised address at the United Nations, his mother said, "They are Ocampans." It took him a few moments to connect the reference, but now, whenever he looked at them, he thought of Star Trek. Their fine features and the ridges near their ears looked like the Tess character.

Cathardi military personnel all wore similar gray tunics over matching pants, making it hard to distinguish the gender of the individual. The uniform's understated insignia required close inspection if one wanted to know the rank of the individual. All wore short 'pixie' cut hair. He now knew that the female officers had a faint cinnamon-like odor. He wasn't sure if it was natural or if they all wore the same perfume.

They reached the beacon in nine minutes, and Josh gave the okay for retrieval and waited for word that the object was onboard.

RRRRRRRR! RRRRRRR! The alarms sounded, and red lights flashed a hull breach warning.

"Engine room report!" Josh called, but no answer came.

"Oxygen levels are dropping," Kim reported.

Josh unbuckled his restraints. "Keep me apprised of the situation below. I'll seal this hatch," he said. Then he ran out of the bridge to the stairs, grabbing a portable oxygen mask from the emergency station at the top of the stairs before sliding down to the lower level. He could feel the air rushing through the passageway, the cold fogged his mask. He checked the engine room. It was clear. He ran to the cargo bay. Two Cathardi crewmen lay motionless on the floor. The bulkhead, near the robotic arm, had a hole in it. Air rushed through the hole, sucking loose objects toward the hole and out into the vacuum of space.

He went to the first crewman and pulled him through the hatch into the passageway. When he went back to the second crewman, he noticed blood on the floor. He pulled him out and sealed the cargo compartment hatch.

"Fauna," he said through the com. "Do we have a visual view of the retrieval arm? A hole has been torn in the cargo hold hull. Both crewmen are unresponsive. I will need help down here."

"I am on my way," she said. "The visual is on camera three. You can access it from engineering."

"Kim, can you shut off the alarm?" He went to the engineering console. The alarm stopped.

"I have the alarm off for now, but we are still slowly bleeding atmosphere."

He checked the visual. The robotic arm had broken loose on one side and ripped away from the hull. It seemed stable for now, but he didn't think it would take any kind of thrust. The inertia could tear a larger hole and maybe compromise any systems running through the wall.

"Captain," Fauna said as she entered. "What do you want me to do?"

"The first thing is to tend to the crewmen. Help me get them into the galley."

They carried the first crewman and laid him on a bench. He was alive but unconscious. Fauna took an oxygen mask and put it on him before they went back for the second. When they laid him on the bench, she said, "This one is dead. From the wound on his head, it appears he either struck something when he fell, or an object hit him as it flew toward the breech."

"Dead?" Josh couldn't believe it. This was just a training exercise. How could he lose a crewman on a training exercise?

"Josh." He heard Kim through the com. "I cannot contact Eagle Station. Somehow, we have lost outside communications."

"Keep trying," he said. "Fauna, you need to see this, since you are more experienced with this ship than I am." He took her to

Engineering, and they looked at the video showing the arm. "I don't think we can move with the arm like that."

"I agree. We need to secure it or cut it loose." She pointed to the monitor. "But it has to be done out there."

"Do we have suits?"

"Yes, they store them by the airlock at the rear of the shuttle. I will show you." She took him back and showed him where they kept the suits.

"Good. I think just to be safe you and Kim need to don suits. I'm going to see if we have equipment to do something about the arm."

"What about the crewman?" she said.

"He should have one as well if you can get it on him. Otherwise, he will have to do with the oxygen mask until he regains consciousness."

Fauna started putting her suit on while Josh went to Engineering, where he found the fusion torch and a metal repair sheet. Using the torch, he cut a square piece from the sheet several inches bigger than the hole. Then he went to the airlock with the torch and the patch. Fauna already had her suit on, and Kim was just putting on her helmet.

Josh got into his suit. "Kim, go back to the bridge and try to determine what is wrong with the communications. Fauna can stay down here and help with the tether. I don't know how long we will be here, so only use the oxygen in your suits when it's necessary. How much time will the suit give me outside?"

"You will have two hours if you do not overexert," Fauna said.

"That's cutting it close, but I think I can do it."

Josh took the fusion torch, the hand grinder, and the patch inside the airlock. "Let me know my oxygen levels about every ten minutes," Josh said over the radio. "I don't want to stay out too long."

"I'll monitor your oxygen levels, Josh," Kim said.

When the door closed, he started the evacuation cycle. When the outside door opened, he hooked the tether and floated out. Using the suit thrusters, he moved around to the breach. This was going to take a while; the arm had bent out the edges of the hole. He would need to grind them flat enough to get a seal with the patch. The arm was another story. There was no way for him to move it into a position where he could secure it. He would need to cut the fasteners still holding part of the base to the ship. If he wasn't careful, the arm could move and hit him. *First things first, I need to remove that arm.*

He made his way to the lower fastener and began cutting through the large bolt using the torch. "Ten minutes." He heard Kim through his helmet.

Moving to the upper fastener, he put both feet on the arm with his back against the hull. He began cutting through the bolt, keeping pressure on the arm with his feet. "Twenty minutes." Just before he cut through, it gave way. His feet pushed the arm away from the shuttle. He was afraid it would spin around and hit the hull or him. But the momentum of the push got it far enough away that it cleared the ship.

Moving back to the jagged hole, he began cutting through the bent metal. Then he started with the grinder. It hummed through his gloves as he worked on the remaining bent metal. He took his time to ensure he could get a seal.

"Fifty minutes."

He thought the surface was smooth enough, so he held the patch against the hull. There was a small gap at the bottom, but he thought the torch would fill it.

He began stitch-welding the plate to the hull.

"Sixty minutes."

He welded in one-inch increments around the patch, being sure the overlapping welds looked good.

"100 minutes. Josh, You won't make it two hours. Your levels are falling too fast!" Kim said.

"Keep me apprised. I am almost finished."

The last stitch at the bottom proved the most difficult with the escaping air blowing through. He started the last weld.

"110 minutes. Josh, get inside!" Kim shouted over the radio.

"Five more minutes." Josh worked to seal the last few millimeters, but it was hard for him to focus. "I'm done," he called.

"Josh, hold on to the tether. Fauna will pull you in," he heard through the com.

"I'm so—" He lost consciousness.

Josh woke on the galley floor. "What happened?" His head hurt and he couldn't push himself up into a sitting position.

"You passed out," Kim said. "Fortunately, Fauna was in the airlock, ready to pull you in. You cut it way too close."

"How is the crewman?" he asked.

"He will survive. His oxygen levels are still low, but he is conscious," Fauna said. "That was very brave of you to go out there. Do they teach hull repairs at the academy?"

"No, my father ran a machine shop. I had some welding experience before the academy, though it was much harder out there. I got drowsy towards the end. We should go check the patch."

Josh staggered back to the cargo bay, leaning on Kim. The patch was holding fine, but he thought he should put a patch on the inside just to be safe. Once he could move better, he got another piece of patching. He had to push broken cables back into the wall space. *I'll bet one of those broken cables is for the radio.*

When he finished welding the patch, he returned to the galley with Fauna. She checked his oxygen levels. "They are still lower than they should be. You need to rest with supplemental oxygen. I will set you in a seat down here and fasten your restraints."

"Will you pilot us back?"

"No. Kim will pilot the shuttle back to Eagle Station. I will man the engine room since she and I are the only two crewmen still functioning."

"I assume the accident was not part of the exercise?" His voice sounded more sarcastic than he wanted. It was just a rhetorical question.

"No, we would never endanger either you or ourselves in that manner."

Of course, she took it seriously. I don't think they have a sense of humor.

Josh reclined his chair. He had to admit that he still felt light-headed. He hoped he had made no mistakes on the inside welds. Across the galley, the other crewman looked to be sleeping. Over the com, he heard Kim and Fauna going through their pre-jump checklists.

"Engines and gravity drive are fully functional. We can be underway at your command," Fauna said.

He sank into his chair as the gravity increased and passed out.

After the two short jumps, Kim made the jump back to the designated return coordinates. When they completed the last jump, Josh felt well enough to return to the bridge. He went over to Kim and put his hand on her shoulder. She got up and threw her arms around him and hugged him so tightly he thought she would squeeze all the air out of him again. "Too tight," he whispered into her ear. She eased up.

Josh held her for a moment. He caught a scent of coconut, probably from her shampoo, since regulations prohibited perfume in the close quarters of spaceships.

She released him. "I was so scared. I thought you would die out there."

"Well, I didn't. You and Fauna handled things, so we're going to be okay. But we may not pass the exercise. We didn't retrieve the target, and we exceeded the time limit. Hopefully, they will consider the mitigating circumstances. Have we had any communications?"

"Nothing yet. I set a repeating transmission and I'm watching the proximity sensors." She sat back down at her console. "We are in the standard shipping lanes, and within sensor range for Eagle Station."

He took his seat but didn't bother with any of the controls. Smiling, he watched her work. Ever since they met at the Academy, he had found her attractive. She was petite, only five feet four inches tall, with long blond hair and deep blue eyes. He thought she felt attracted to him as well, but when he tried to get her to share a hotel room with him last Christmas break, she refused. She's straight-laced and wouldn't break the school rules then or service rules now.

***

After they docked at Eagle Station, medics and security officers boarded the shuttle before the crew could leave. They took Josh's vital signs, and then escorted him off the ship. Inside the station, a small crowd had gathered. He recognized some of his classmates who stood toward the back along one wall of the passage leading to the main part of the station. He could see the worry on their faces. But his escort didn't slow down. They rushed him to a treatment room in the medical area where they helped him out of his suit and made him lie down.

When the medical team left, the security officer stayed at the door. "What's going on?" Josh said.

"You are being held until they complete the initial investigation of the incident," the guard said. "You may not talk with or see anyone until they get statements from the entire crew and examine the physical evidence."

While he was talking, medics carried the body of the dead crewman by the door. *They're blaming me for the crewman's death. Is it my fault? Could I have checked the arm when I had the chance? How could I be so stupid?*

"Am I under arrest?"

"No, just detained until the investigation is complete." The guard closed the door to keep the curious from peering into the room. "The investigators don't want your version of the events to influence the statements of the other crew members, especially the other cadet."

There was a knock at the door. The security officer opened it for a Cathardi medical officer. "Cadet, I'm Doctor Kolvar. You are a very lucky man. You almost died out there and you still have some lingering effects from the low blood oxygen. Rest and you will recover."

Josh leaned back against the raised head of the bed. The doctor worked behind him and brought tubes around that he put into his nose. When he was done, Josh said, "What about Kim and the other crew members?"

"They have no medical issues and are just being detained until the investigators can get a statement. They should return to Earth on the next shuttle." He turned to leave but stopped. "You have created quite the uproar on the station. There has not been an accidental death in this sector since we arrived. Now rest." He left, and the guard went out with him, closing the door behind him.

They kept him in the room for three days. Each day, an investigator came in and had him repeat his recollection of the mission. The only thing he regretted was not checking the arm before the shuttle left. But even if he had, the flaw may not have been apparent. He struggled with his feelings about the crewman's death. He didn't even know his name, so he didn't feel any personal loss. But the image of him lying on the floor of the bay with blood pooling around his head haunted him.

On the fourth day, they brought him a clean uniform and escorted him to a shuttle for Earth. After landing, they took him to the academy and led him to a room in the administration building. The room arrangement resembled a courtroom. The academy superintendent sat at a table in the room's front. A Cathardi commander flanked him on his right and an Air Force colonel on his left. Josh's escort took him to another table just in front and to the left of the head table, where he sat facing the tribunal with his escort. At a second table to his right sat two Cathardi officers. He recognized them as the investigators who had questioned him at the station.

This is a trial. They are blaming me for the crewman's death. I might go to jail, and they will probably expel me from the academy. Reaching for the pitcher of water on the table, he poured himself a glass and gulped it down. Then took several deep breaths, and let his shoulders fall, while the Cathardi at the head table recited the formalities of the hearing. *I can accept their decision. Even though I did nothing wrong.*

Then one investigator, Captain Tanat, stood. "Members of the tribunal, as you know, commanders of vessels have great discretion in the decisions they make during a voyage. This puts them in a position of responsibility for the safety of the crew and passengers affected by the commander's decisions. This is a documented and traditionally accepted responsibility." He turned to face Josh's table. "Cadet Albertson, do you understand and agree with this statement?"

"I do." Josh slumped back into his chair. *There is no way I am getting out of this.*

The captain faced the tribunal and continued. "During the investigation, Lieutenant Lykor and I questioned Cadet Albertson on three separate occasions. In each instance, he stated he did not check on the condition of the retrieval arm prior to proceeding with the flight. He merely asked the now-deceased crewman if the arm was functional. It is now apparent that the arm was faulty. We could consider the failure by Cadet Albertson to examine the arm as negligence."

This just gets worse and worse. Why didn't I check the arm? That was the question he had been asking himself since the accident. The icy stares of the tribunal pierced him like daggers. *I screwed up.*

Tanat then turned toward Josh's table again. "These facts come directly from the testimony of Cadet Albertson. Further investigation into the physical evidence available on the shuttle revealed a material flaw in the fasteners holding the arm in place. The fastener broke while the crewmen prepared to deploy the arm. When the fastener broke, the force of the arm tore a hole in the hull of the ship. A metal tool from the storage rack behind the crewman struck him in the head as it flew toward the hole, knocking him to the floor. The autopsy of the crewman determined the cause of death to be blunt force trauma to the head from either the tool, the floor, or both. However, the rapid evacuation of atmosphere from the compartment causing low oxygen levels could also have contributed to his death."

Josh sunk deeper into his chair. Behind him, the people assembled in the room murmured.

"The metallurgical analysis of the fastener determined the flaw was not visible and that the arm could have given way at any time. The defect could not have been visible during a routine examination," the investigator said.

Did he just say I wasn't at fault?

"Additional testimony from the other surviving personnel show that the cadet performed in a more than satisfactory manner concerning the safety of the crew." Tanat picked up a sheet of paper and started reading. "I have flown for many years and under various conditions. The actions of the Earth Cadets, especially Cadet Albertson, were of the highest caliber, as good as or better than any Cathardi with which I have flown. As Proctor of the flight, I recommend nullifying the disqualification from the exercise given to the Cadets. Cadet Albertson saved the lives of his remaining crew once we detected the hull breach. He nearly sacrificed his own life to repair the breach." He laid the paper down. "That is an excerpt from the testimony of Lieutenant Fauna who oversaw the flight as proctor. Based on the testimony and physical evidence the investigators recommend no charges against the cadet and that the tribunal should accept Lieutenant Fauna's recommendations concerning the results of the exercise."

The three senior officers spoke amongst themselves before the superintendent said, "The tribunal agrees with the recommendations of the investigators. Cadet Albertson, you may rejoin your class. The tribunal also wants to thank you for your heroic efforts to save your ship. I adjourn this hearing."

Everyone stood until the senior officers left. Then his classmates surrounded him. Kim hugged him. "My hero." She kissed his cheek.

Ray slapped him on the back. "Good job, dude."

Even Carla hugged him. "I knew they would clear you. All they had to do was listen to Kim and the Cathardi lieutenant."

He looked around to see if Fauna was there. She stood just behind his friends. He stepped over to her and extended his hand. "Thank you."

"There is no need to thank me," she said and took his hand. "I merely told the truth. I will fly with you anytime the opportunity presents itself. Now go enjoy your friends."

He walked back to the housing unit with his roommates. They laughed and teased him about facing a 'court martial'.

"You guys laugh," he said. "But I thought they would at least expel me from the academy. "

"They can't expel the best pilot in the academy," Bruce said. "Now, I'm hungry. Why don't we go into town and have a celebratory dinner?"

CHAPTER 2

Liria heard a knock at the door while she was studying some reports.

"Ompresti." Myra bowed as she entered. Her assistant wore an orange and yellow floral scarf tied loosely around her neck. The splash of color, an adoption of Earth custom, offsetting the long gray robe of the Order. "Pardon the interruption, but the Ambassador would like to meet with you at the embassy this morning. He needs your advice."

"Thank you, Myra. Let him know I will be at the embassy in one hour. Will you put these away for me?" She sighed and began collecting the papers from the work table. The Ambassador was not one to make tough decisions on his own. She handed the papers to Myra. Liria went to the window and looked out at the Embassy located a short distance away. The Cathardi ship was once part of the original arrival forces, but now it housed the embassy to Earth and sat, supported by steel and concrete pillars, above the city and overlooking the Capitol and the mall in the distance.

When Liria arrived at the Embassy, the ambassador's assistant took her directly into a conference chamber. The ambassador and several officials stood talking around a large table in the center of the sparsely furnished room.

"Ompresti." The ambassador walked toward her. He wore the traditional diplomatic service gray and gold tunic which hung down below his waist over dark gray pants. His close-cropped blonde hair revealed a bald spot at the top of his head when he bowed. "Ompresti, we have a decision to make. As I am sure you are aware, the high council has requested your presence at a convocation on Cathardi."

"I am aware of the request. I have yet to decide if I will attend."

"They have also asked for a delegation of religious leaders from Earth to attend."

"The leadership of Earth can determine their delegation. Why did you need my input? Why have you brought me over? This is all trivial and does not require my input." She sensed there was something more that the ambassador had yet to disclose.

"The Earth leadership has requested we allow some of their pilots to fly the delegation to the convocation," the ambassador said, shaking his head.

"I was not aware they had any pilots."

"That is the quandary." He shook his head. "Technically they do not, but by the departure time for the convocation, their first class of pilots from the jointly run academy will have graduated. They want some of them to fly as a show of good faith and a demonstration of our sincerity in training them."

"Are the trainees qualified?"

"Qualified? Yes, Ompresti, but not experienced in the distances that will need to be jumped. Commander Kyrio is skeptical of their ability. But many on Earth do not trust us, even after all this time."

"What do you suggest, Ambassador?"

"Perhaps we could evaluate the best of the class. If we deem them suitable, they could be part of the shuttle crews. If not, then we have given them a chance which should satisfy the critics."

"Commander Kyrio, do you agree?" Liria looked directly at the commander who was standing with a small group at the side of the table. The commander was in his plain gray uniform with only the small red and blue buttons on the chest, denoting his rank.

"I do not." He strode around the table. "They are untested and inexperienced. If anything goes wrong, it will be a disaster. I cannot agree to their manning any of the shuttle posts."

"Spoken like a true soldier," the Ambassador said. "Ompresti, we need to at least give the appearance of considering the request. However, I will defer to your judgment if you agree with the commander."

"Commander, will you accept my judgment as well?"

"Of course, Ompresti."

"Very well. You will have my answer in the morning. Have the files of the Earth candidates delivered to my apartment. We will meet back here after we have reviewed the candidates."

Liria looked at each of those in attendance, trying to get a feel for the direction they thought best. The majority seemed to not favor the Earth's request. She walked out and took the elevator to the ground floor, then went to a nearby park, where she sat on a bench to think. The air was cool, but not cold as the big orange disk of the sun hung in the eastern sky. Kids ran around the playground near her. Mostly humans with a few Cathardi scattered amongst them. She closed her eyes and cleared her mind. The noises of city traffic were broken by the voices of children. The humid air smelled of exhaust, dirt, and hotdogs from the nearby cart, unlike the clean air she remembered from Cathardi.

She thought to herself as she watched the children play. *Amazing how children accept each other when they are young.* She looked at the parents. A few seemed unconcerned and mingled together, but many of the human parents seemed to fear or dislike the Cathardi's presence and clustered at a distance from the Cathardi's parents.

She rose and returned to her apartment, determined to have an open mind as she reviewed the files, and to spend the night in prayer, asking for guidance. *Creator, I came here six years ago to find the one from the prophecy. The one that will save both my world and his. And, for those six years, you have not given me a sign or a dream. Help me tonight to know your will.*

Liria arrived at the embassy early the next morning. She waited at the table, drinking a cup of hot tea. Though not as good as the Cathardi tea, it sufficed. Even with the new orbiting space station, the cost and time required to get supplies from the home world were steep.

Commander Kyrio was next to arrive. He appeared smug as he strode into the room, confident the decision would go his way.

"Ompresti, I hope all is well."

"It is well, Commander."

The Ambassador was late. He rushed in, shaking his head and mumbling to himself, before bowing and greeting Liria. She knew he was grateful just to have someone else decide.

"As you both know," Liria said, "we came here because of a vision I received while serving the Sisterhood in the capital. I believed we would find specific fulfillments of that prophecy. However, I have found no fulfillment. Despite the Sisterhood's confidence in my prophetic abilities, I think it is time to admit I was wrong." Liria walked to the window and looked out at the morning sunshine. "You have both had enough time to review the files from the academy. Do you believe the cadets can pilot the shuttles?"

"Ompresti, I do not. During a routine exercise commanded by one cadet, a Cathardi crewman died. We cannot put the lives of yourself and the other dignitaries in jeopardy by allowing inexperienced pilots to fly the ships," Commander Kyrio said.

She spun. "Did you read the entire report, Commander?"

"I did, Ompresti."

"Then tell me, what would your suggestion be if the pilot of that ship was a Cathardi?" She walked back to the table. "The Cathardi officer aboard that vessel recommended the pilot for a citation for bravery."

"I cannot say, Ompresti. It would depend on the circumstances."

"I have decided we need to allow the human cadets to fly the shuttles," Liria said. "I may not have found the fulfillment of the prophecy, but the people of earth are spiritually closer to the Cathardi than any other species we have encountered. Their beliefs and traditions mirror ours in too many ways for it to be accidental. I think this is the time to show our confidence in them and prove the truth of our words." She walked to the doorway and paused. "For the last six years, we have tried to earn the trust of these people, while we have secretly felt them to be inferior to us because they lack the same level of technology. My decision is final."

"Ompresti—" Liria held up her hand to signal the discussion was over. Kyrio glared at the Ambassador. As she left, she heard him tell the Ambassador. "Now, look at what you have done. When the ruling council receives my report, they will not be pleased."

"Then perhaps they will call me home," the ambassador replied.

Liria walked back to her apartment without noticing the people rushing by. *Commander Kyrio will have his report sent to the home world by the time I reach my apartment. He objects to my leadership here. Unfortunately, the last report from Moira hinted at a significant change in the ruling council. Marlon is the new civilian faction leader and his well-known misogynistic views toward the Sisterhood could mean trouble. Perhaps it is time I returned home to see the situation myself.*

***

Two weeks after graduating from the Academy, Josh and seven other members of his class sat at the conference table in their commander's office. Across the table from Josh, Carla asked, "Does anyone know why we're here?"

"Not really." It was Steve who always seemed to know the latest scuttlebutt. "There's a rumor they have a special mission planned. But I don't know any details."

Just then, the commander, an Air Force Colonel, came into the office. They all stood and saluted. He returned their salute. "Welcome, at ease." When everyone returned to their seats, he continued. "You have all achieved many awards, both as individuals and as a team. You are the most proficient cadets to graduate from the Academy, with more successful space jumps than any of the other cadets. Because of your capabilities, we chose you as the first group to fly a special mission that will take you out of our solar system. You will be the first humans to accomplish this task."

Finally, a chance to fly into space on an actual mission. Josh hoped his excitement wasn't too obvious. This was his chance to fulfill his dream.

"What is the mission?" Carla asked. She was very detail-oriented and finished at the top of the class. They would probably make her the commanding officer of the mission.

"You will receive the mission parameters just before you leave Eagle Station." He looked at the stunned cadets. "Lieutenant Ruiz please stand."

Carla stood, and the commander walked around the table to her. "You are now, Captain Ruiz." He pinned the rank insignia to her uniform jacket. "You will be the pilot for one shuttle, and the commanding officer for the mission." He shook her hand.

"Thank you, sir. I am honored."

The commander turned and walked back around the table and stopped beside Josh. "Lieutenant Albertson, please stand." Josh stood and faced the commander. "You are now Captain Albertson. You will pilot the second shuttle and be second in command of the mission." He shook Josh's hand and pinned on the rank insignia.

"Thank you, sir." *Well, I was right. Carla is the mission commander.*

"As for the rest of you, Captain Ruiz will give you your assignments. Once you arrive at Eagle Station, you will meet the Cathardi members of each shuttle's crew. A Cathardi officer will be the second in command of each shuttle. Do you have questions?"

"Sir, how many Cathardi are on each shuttle?" Josh said.

"The total crew for each shuttle is eight, evenly divided between Earth and Cathardi crew."

"If there are no additional questions, you are dismissed. A security detail will meet you in the mess at 0630 tomorrow morning. Good luck."

Walking back to their quarters, Carla said, "How cool is this? We might be the first humans to pilot a spacecraft to another world."

"I don't know," Josh said. "I'm not sure about having Cathardi as half the crew, and a Cathardi executive officer could cause conflicts. We haven't worked with any of them."

"Don't be such a downer," Bruce gave Josh a light push on the shoulder. "You're the best jumper in the school."

"Yeah. I want to pilot as much as anyone. Since I was a boy, I've dreamed of flying a spaceship, but I just don't trust the Cathardi, and I don't want to count my chickens."

"Speaking of chickens," Jason said. "Weren't they serving chicken and rice for dinner in the mess tonight?"

"Yeah," Ray said. "It's one of my favorites. Who would have thought service cooking could be so good? I thought it would all be MREs or chipped beef on toast." Everyone laughed.

At dinner that evening, Josh joined the others. They found a table in the rear where they thought they could have some privacy. But others kept coming to the table to congratulate them on their selection for the mission. When things finally settled down, Carla pulled out a piece of paper. "The Colonel gave this to me and told me to use it for crew assignments."

She opened it and read, "Captain Ruiz, you and Captain Albertson may assign the remaining members of the group to your crews. You are both more than capable, as are the other six. Once you have them assigned, give the list to the security detail in the morning. They will get it to me." She looked at Josh. "How do you want to do this?"

"I think we should just take turns picking someone. I agree with the commander, any of them will work well. You pick first," he said.

She looked at the others who all nodded in agreement. "I will take Ray." She wrote Rayquan Johnson on the sheet of paper under her name.

"I'll take Kim. We make a good team."

Carla wrote Kim Anderson under Josh's name. "I pick Bruce."

"I'll take Jason," he said.

"My last pick is Sean. That means Steve is your last crewman."

The last list showed: Rayquan Johnson, Bruce Greenberg, and Sean Donlon on Carla's crew. Josh had Kim Anderson, Jason Baylor, and Steve Mack. *That is a good crew. I trust all of them and I can work with them.*

After a few minutes, Jason said, "I think I'll head over to the Officer's Club for a nightcap. Anyone want to join me?"

"Count me in," Bruce said.

"Me too," said both Sean and Steve.

"Remember, we have an early departure tomorrow," Carla said as they stood to leave.

"Yes, sir." They saluted and left.

Kim and Ray both left a short time later, leaving Josh and Carla alone at the table. "How do you think that worked? Are you happy with your crew?" she asked.

"I am. Though I would have liked to have Ray."

"I'm sure you would. It surprised me you picked Kim."

"I trust her. She did an exceptional job during the exercise where we had the hull breach. And she gets along well with the Cathardi. You know I have a hard time trusting them." He leaned back in his chair.

"Why don't you trust them?"

"My father always said they appear to be friends, but once they get what they want, they will desert us. I also worked with them a little before the academy when my father's shop was making parts for Eagle Station. The engineer I worked with was demanding and arrogant. He didn't think we could meet the requirements. But we proved him wrong. The interpreter; was nicer but still aloof. She belonged to the sisterhood."

"But after the accident on the exercise, the Cathardi officer gave you considerable praise. It seemed to me she liked you."

"Fauna, she was different. Unlike the engineer and the interpreter, she wasn't aloof. I like her and have seen her around the base periodically. She is still friendly."

Carla smiled. "You trust them more than you think. If the only people you knew were career military, how would you feel about our people?"

"Ha! I wouldn't trust them either. Anyway, only time will tell." He took a drink from his glass and smiled. "Changing subjects, are you Captain Kirk or Han Solo?"

"Neither, I'm Ripley."

"Ooh, from *Alien*. Good choice. Capable, independent, and tough, but follows regulations. I think it suits you."

"Who are you, Josh?"

"I think I'm Han Solo, but the truth is I'm probably more Captain Kirk. And don't laugh, but I have given it some thought. This mission fulfills a boyhood dream of mine."

"I've thought about it, too. But my dream wasn't to go to space but to be a fighter pilot and outperform the boys. I have five older brothers and had to fight for my place since I can remember." She finished her water. "I'm heading back to my quarters. I'll see you in the morning."

Josh sat there alone for a few minutes. *Carla is smart. I won't have any trouble following her lead. Ripley? Who would have thought of that? I'm impressed.*

CHAPTER 3

Once at Eagle Station, they took Josh and the others to their assigned quarters before assembling for a briefing. An aisle down the center of the room separated rows of chairs for forty occupants. On one side sat eight Cathardi. Josh joined his friends on the other.

Kim came in after Josh had found a seat. "I see we're off to a good start."

"What makes you say that?" Ray said.

"We are going to have mixed crews. Maybe we should all look and act like one team instead of two," she said. But before they could do anything about the obvious separation, the station commander came into the room.

"Attention," an officer who accompanied him said. Both groups stood at attention.

"Welcome to Eagle Station," the commander said. "Take a seat. You are here for your mission briefing and crew assignments. This is the first interstellar mission for the newly created Earth Space Force. You will fly shuttles carrying a diplomatic mission to the Cathardi home world. I know none of the ESF personnel have been beyond our solar system and the Cathardi have restricted access to their space. This means you will receive the jump coordinates for each leg of the journey just before takeoff." He paused.

"You will launch tomorrow at 0600 station time. That gives you the rest of the day to acquaint yourselves with your fellow crew members and the shuttles. Captain Ruiz, stand, you will command shuttle one. Captain Albertson, stand and move to the other side of the room." He gave Josh a minute to move. "You will command shuttle two. The rest of you will now join your captains. Take time and get to know each other."

Josh stood by the far wall. Four of the Cathardi stood and lined up on his left, while Kim, Jason, and Steve lined up on his right. He turned and saluted the Cathardi captain standing next to him. "Captain Josh Albertson." He extended his hand.

"Captain Taral," the Cathardi said and took his hand.

He moved down the line and introduced himself to each of the Cathardi, Lieutenant Ayrl, Ensign Elas, and Ensign Wyn. The other Earth crew members followed his lead. When they finished, Josh returned to Captain Taral. "I suggest we reconvene on the shuttle in twenty minutes if that is acceptable to you?"

"As you wish, Captain," Taral said.

After they left the briefing room, Jason said, "A diplomatic mission. That sounds pretty cushy. Still, for us, we will explore strange new worlds to quote the old television show."

"That's why we joined, isn't it?" Josh said.

"I wonder what kind of diplomats we will carry?" Kim asked.

"It sounds like we will find out tomorrow morning. But it will probably be an ambassador or a trade delegation. Like Jason said, it sounds pretty cushy.

When they got to the shuttle, there was a marine sergeant guarding the entry. He saluted smartly as Josh approached. "Has Captain Taral arrived yet?"

"No, sir," he said. "Will you wait for him, or do you want to board?"

"We will board, sergeant. Tell Captain Taral and the others we will meet them in the galley."

"Aye, sir."

Once inside, Josh realized the vessel was at least twice as big as the shuttles they were used to flying at the academy. The lower deck housed the same compartments as the smaller shuttles, only each was larger. There was also an extra compartment at the bottom of the forward stairs across from the galley.

"This thing is huge," Jason said and took a seat at the closest table. "Maneuvering this away from the station could be a challenge."

"But once we are away, it won't fly any different," Josh said.

They sat and talked until Captain Taral arrived. "Captain, is this your first time aboard an Ebry class shuttle?"

"Yes, it is larger than the ones we normally fly."

"The controls are identical. It will not take long for you to become accustomed to handling it."

"Thank you, Captain. Why don't you give us a tour and explain the differences between the two?" Jos said.

"Very well, but maybe you should address me as Taral rather than Captain, to avoid confusion, since you are the captain of the ship."

They spent the next several hours going through the ship. The engine room and bridge took most of that time. When they returned to the galley, Josh felt that even though Taral had been very helpful, he seemed to resent the fact that Josh was his superior. Once he dismissed the rest of the crew, he asked Taral to stay.

"We need to discuss the shift assignments," Josh said and sat. He pointed to a chair across the table. "We are used to our normal twenty-four-hour days. But I believe you are more accustomed to the standard twenty-two-hour days from your home world."

"That is correct, sir."

"My suggestion is we run two eleven-hour shifts, with the Cathardi taking one shift and the Earth crew taking the other. Would that be acceptable?" He watched to see the Cathardi's expression.

"That would have been my suggestion, Captain."

"Good." He leaned forward. "Now Taral, I need to know if you will have any problem obeying my orders since I feel you resent the fact that I am the commander."

"I will obey. You are the captain." Taral leaned forward with his face inches away from Josh. "I resent they appointed you captain over me. I have served for three years and commanded ships this size on several occasions. We both know your command is a symbolic gesture. But I am a military man, and I will obey orders even if they come from you." He leaned back. "Is that all?"

"No. I have one more request. When we depart tomorrow, I will pilot the ship away from the station, but I would like you to sit at the co-pilot's station in case I have problems. Once we are away, you will be relieved by Lieutenant Anderson."

"Yes, sir." The sly smile that creased his face was the only reaction Josh could read.

"Very well, Taral. That is all I have. You may leave." Josh watched him leave. *This will be interesting. He reminds me of Ondal, the Cathardi engineer I worked with at Dad's shop. It won't be a pleasure cruise. I hope we don't have problems with the other Cathardi. I'm sure they will sense his resentment.*

He left the shuttle and headed toward his quarters.

"Captain." He heard a familiar voice. When he turned, Lieutenant Fauna was coming up the intersecting passageway.

"Lieutenant," he said.

She saluted. "I am glad I got the chance to see you. There were rumors that Earth pilots would fly soon. Are you one of them?"

He returned her salute. "I am."

"What about Kim and the other cadets?"

"Kim is on my crew, as are two of the others. Carla is also commanding a ship with three others."

Fauna smiled. "You deserve it. Are both crews only from Earth?"

"Unfortunately, no. There are four Cathardi on my crew as well. A Captain Taral leads them."

"Taral, I know him. He is old school. How is he taking being under your command?"

"As good as can be expected. I think. He resents it."

Fauna laughed. "I am sure he resents it. He even dislikes flying under female Cathardi officers. But he will follow orders." She put her hand on his shoulder. "I would like to talk more, but I have a briefing. Good luck."

Why can't more Cathardi be like her?

***

A young marine lieutenant with short brown hair and dark eyes sat behind the desk when he walked into the station commander's office. He greeted Josh. "May I help you, Captain?"

"Yes. I would like to speak to Colonel Mack."

"Do you have an appointment? Colonel Mack is very busy."

"Yes, I'm Captain Albertson. He is expecting me."

"I will let him know you are here. You can sit over there." She pointed to the chairs along the wall and then tapped the headset she wore. "Sir, there is a Captain Albertson here to see you."

Josh sat with his hands in his lap. *I hope I don't get into too much trouble for this, but I don't think I am the right choice for this mission.* He took a deep breath, trying to remain calm.

The door behind the lieutenant's desk opened and a short, barrel-chested man stepped out. "Captain, come in."

In the office, the colonel sat behind his desk while Josh stood facing him. "Relax captain. Have a seat." The colonel picked up a pen and wrote in an open notebook on his desk while Josh sat. "What can I do for you?"

Josh opened the paper he held. "I think there is probably a mistake in the crew assignments for the shuttle mission, sir."

"What makes you think that?" The colonel leaned forward; furrows appeared on the high forehead. He was completely bald except for the short-cropped hair above his ears.

Not a good start. He doesn't look pleased. "Sir, according to the manifest my shuttle will transport only members of the Cathardi Sisterhood. Wouldn't it be better to have a Cathardi crew man their shuttle?"

"It might appear that way, son. But this mission has been in planning for some time with consultations between the Earth Space Force and the Cathardi. The crew assignments were determined during the planning. Are you telling me you don't want to fly the mission?" He kept eye contact with Josh, waiting for his answer.

"No, sir. I want the mission, but I know little about the sisterhood and their requirements." He broke eye contact.

"Captain, if it was up to me, I would gladly change the crew assignments. However, the Ompresti herself specifically asked for you to pilot her shuttle." He leaned back in his chair and rolled the pen between his fingers. "You may not be aware, but the Ompresti is the commander of all the Cathardi forces on Earth. She led them here. So, if she wants you to pilot her shuttle, you will pilot her shuttle. You should consider it an honor."

"I am honored. But..."

"You don't trust the Cathardi." The colonel completed the thought. "I've read your file and I am aware of your feelings. You may want to bury those feelings if you can. Rumor is that the Ompresti can sense your thoughts and emotions. Try not to upset her."

Looks like I'm stuck. How will I be able to keep my thoughts to myself? "I will do my best, sir."

"I'm sure you will. Now, go get your ship and your crew ready for departure." He stood and moved toward the door.

After leaving the colonel's office, Josh went to his ship. The rest of the crew had already boarded and were performing standard systems checks. He took the nearest com and asked that the crew meet him in the galley.

Kim was the first to join him. "What's wrong? You look troubled."

"Nothing's wrong. I just came from the colonel's office, and I'm not pleased with how the conversation went. But it doesn't affect our mission." He went to the hot beverage dispenser and pressed the button for a cup of coffee with cream. "I assume all the stores are on board and everything is functional," he said as more of the crew entered.

He sat on a tabletop, waiting for everyone to make it in. They seemed excited. There was a buzz of conversation. Taking a drink of his coffee, he stood, signaling he wanted their attention. *This is excellent coffee. It tastes like real cream, but I know it isn't.*

He held up the passenger manifest. "I know many of you have been eager to know who would fly with us. Eight members of the Cathardi Sisterhood including the Ompresti Liria, will be aboard later this evening. The Ompresti requested this shuttle. You should all accept this as an honor." An excited hum returned as they talked about the news.

He gave them a few minutes, sipping more coffee. "Lieutenant Taral, I will need your help. I am not, and I doubt the other Earth crew members are familiar with the protocols for dealing with the Cathardi Sisterhood. Can you help us with that?"

"Yes, sir." He moved up to stand by Josh. "This is a tremendous honor. The Ompresti is a revered figure for those of us from Cathardi. The key thing you will need to do is address her by her title, Ompresti unless she gives you specific instructions not to do so." He smiled and looked at the Cathardi crew members. "We Cathardi must remember that we are part of the crew first and not bow or prostrate ourselves while she is near. She will expect us to always perform our duties." He paused, appearing to debate whether to proceed. "If you would not object, we could construct a prayer cubicle for them to use in their devotions. We could construct it in the empty compartment across the passageway. It would only require a bench or small table, and I think Ensign Aryl could acquire a suitable cloth for covering it. Ensign?"

"Yes, sir," she said. "There is a chapel on the station, and they can supply us with one."

"Do you have any other suggestions, Lieutenant? Or anything else to add?" Josh asked.

"No, sir. The sisters are not demanding and will most likely stay to themselves. I would warn you to be aware of their abilities to sense feelings from those with whom they are in contact."

"Great, does that mean they can read our minds?" Steve said.

"No." It was Aryl who spoke. "They can sense feelings, emotions. The sisterhood trains them to be counselors. I attended the sisterhood school on Cathardi for several years but chose to serve in the military. They cannot read minds."

"Thank you, Ensign." Josh dismissed the meeting but asked Taral to stay. When the others were gone, he said, "Show me what we need to do in the compartment."

Taral told him what he thought would be appropriate and showed him how much room they needed. He didn't expect over two or three sisters to be there at the same time. It would require them to move some cargo, but they could do that easily.

They had only stored it there because it wasn't in use. He also suggested a curtain over the hatch, which would remain open.

"Okay," Josh said. "Have Aryl get the items she needs from the chapel. How are the preflight checks going?"

"They are nearly complete. Only the engine room still has some items to go through."

"Have Jason give you a hand moving stuff in here, and when the engine room is complete, Steve can find you a table or bench to use. He's a good scrounger. I will be on the bridge if you need me." He left Taral and when he got to the bridge, he sent Jason down to help him.

On the bridge, Kim was talking with Elas and Wyn, the other two Cathardi crewmen. They all stood to attention and saluted when he walked in. He returned their salutes. "We won't need that kind of formality from now on. Are the ship-to-ship communications working?"

"Yes, sir," Kim said.

"You are all dismissed for now. The passengers will not be on board until after the reception. You may leave the ship or help Taral and Jason below, but be in the mess for the start of the reception."

"Shuttle two to shuttle one, come in," he said over the ship-to-ship com.

"Shuttle one, here," a female voice answered.

"Is that you Ripley?"

"It is. Am I speaking to Kirk?"

"Kirk here. How is the preflight going? We have nearly finished over here," he said.

"I saw your passenger manifest, Josh. That's how I knew you were Kirk and not Solo." He heard her chuckle. "We are also nearly complete. It goes fast when you have two crewmen per station. Do you want to meet and go over the route for the first leg? I can meet you in the Officer's Club in twenty minutes."

"See you there. Shuttle two out."

Carla would get his mind off the passengers and back on the mission. She had that sort of single-minded focus. He needed to focus on the mission.

CHAPTER 4

When they docked at Eagle Station, Liria was the last passenger off the ship. Though she had done it several times, she did not like space travel. It always felt cold, even though the ships maintained a comfortable ambient temperature. It also brought back painful memories from her childhood. Her parent's deaths and the feelings of being an outsider. She did not look forward to returning to the Melal station where they died. But it was time to return.

Now, she stood outside the door to the station mess hall, waiting to meet the crew of the shuttle that would transport her and her sisters to Cathardi. She had spent the last two weeks studying the records of the crew members but still did not know any of those from Earth. They represented a fair cross-section of the North American population, except the majority were from small towns and there was only one Hispanic and one Black among the crew. Though she was eager to meet them, she did not enjoy these formal functions.

"Ompresti, they are ready for you to enter," the attendant at the door said.

She entered, leading the seven sisters who accompanied her on the trip through the door, where the crew stood in line to greet them. The first offered her hand. "I am Carla Ruiz."

"Liria." She took her hand and bowed. "It is a pleasure to meet you. Your parents are very proud of you. If I remember correctly, you finished at the top of the class."

"Thank you, Ompresti."

Liria continued down the line, greeting each and recalling some fact or story from her studies or her conversations with their parents or acquaintances to personalize the interaction.

"Kim Anderson, Ompresti." The petite blonde blushed.

"Kim, so nice to meet you. I met your family earlier this week. Your mother looked so vibrant. She beamed when she talked about you."

"Thank you, Ompresti. I am grateful the Cathardi doctors could help her."

"As am I. Captain Kel tells me you are an exceptionally devout young woman. Perhaps we will have time to talk during the trip." If possible, Kim's face grew even redder.

When she reached Josh, the last in line, she held his hand a long time, staring into his eyes. Josh shifted his feet but didn't break eye contact. *There is something different about this one. I sense a connection I did not feel with the others.*

"Josh Albertson, Ompresti," he said, breaking the awkward silence.

"Liria, you may call me Liria. I was unsure about the decision to have Earth crews take us to the home world. But now that I have met all of you, I believe it was an excellent decision. I am honored to travel under your care."

After going down the line of Cathardi crew members, she mingled with the other attendees for an appropriate amount of time. Then she went over to join the shuttle crews who sat together at a table near a window looking out into the blackness.

"May I join you?"

"Yes, Ompresti. Please do." Carla said as the male crew members stood.

"Please, do not allow me to interrupt your conversations. I do not enjoy meeting these self-important officials and you offer me an excuse to separate from them."

There were a few minutes of silence before Rayquan stretched and spoke. "What a crazy day. If we were still at the academy, we'd be cramming for the finals that start next week instead of being wined and dined like celebrities."

"You would cram. I would relax, knowing I was ready," Carla said. "Though I'm not looking forward to the first long jump."

"It'll be an unfamiliar experience for all of us," Sean said.

"I'm not looking forward to it either," Kim said. Then turning to Liria, "Ompresti, how long has it been since you have been back to your home world?".

"I have been on Earth for over six of your years."

"Don't you miss your family?" Kim asked.

"The sisterhood is my family. As you can see, I am surrounded by family. The other sisters sat at a table just behind her. But I assume you meant my biological family. My parents died when I was quite young, and I have no siblings."

"I am so sorry. I miss my family and I have barely left Earth."

"Hey, aren't we your family?" Steve said, laughing.

They continued talking until the party ended. Before she left, Liria had a moment alone with Josh. "You have a unique gift. I cannot tell you why, but I feel safer with you than with any non-Cathardi I have ever met. Fauna's report was very complimentary of your actions during the exercise she flew with you and Kim."

"Thank you. But I lost a member of my crew. That's not something I feel good about."

Liria sensed his sadness. "Nevertheless, I trust you will perform your duties well." She offered her hand to him. "Good night."

"Good night, Ompresti," Josh said and shook her hand.

Liria returned to her sisters, contemplating her return to Cathardi. *The reports from Moira are disturbing. The balance of power in the Council is changing. What will I find when I return?*

She remembered when news first leaked out about the discovery of the planet. Many Cathardi faithful looked upon me as an icon, treating me with reverence, and calling me the chosen of God, a prophetess (Ompresti). It became difficult for me to concentrate on my duties in the sisterhood. Now, after six years on Earth with no answers, will they still feel the same? I am still convinced Earth was the planet of the prophecy and want to report my findings to the ruling council. The trip will give me time to think and pray.

But, the Earthling pilot, Josh, why does he unsettle me? There is more to him than I currently know. I sense a strength and singleness of purpose in him, a strong sense of right and wrong, and a reassuring confidence. Yet there seems to be this wall of distrust or fear. This will be an interesting trip. Could he be the one?

***

Josh was relieved as he walked in the station's artificial gravity to the shuttle bay after the reception. *No more social functions to endure, only my ship, my crew, and the passengers. No pressure to fit in, just the freedom of space. This is where I belong, what I dreamed about as a boy.*

With over an hour before departure, he took his time to check each of the ship's systems, and the modifications Taral had made to the forward compartment. The rest of the crew would board over the next half hour to conduct their pre-departure duties and checks. Thirty minutes before departure, the passengers would board. Josh wanted everything completed so he could greet the passengers. He loved the pre-flight routine, especially since it was his first ship. In his element, his ship, he needed to get to know her. He stopped first in the aft stowage hold, no larger than an oversized closet, and examined the rigging used to secure the passenger's luggage, supplies, and ship's spares. Everything would need to be secured and clearly labeled.

He continued down the lower passageway, past the aft staircase to the environmental control room. There he examined the life support systems and spent several minutes ensuring optimum comfort for their Cathardi passengers. Touch-controlled biometric scanners provided access to the individual compartments aboard the shuttle. Only he and Taral, the first officer, could access every compartment on board.

Across the passageway, from the environmental control room, was the poorly named engine compartment, the largest on the shuttle. It contained the Cathardi gravity field generator, the largest and most prominent feature within the shuttle. Located directly in the center of the vessel, it not only generated the gravity fields used to create the gravity well that allowed for interstellar travel but also the simulated gravity aboard the shuttle. They had mounted the engines that powered the ship during normal space flight on short wings extending from the hull. They used compact fusion reactors to create enough thrust to produce speeds of over 40,000 miles per hour.

Between the environmental control room and the forward staircase, the galley and dining area contained pre-packaged foodstuffs, beverages, and a drinking water recycling unit. Nearly as large as the engine room, it provided space for sitting and moving around with exercise equipment along the aft wall that the limited personal quarters on the upper deck could not contain.

The front compartment that Talar had modified was on the other side of the lower level next to the forward staircase to the upper deck. Before the Taral's efforts, it seemed to be wasted space. Josh thought they originally designed it for cargo or another purpose. Taral had covered the hatch from the passageway to the compartment with a sheer orange and yellow tie-dyed curtain. He had it furnished with a bench covered in a piece of blue and red fabric and attached pillows to the floor in similar colors. Josh guessed it would serve well as a chapel for the Cathardi sisters.

On the upper level, the forward staircase ended in the passageway between the bridge and the individual quarters. The sparsely fitted crew and passenger quarters, on both sides of the central passageway, contained a bunk, a small storage area for belongings, and a communications center. Two individual compartments shared a head with a sink, toilet, and recycling shower, allowing for five minutes of warm water. All the water on the ship went through the purification and recycling unit. Quarters were the same for both the crew and passengers, except for the slightly larger captain's quarters, which also contained a small desk, a chair, and monitors of the ship's primary systems.

Forward from the stairs, the bridge featured the pilot's station, centered in the U-shaped command center, with the controls and monitors for all the ship's systems, including communications. The co-pilot's station on the left had identical controls. Behind and to the right of the pilot's station was the engineering console, with the communications console behind and left of the co-pilot. The ship was designed for a crew of eight, but in an emergency, could function easily with a crew of four. Josh's crew would alternate twelve-hour shifts during normal space flight. The Earth crew would work one shift and the Cathardi crew the other. During jump cycles, both crews were available.

As Josh finished on the bridge, Kim came in for her pre-flight checks. He watched her as she snapped to attention and saluted smartly. "Permission to come aboard, *sir*?"

Her smile reminded Josh of how attracted he had been to her at the Academy. He had often wondered if they could be more than friends, but the rules prevented them from exploring that possibility. However, he had invited her to share a room with him during an unexpected layover after the Christmas break two years ago. She declined, not wanting to risk expulsion from the academy. Now, as her senior officer, the protocol still constrained their relationship, at least for this trip.

"Permission granted. And we won't require that much formality this trip, Lieutenant." He returned both her salute and smile. "Has anyone else come aboard?"

"Not yet, *sir*," she laughed. She seemed excited, and full of energy.

"The bridge is yours, lieutenant." Josh stood to leave the bridge. He went to the boarding area, double-checking some systems on his way. When he reached the main airlock, he saw Steve coming down the ramp to the shuttle. Before entering, he stopped, saluted, and asked permission to board. They talked briefly before Jason, who repeated the formality, joined them. Taral and the Cathardi crew also observed the formal boarding request.

"Is this some kind of conspiracy?" Josh asked Jason when the others had boarded.

"Yes, sir!" he said. Laughing, he made his way onto the ship, leaving Josh on the ramp.

Josh stepped out into the passageway to where a veteran marine sergeant stood and saluted him. Josh returned his salute.

"Permission to speak freely, sir?" The marine asked.

"Permission granted, sergeant."

"All of us at the station are proud that you are making this trip. We have never really trusted the Cathardi. They're too easy, too friendly, and too secretive about their home world. But maybe we have misjudged them. We..." He stopped and snapped to attention.

Josh turned and saw the Cathardi sisters making their way down the passage. He also snapped to attention and returned their bows when they arrived. The Ompresti offered her hand, which he clasped, and they exchanged greetings.

"May I escort you to your quarters?" Josh asked. "May I give you a tour?"

"You may certainly escort us. We desire your company, but a tour is unnecessary. We have been on shuttles before," the Ompresti said.

Josh offered his arm to her. She accepted, and they started down the passage to the forward stairs. The remaining sisters followed silently. When they got to the forward stairs, the Ompresti stopped suddenly, pulling Josh back. She stared at the chapel area. Taral had moved the curtain, allowing the inside of the compartment to be seen from the bottom of the stairs. He wondered if there was something wrong. Did they miss something?

"Taral had the space converted for you and your sisters. I hope it meets your approval." Josh said.

"How considerate you are. This is unexpected and truly kind. Your thoughtfulness honors us. We will put it to good use, Captain."

The other sisters murmured in subdued but excited tones. They took turns kneeling at the altar before accompanying Josh up the stairs. He offered the Ompresti his quarters, which she adamantly refused.

"I am quite comfortable in standard quarters, captain. You will require the monitors."

He escorted each of them to their quarters and turned to head back to the bridge to go over his jump calculations. As he passed the Ompresti's room, she stopped him. "Your presence at the first meal would honor us, Captain."

"The honor would be mine, Ompresti." He turned and continued to the bridge.

She intrigued him. The other sisters called her 'elder', but she did not appear any older than the others and probably younger than a couple of them. Though it was difficult to judge Cathardi's ages by appearances. Josh guessed she was not much older than he. In addition, every time she touched him, he felt she could read his thoughts. He would have to keep his head when around her.

Sitting in the pilot's chair going through his calculations, Josh felt the crew's excitement growing. Their conversations buzzed as they went through their checklists and noted system readings. Jason interrupted, "Sir, the station command center has given us permission to launch."

"Thank you. Inform Carla we will leave ten minutes after them and meet them at the rendezvous. Announce our departure to the passengers and have them secure themselves for launch."

A few minutes later, he heard Jason announce, "Shuttle one has departed."

Ten minutes later, Josh began the launch sequence. "Release docking clamps. He maneuvered the shuttle back slowly using the joystick at the command console." There was a loud clunk and a slight jolt as the clamps released and the engine's reactors started. The shuttle trembled slightly as the engines began backing the shuttle away from the station, maneuvering the ship into the departure position. Even though it was twice the size of the other ships he had flown, the shuttle handled easily. Josh watched his monitors closely and piloted the ship clear of the station. Once clear, he used the thrusters to turn the ship and increased engine power until the ship achieved cruising velocity. He inputted the rendezvous coordinates and activated the autopilot.

"Well done, everyone," he announced.

Taral stood. "Permission to leave the bridge, sir?"

"Permission granted," he said. "I will see you at shift change."

"You did well, sir." Taral left the bridge and Kim took the copilot's seat he had occupied.

They would cruise for just over sixteen hours to reach the rendezvous with Carla's ship to begin their first jump through folded space. They needed to be away from gravity fields that could jeopardize the jump by distorting or preventing the formation of the jump singularity. This made jump-starting locations more critical to success than the ending locations unless the jump put them in direct proximity to the gravity field of a large planet, star, or black hole.

Cruising, especially on autopilot, required only minimal attention. The crew used the time to rest, recreate, and perform system diagnostics. The passengers used the makeshift chapel continuously. Whenever Josh came down the stairs, at least one sister knelt in front of the altar in prayer. He got a strange sensation as he passed and almost believed that a spiritual presence surrounded the sisters.

At dinner the first evening, Josh dined with the eight Cathardi sisters. He sat across the table from the Ompresti. "Thank you for inviting me to join you, Ompresti."

"You are welcome. But please call me Liria. We are grateful for your thoughtfulness. Your kindness is surprising. How did you manage to add the chapel?"

"Fortunately, all the credit belongs to Taral and others of the crew. Aryl brought fabrics and pillows. Jason found the bench. I had little to do with it."

"I will see that we thank them as well. Do you mind if I pray over the meal before we eat?"

"No, please do."

Liria blessed the meal, and they all ate quietly for a few minutes before she asked, "Why did you become a spaceship captain?" Though Liria had insisted he call her by name, she would not consent to call him anything but captain.

"As a boy, I used to watch movies and television shows about the future and space flight. Then I started reading what we call science fiction books. I would dream about one day flying a ship through space. When the opportunity arose to join the Academy, I had to try, and here I am in my dream job."

"Is it everything you have imagined?" She sensed a note of sadness. What about the academy made him feel so sad?

"Not everything, but close."

They spent the rest of the meal in light conversations, and Josh learned more about his passengers. It turned out all the sisters were in their late teens or early twenties, in Earth equivalents, and schooled by their order since childhood. They seemed 'human'. They teased one another, joked, and laughed. Their fervent belief in the existence of an eternal, omniscient, omnipotent, omnipresent God reminded him of some of the 'holy rollers' in his parent's church. They bubbled at the kindness he showed by providing them with the chapel and said it would guarantee a safe journey to the home world. After the meal, Josh excused himself rather early since he wanted to get a full sleep cycle before the rendezvous and first jump.

Chapter 5

After Josh left her and her sisters, Liria asked Myra, her assistant and confidant, to stay with her. "What are your impressions of the captain?" She said once the others had left.

"He seems to be a kind and capable young man, but there is a sadness underneath his confidence," Myra said. "He is good at hiding his feelings, but when he talked about going to the academy, his sadness was clear. Why are you asking me? You are better at sensing these things than I am."

"He confuses me. I have sensed something different about him since we met." She stared at her hands while Myra sat silently, waiting. "I have also sensed the sadness. I think there is a deep hurt or trauma associated with the academy. Maybe it has something to do with the death of his father who died in an automobile accident before he went to the academy. There is also resentment or distrust of us. I am not sure if it is connected to the sadness or just the residual feeling many on Earth have that we are conquerors."

"Yet," her assistant said. "He allowed the setting up of the chapel. He seems to want to do the right thing. Even with the repressed feelings, I like him. He was a good choice to command our shuttle. Why did you select him instead of the young woman?"

"When I decided to allow the mission to proceed with the Earth crews, it was because of the report that a Cathardi crewman wrote after the accident our captain's ship suffered during an exercise. She felt he was willing to sacrifice his life for his crew." She paused and sat back.

"You know that I have studied the spiritual beliefs of Earth since we arrived. Their Judeo-Christian beliefs are so like our traditions, that it cannot be an accident. The Creator led us here. I believe because the chosen one will come from among them," Liria said. "One saying from their tradition that the Christian leader, Jesus, told this to his disciples: 'Greater love has no one than this than to lay down one's life for his friends.' The captain shows this type of love even for those he may not like. He is the type of person I can see the Creator using to save our people. Is it possible that our captain is the chosen one?"

"It is possible," Myra said. "But how can you be sure? Have you asked for a sign? Has the Creator spoken to you?"

"I have prayed. But I have not received a sign or a word. How am I to know?"

"You have been patient for six years, Ompresti. You can remain patient. We will be back on Cathardi soon where you can consult the leaders of the order. Perhaps Moira or another can guide you."

"Thank you, Myra. As usual, you are a help to me. I will contact Moira before we arrive. She will make time to listen to me." Liria finished her tea. "I think I will try to sleep. It has been a hectic day."

Myra got up from the table with Liria. "I will walk with you, Ompresti."

They walked to the forward stairs, and Liria stopped. Two of their fellow sisters kneeled at the altar in the makeshift chapel. She could hear them praying and sensed their devotion. She had to wait for a few minutes before she continued. The presence of the Creator was there. *I should come down later and use this myself.* "It was kind to provide this space for us," she said to Myra. "It is already in use, and I feel the Creator's hand on our shuttle."

"I feel it too, Ompresti." Myra walked with her to her quarters before continuing down to her own.

Once in her quarters, Liria went to bed and dreamed of the home world.

***

Josh rose from his sleep cycle, at 0400 Earth time, two hours before the rendezvous with the other shuttle. He expected everyone but the Cathardi crew to be asleep, so he dressed quickly and started down the forward stairs on his way to the galley to grab a light breakfast before making his way to the bridge. The smell of cinnamon filled his head as he descended. He felt strange, unsettled, like a fog descending around him. Then, when he neared the bottom of the stairs, erotic visions flooded his mind. His flesh pressed against the naked form in his arms, kissing her neck and shoulders as they made love. He stumbled, but the railing prevented him from falling into the bulkhead as he missed the last step.

He stood dazed at the bottom of the stairs, shaking his head, trying to clear his mind of the visions. "Captain!" he heard someone say.

He turned his head and saw Liria stand up from kneeling before the altar. She stared at him with wide eyes and her mouth agape in apparent surprise. Her silky gown, though modest, draped over her youthful body, accentuating her figure, and reigniting the vivid images of the two of them embracing. He could see into her pale blue eyes and feel her moist lips, her warm smooth skin against his.

"Captain!" She clapped her hands, interrupting the visions, and wrapped her cloak around herself. "Are you all right, Captain?"

Josh shook his head, "I... I am sorry. I am sorry for disturbing you. I didn't think anyone else was up. Forgive me. I just wanted some coffee." The blush burned his face. He turned and hurried into the galley. There he stood at the beverage dispenser. Moving on autopilot, he pushed the button for coffee and cream and waited while the cup filled. *What just happened? Where did those thoughts come from? Why do I feel like I just did something wrong? Was I sleepwalking?* He sat at one of the small tables.

Liria entered the galley and got a cup of Cathardi herbal tea from the dispenser, then sat across the table from Josh. He didn't meet her gaze and tried not to blush as the images still popped in and out of his thoughts.

"I need to apologize to you," Liria said. "The first time we met, I sensed a connection between us, but I did not realize how strong it was. Since you are not Cathardi, you may be unaware that everyone in the sisterhood possesses a certain sixth sense, a heightened level of clairvoyance and spiritual insight. The sisterhood nurtures and encourages these talents. We sense the thoughts and emotions of others, allowing us to be more empathetic when ministering, and can transmit our calm reassurance."

Josh fidgeted, still not looking into her face. *What is she talking about? Does she know what I saw?*

"When we are in fervent prayer," she continued. "We reach a heightened state of awareness, like sexual arousal in your species. During these times, our bodies release pheromones. Because of this, Cathardi men and women do not worship together. Significant incidents of failure and debauchery mark our history. But you are the first non-Cathardi I have ever encountered who reacted to these pheromones. I apologize. It was not your fault. You were only reacting to the chemicals and the mental connection we have."

Josh looked at her. "But you don't understand."

She lowered her eyes. "I do," she said. "I saw the same images you did, and I felt what you felt. I am still feeling what you are feeling." She paused and looked up at him. "It will pass in a few moments as your reaction to the chemicals subsides. My sisters and I will no longer allow ourselves to be so fervent in our prayers." She took his hand and immediately the vision returned. She let go and clapped. Again, the vision left. Then she tried to explain the Cathardi practice of gender separation in worship.

Josh sat there silently and drank his coffee, not quite hearing or comprehending what she was saying. Trying to understand what happened. Eventually, the arousal diminished, and his mind cleared. When he finished his coffee, he excused himself and left for the bridge. Not wanting to risk another disturbing encounter, he determined to use the aft staircase.

On the bridge, he was so unsettled he had to go through his jump calculations several times before he was sure of their accuracy. It would be the longest jump any of the Earth crew members had ever attempted. When he was sure of his numbers, he contacted Carla to compare the calculations and the spacing information. Both shuttles would jump through the same fold, making timing and separation critical. Too close, and the gravity field could pull them into each other. Too far apart, and one might miss the field entirely or miss their destination. Carla checked the calculations and relayed her confirmation.

Jumping could cause unconsciousness, disorientation, nausea, or dizziness. Once completed, the recovery time for crew members could be several minutes. Unlike most people, though, Josh typically recovered quickly without nausea and little disorientation, an ability that had factored into his and Carla's selection for command of the shuttles.

"Captain, the other shuttle is ready to begin the jump sequence," Kim reported.

"Very good. Make the announcement."

The crew took their seats and fastened their harnesses while the passengers went to their cabins, where they sat in jump seats provided. Once Josh saw all the restraint indicator lights were lit, he had Kim relay their readiness so they could simultaneously begin the jump.

"Everything is a go." He heard Carla over the speaker.

"Roger that," Josh responded and put his hand on the gravity engine activation switch.

"Singularity in, 5, 4, 3, 2, 1, now," Carla counted down, and both shuttles started the jump sequence.

When Josh recovered his senses shortly after the jump, he put his hand on Kim's shoulder. "Kim, Kim, Kim." He gently shook her shoulder until she was alert. "Contact Carla, to ensure everything is okay with them. Then broadcast our arrival notice and alert me when we receive a response. I will check on the passengers." Josh unbuckled his restraint and got up to leave the bridge. "Taral, you have the controls."

Kim let Josh know, over the com, when the other two crew members regained their senses. He also heard Carla's reply as he walked down the passageway to the passenger quarters. Both shuttles had completed the jump. He was on his way back to the bridge when Kim paged him.

"Captain, we received a request from the Cathardi to hold our position and await visual confirmation of our identity," Kim reported.

"We are in the right place," Josh said as he entered the bridge. "How long until the Cathardi ship arrives?"

"If the sensors are correct, it looks like three hours," Taral reported.

"Have the crew take a break. I will watch things until they arrive. And can someone bring me a cup of coffee?" Josh said as they left the bridge.

He sat alone on the bridge, watching the monitors and drinking the coffee Kim brought him. Less than an hour after their contact, the proximity sensor alarm went off. Two small, fast-moving vessels appeared on his screen. They would be on top of the shuttles in minutes.

"Unidentified craft approaching. Please identify yourselves. This is a Cathardi shuttle on a diplomatic mission. Please respond." Josh transmitted in Cathardi and immediately called the crew back to their stations. *This better be the Cathardi. Otherwise, with no weapons or shields, we are in trouble.*

"This is group leader, Amala of the Cathardi forces. Transmit your clearance code and hold position while we conduct visual verification."

"Kim, contact Carla's shuttle to see if they have any additional information on the two approaching ships."

When Taral entered the bridge, Josh said, "Will you be able to identify the two ships when they come into visual range?"

"I believe so."

Josh drummed his fingers on the control console while they waited silently. The two ships zoomed past the waiting shuttles, passing within a few hundred feet. Smaller than the shuttles, they bore typical Cathardi markings on their hulls. But to Josh's surprise, they appeared to be heavily armed fighters.

He looked at Taral. "Are they Cathardi?"

"Yes, and they are fighters. You must understand, that not all races we encounter are as peaceful as you. Your concern, though prudent, is baseless since they are expecting us. A larger vessel, also a warship, acts as their base."

The lead scout ship communicated back in Cathardi, "We confirmed your identification code. Here are your course and docking instructions," the scout ship replied to the shuttles. "We will escort you. Do not deviate from your prescribed course. The automatic defenses of the mother ship will activate if they detect deviations. The commander of the mother ship will formally receive you on arrival."

Kim acknowledged the instructions. Carla and Josh piloted the shuttles into formation behind the lead scout ship for the flight to the mothership.

Josh said. "Is there anything we need to know before we enter the lion's den?"

"I do not understand your question," Taral said. "The Cathardi vessel will receive you as guests aboard. Shall I remain here on the bridge, sir?"

"That won't be necessary. You may return to your previous activity. Thank you."

Taral left the bridge.

"What was that about?" Kim asked.

"Too many surprises." It was hard to trust people who constantly did things outside expectations. Especially after his personal experience from the morning and the continuing struggle with his thoughts whenever Liria was around.

***

The Cathardi mother ship was the biggest vessel Josh or any of the humans had ever seen. Bigger than the space station orbiting Earth, bigger than any of the ships in the initial Cathardi contact. At first sight, the vessel appeared as an elongated oval. Protrusions on the surface of the main body showed the locations of weapons stations. Its short wings ended in large engine nacelles. Scout ships and shuttles entered and left the larger ship from bays near the underside of the vessel. The shuttles followed the scout ships into a bay near the center of the warship. Josh saw a dozen scout ships lined up to leave. He docked his shuttle next to Carla's near the giant airlock at the innermost point of the bay. Jetways extended and sealed to the shuttle's rear hatches. Once pressurized, the airlock doors opened to a passageway lined on both sides with Cathardi in full military uniform. The Commander and senior officers of the ship greeted the passengers and crew as they disembarked and escorted them to a large room where more of the ship's officers had assembled.

"Would you like refreshments?" Their escort pointed to tables arrayed with fresh food and beverages. "The commander has given most of the officers leave so they could meet our honored guests."

"Thank your commander for us," the head of the Earth delegation answered in the rather formal Cathardi taught to diplomats. "We appreciate the opportunity to meet all of you and you honor us with this reception."

Josh saw the crowd of officers around the Ompresti. *She looks to be the real honored guest, not us.*

The curious Cathardi officers asked a lot of questions about Earth and their mission. About two hours after it began, an announcement ended the reception, sending the officers back to their duties. Liria approached Josh and the other shuttle crewmen with a female Cathardi officer. "May I give you a tour of the vessel?" the Cathardi officer said in English.

"Yes, thank you," Carla said in English as well.

"You will only see the major sections of the ship because of time limitations," the escort said.

They left the reception and walked down a short passageway, entering what Josh thought was an elevator. But when the Cathardi officer entered the destination into the control console, the compartment moved suddenly to the right, forcing the passengers to grab the rails provided along each wall. She tried to explain in English where they were, but she eventually apologized and explained in Cathardi, which Liria translated to English for the civilian delegates. They stopped first in the stern hangar like the one the shuttles entered. Each hangar the officer explained housed twenty of the smaller scout ships, fighters, and an assortment of larger vessels remarkably like their own shuttles, except these vessels appeared heavily armed with missiles and other weapons similar in appearance to cannons but probably energy weapons or rail guns, extending from the forward section. The mother ship had a crew of over four thousand and, along with the smaller vessels it housed, it had an array of weaponry.

"We patrol along this section of the frontier of Cathardi-controlled space. We watch for any contact with unknown races and provide help when needed to civilian craft traveling through the sector," their guide said.

Josh listened. *So much firepower for the 'peaceful' race the Cathardi claims to be. Even their shuttles have weapons.*

The size and might of the Cathardi vessel impressed the civilian passengers, who kept saying how fortunate Earth was that the Cathardi were friends.

After the tour, the escort returned them to their shuttles.

"Here are the documents containing the start and end coordinates for your next jump." She handed the documents to Carla and Josh. "Please remain on the shuttles until you receive clearance to leave. Remember to follow the exit flight plan, just as you did when arriving. The ship's automated defenses are still active."

Once their shuttles were out of the bay, Cathardi scout ships escorted them clear of the warship's defenses, and the shuttles began their cruise to the next jump point.

After the escorts disappeared, Josh walked down the passageway past the crew quarters to Liria's berth. He knocked on the hatch. "Liria, it's Josh. Can we talk?"

She opened the hatch. "Certainly, Captain, come in."

He immediately flashed back to the encounter in the chapel. He focused on the purpose of his visit and blocked the images from his mind.

"I think I will remain outside for now," he said. "That was a rather impressive show of force by the Cathardi warship. I assume there was a purpose to it."

"Your assumption would be correct."

"And what exactly was the purpose?"

"I cannot say, but I believe it was to show that our friendly intentions toward your planet were genuine. We could have easily come as the conquerors that many of your people think we are, instead of friends."

"If you are friendly, why do you need such strength?"

"Not all the races we have encountered are as friendly, or as backward as yours." Josh sensed she was holding something back.

She looked him squarely in his eyes. "I will not tell you more. Only time can provide the answers you seek."

Josh started to leave, then stopped. "Will the discomfort I feel around you ever leave?"

"It may never leave," she broke eye contact. "It is a powerful connection, but the urgency and force should decrease."

Josh walked back to the bridge. "Taral, how long until we reach the jump coordinates?"

"Several hours, sir."

"I will be in my quarters if you need me."

This thing with Liria is affecting my thinking. Not only do I have these strong sexual urges around her, but now when Kim smiles at me, I have similar urges around her. I must get control of this.

Exhausted after the brief night and busy day, Josh lay on his bunk and fell asleep. He dreamed of the Cathardi warship orbiting Earth. On his knees, with his hands tied behind his back, he watched as the warship fired upon Earth.

"I thought you were our friends!" he said.

"We are your friends." He heard Liria's voice beside him. He turned. She stared down at him with icy blue eyes. "This will keep you from destroying yourselves." Her laugh sounded like an alarm. She opened her robe and pulled his face into her body. "You need me. And I need you."

He felt a hand on his shoulder. "Captain." He jerked and saw Kim standing next to his bunk. "We are at the jump location," she said. "Are you okay?"

"Yes, thank you. I was having a strange dream," he said. "I will be on the bridge momentarily, lieutenant."

CHAPTER 6

After completing their second jump successfully, the shuttles broadcast their arrival and two Cathardi scout ships met them, but this time the fighters escorted them to an immense orbiting space station. Josh stared out through the front viewports at the station, which was the size of a small moon and constructed of seven counter-rotating cylindrical bands. Two large bands formed the upper section. Enormous ships, probably commercial vessels, docked at various points around the rings. More orbited around the station, waiting to dock. Two smaller bands formed a central section that contained docking bays for smaller non-military vessels, and a lower section, formed by three rings, serviced military vessels with several warships, as large as the one the shuttles had left, docked in the larger bottom band. Smaller warships docked in the rings above. The bands were all connected to a large central tower that extended above the upper ring and below the bottom ring.

His and Carla's shuttles were to dock in the bay just above the military level.

Approaching the station, Josh watched as the large commercial vessels docked and departed at a rate of about one every thirty minutes. With military vessels docking about every fifteen minutes, and smaller vessels every ten minutes. It reminded him of a giant beehive.

Once they docked, everyone disembarked from the shuttles into jetways that led to a large corridor where several Cathardi officers and a small contingent of a new alien race, the Melal, received them. The short, stout, dark-haired, and round-faced, humanoid Melal in their brightly colored clothing provided a stark contrast to the Cathardi in their gray uniforms.

"Welcome aboard the joint Cathardi-Melal transfer station," the ranking Cathardi officer said. "I am Commander Agal. You will spend the next two days with us. We will service your shuttles while we meet with the Cathardi delegates. Kai Bora of the Melal station council has arranged for your quarters and guides during your stay." The balding, jolly-looking Melal in a bright purple shirt bowed at the mention of his name.

"Now, if you will follow me." The Commander walked down the passageway, not waiting for a response.

He led them to a transport tube like the one on the warship. Josh, his crew, and the Cathardi sisters went into the first unit, along with a mix of Cathardi and Melal from the reception party. The unit stopped and exited at a hub where several tubes met. They waited there for the rest of the delegation. The hub was without adornment except for the tube control panels, which provided the only color.

Once the rest of the party joined them in the hub, Commander Agal turned and entered a tube that had just arrived. "Ompresti, you and the other Cathardi will go with me as we have business. Kai Bora will escort the rest of you to your quarters."

The Cathardi sisters and most of the Cathardi military personnel followed him into the car, leaving the shuttle crews and the other Earth passengers with the Melal and a couple of Cathardi junior officers.

"If you will follow me." Kai Bora turned to another tube and gestured for them to enter. The transport tube took them to the central hub. Josh stepped through the large sliding metal doors and into a crowded commercial area. *Just like a beehive. It looks like the cantina scene in the old Star Wars movies I watched as a kid with my dad.*

The crowded halls buzzed with activity accompanied by a constant hum of conversations from an enormous variety of humanoid races in every imaginable style and color of clothing. Overwhelmed, Josh stopped to give himself time to adjust. *This is incredible. The crowd is amazing, even worse than the Christmas rush at the mall. Who would have imagined so many variations on the human form, so many sizes, shapes, and colors?*

One of the Melal officials interrupted Josh's thoughts. "The Cathardi and Melal authorities co-manage the station. The Melal people inhabit the planet that the station orbits. Our alliance with the Cathardi has existed for several generations.

We share a common economic system, and we provide for the needs of the non-Cathardi inhabitants and visitors. You will find dining, shopping, and entertainment facilities on the levels above this one. You are free to explore and enjoy everything on this level and the three levels up. The lower levels, occupied by the Cathardi military, are off-limits. Follow me and I will lead you to your quarters."

The Melal led the crew to their quarters. The colorful décor of the room, which contained a sleeping berth recessed into a purple wall, surprised Josh. A small table with two bell-shaped stools and a red futon-style sofa in front of a large video monitor completed the decor. The guide showed them how the communications system incorporated into the monitor worked.

"Your rooms show in the lower right corner of the screen. You may contact any room by touching the solid blue icon. You may contact a guide, available to take you wherever you desire, either individually or as a group, by touching the bottom left icon. The personal needs closet is through the door next to the sleeping recess. I will leave you now. Use the blue icon if you desire anything."

He examined his quarters and found the personal needs closet was the head, which included an unlimited running water shower.

"Hey Josh," he heard Carla's voice through the monitor. "Can you hear me?"

"Loud and clear," he answered.

"I'm going to get a guide to show us around, then take us somewhere we can eat and relax while we have the time. If you want to join us, we will meet you in the passageway in ten minutes."

"Make it twenty and I'll be there. I want a quick shower first."

"Let's make it thirty. A shower sounds great right now."

Josh joined the other crew members in the passageway where a young Melal female in a long, flowery low-cut dress would guide them on a tour of the Melal sections of the station. She was approximately five foot four inches tall and round, with shoulder-length brown hair and dark brown eyes. "Most of the middle levels of the station contain housing for inhabitants and travelers, shops, and eateries. Gambling halls, saloons, and pleasure houses, frequented by the constantly arriving freighter crews, also occupy several large sections on these levels. Melal and Cathardi provide a visible police presence in these sections. Some of the visiting crews can get quite rowdy." She grinned.

When the tour ended, Steve asked, "Is anyone else hungry? I'm starving."

Carla looked at their guide. "Where would you recommend we go to eat and relax?"

"Do you desire off-world food or a more traditional Melal offering?"

"Melal," they said almost in unison.

"A place on the next level serves traditional Melal food with live entertainment you might enjoy since you are not Cathardi. The shortest route is through here. Follow me."

The guide led them down a rather narrow, dimly lit corridor filled with strange music. Josh was talking to Carla when Kim gasped and turned right into him. He knocked her over and nearly fell himself.

"Are you okay?" Josh helped her up. Behind him, he heard Steve and Jason laughing.

"No! We need to go another way." Kim said.

"What's so funny?" he asked Steve. Then he saw the tall, shapely female standing in the door on his left. Barely clothed, she smiled at him and beckoned him in with her long-fingered hand. He could not help but stare until he felt the sharp pain in his arm where Carla hit him.

"We need to go another way," she said to the guide.

"My apologies. I forgot you are not familiar with life on an off-world trading station. We will go this way." She led them back in the direction they had come.

"What was that?" Jason asked her.

"She is an Elorian, a pleasure worker," the guide explained. "Most of the establishments down that passage are pleasure houses."

"You mean a prostitute?" Carla asked. The guide looked confused. "She performs sex acts for money?"

"Yes." The guide looked relieved that they understood. "She is a pleasure worker."

She led them to the center of the level, where they took a transport tube up to the next level. There they meandered through the crowd to a large establishment where the host seated them on stools around a circular table next to the stage. The guide spoke briefly to a flashily dressed Melal, whom she said was the proprietor. Soon a young Melal female brought them a large platter of fresh cut fruit. The stoutly built server stood only five feet tall, with broad features and a curvaceous figure highlighted by a bright red, low-cut floor-length gown. She seemed to take an immediate liking to Jason. With each course, she served him first and gave him larger portions than the others. She especially enjoyed Jason's blushing when she would rub against him as she served. She practically ignored Carla and Kim. Josh saw the creases in Carla's forehead and irritation flashed in her eyes.

The meal was excellent. After the fruit, they ate some type of grilled meat served like shish kabob on a stick with grilled vegetables. The servings were large and more than any of them, including Ray, could eat. It relieved Josh when the conversation turned away from the incident on the lower level to Jason's new admirer. A musical comedy, the show parodied the Cathardi, making a lot of jokes about their strict religious beliefs, their insistence on abstinence, and their apparent xenophobia. The show's risqué humor made them laugh, though some of it was beyond them. The crew relaxed together for the first time since the mission had started. Still laughing when they returned to their quarters for the night, Carla stopped Josh.

"We are staying here for two days, and I think we need to agree on some rules of conduct. Certain sections of this station need to be off-limits. We are too naïve for such a strange exotic place." She stated emphatically.

"Don't you trust us?" he said.

"Not after what I saw earlier in the passage. And not after the behavior of the server during the meal. It will be too easy for us to get into trouble here."

Josh relented. Together, they went into Carla's quarters and called the rest of the crew members. "Josh and I have agreed we need some restrictions on our conduct while we are here. We can visit the shops and other public areas, but not the saloons, gambling halls, or pleasure houses during our layover at the station."

"But we are adults and responsible for our behavior," Steve objected.

"Besides, Jason can get into as much or more trouble by just seeing that server from the restaurant," Sean chimed in.

"As your senior officers, this is an order, not a request," Carla answered.

"You heard Carla. We will, for the duration of our stay, abide by these rules," Josh said to support Carla.

Josh slept well that night and rose early. He met the others and the same guide as the previous day in the hallway after Carla let him know they were ready.

"What is your preference this morning?" the guide asked.

"Nothing so raucous as last night. Maybe we can go someplace smaller." Carla looked at the other crew members, who nodded in agreement.

The guide took them to a Gnoshian café where they served pastries and hot beverages, mostly for loading bay workers and Cathardi soldiers. "Inhabitants of the station are normally late risers. Only a few eating establishments are open this early."

The only table that provided enough seating for them all was in the corner, near a window overlooking the central area. A large burly male, who appeared to weigh three hundred pounds and was taller than Ray, came to the table and greeted them in Cathardi. "Welcome strangers, I am Corvosincovo. May I interest you in some of our kalich fruit pastries?"

The earthlings looked at the guide quizzically.

"It is the bright red fruit you ate last night. Extremely sweet when baked in the light bread here."

"That will be perfect," Carla said. "Do you serve lattes here as well?" The server stared blankly. "A hot beverage made from a slightly bitter roasted tree nut. Mixed with steamed bovine milk and often flavored with various syrups."

"I must apologize, but I don't make lattes, but I do have a hot fusion of orba bark and the milk of domesticated Gnoshian kafkafs. I think you will like it."

"Sounds good. Bring some for all of us," Carla said.

"Did you see the size of his arms?" Ray asked. "I would hate to bump into him in a dark alley."

The big man returned with a tray piled high with pastries and a large steaming jar of dark liquid. The pastries had a bite that offset some of the sweetness of the fruit, and the orba bark drink was smooth and tasty without the bitterness of coffee.

Josh finished his drink and looked around the table. Kim and Carla were smiling and talking about the station. "We have the rest of the day to ourselves," Josh spoke up. "What do you plan to do? Remember, the pleasure houses and gambling establishments are off limits."

"Kim and I are going shopping," Carla said.

"With all these shops, we have to buy something," Kim added.

"I'm going to the area with the acrobats and games," Ray said. "Who wants to join me?"

"Count me in," Steve said.

"Me too," added Jason.

"Okay then, we will meet outside our quarters at 1900 hours for dinner. Stay out of trouble. I am going to explore the docks," Josh said.

Josh walked to the first of the shops with Carla and Kim. When they went in, he continued through the metal doors that led to the central tower and took an elevator to the topmost section of the station. He found a café overlooking the bay that was attended by a Melal, where he sat and watched the activity below. Equipment moved cargo around the bay, often from one freighter to another. People disembarked while others boarded various ships. The noise of the equipment warning beeps and men hollering echoed around the huge open area.

Freighter crews came into the café and drank what Josh assumed was an alcoholic beverage. After one or two rounds, their conversation would get animated and occasionally loud. Most spoke Cathardi, so he listened to the conversations he could understand. He sipped his own hot, sweetened Cathardi tea in silence.

"The Cathardi are so paranoid. I cannot believe their security requirements. They make it as difficult as possible to get here, especially from the frontiers. It took us three jumps just to reach this station." A Melal officer complained to another alien. Josh didn't recognize the species.

"I know just what you mean," the alien said and gave a detailed description of the location of the frontier mining planet where his ship had picked up their cargo of refined platinum. "Then they won't allow us to carry it any closer to their home world."

"I don't know of a single non-Cathardi who has taken cargo to their planet. They bring all of it into this station or another one. Then they load it onto smaller Cathardi ships for the last leg. It is such a waste of time," the officer continued.

Josh listened as they complained about the Cathardi not allowing off-worlders on their planet and the security issues and unnecessary jumps. After a while, the complaints got repetitious, so Josh walked to another gathering spot. He spent the rest of the day listening to conversations and trying various refreshments. Occasionally, he would talk to other customers. The Melal were friendly and talkative if given the chance and spoke Cathardi. As he listened, he began gathering information on other planets and races that frequented the station. And, since he was the first of his race they had seen, they were full of questions about him and Earth. Unlike the Melal, the Cathardi were tight-lipped and did not offer any information, barely speaking in public settings.

That afternoon, Josh sat alone at a small table in a crowded café listening to the surrounding discussions when a Melal stopped at his table. "May I join you? The place is nearly full," he asked in Cathardi.

"Please do. My name is Josh. And yours?"

"Faili, I am the commander of the large freighter you see down there." He pointed to the left, where Josh could see the top of the freighter over the smaller one in the nearer bay. "Where are you from? I don't think I have met anyone of your race."

"I am from a planet we call Earth. We are new to interstellar travel. I am one of the first from my planet to travel this far. I pilot a diplomatic shuttle."

The Melal's head tilted to the right and his brows scrunched. "Where is Earth located? I haven't seen it on any of the star charts I use."

Josh explained Earth's location in terms of jump coordinates. "It is new to the Cathardi. We just completed our first orbital station, so it may not be on the charts yet."

"From the coordinates you gave, I can understand that. It is a long way from most Cathardi outposts. Are you enjoying your stay at our station?"

"So far. We are only going to be here today and tomorrow before we depart. Can I buy you another drink?"

"Thank you." Faili signaled the server, who made his way over to the table.

Josh looked at his new friend. "What are you drinking?"

"Melal Lingal Ale."

"Bring two." Josh handed his voucher to the server. Then, wanting to know more he asked, "Where did you pick up your cargo?"

"Out on the frontier, a planet called Bapto. It is one of the few planets where they found a stable isotope of the super-heavy element used to power the gravity drive. There is no orbiting station, so shuttles bring everything to the ships from a space-port on the surface. It is a wild place with limited Cathardi control. They have a cruiser orbiting and a small force on the surface used to keep order among the miners. You see all the different races here in the café, on Bapto there are at least three times that many. Lonely miners wanting some fun fill the pleasure houses. My friend Taibon owns the largest pleasure house on Bapto. If you ever make it there and want to know what is happening, he is the one to ask."

"Is Taibon a Melal?"

"Yes, he is Melal. He ran a similar business on this station for years but was tired of all the Cathardi restrictions and immi-grated to Bapto. If ferrying diplomats around becomes boring, you can sign on to a freighter and go to Bapto. I will give you a letter of introduction to Taibon."

"I just might do that."

Before Josh could ask another question, two Cathardi military officers interrupted him. "Captain, you need to come with us."

"But I have to meet my crew."

"We have already taken them to the Commander. You will come with us now."

They escorted Josh to a briefing room on one of the military levels of the station. The shuttle crews were standing before a table occupied by the senior station commander, several additional Cathardi officers, along with a couple of Melal officials, and Liria. All stood around the table.

The ranking officer greeted the crew formally and asked them to be seated. "You must understand our position," he began. "The Cathardi have survived and thrived in the universe because we guard against the incursion of foreign beliefs. We have seldom allowed anyone who is not a Cathardi to approach our home world. The only time we permitted an alien to pilot a jump into our space, resulted in a forty-year war. Since then, we have not allowed other races access to the location. However, against my strong objections, you will be the second. If the Ompresti had not insisted, we would have prevented you from proceeding with this ill-conceived mission. She overruled us. So, you may continue the mission as planned. But you will spend the rest of your stay being briefed on protocols for entering Cathardi space. You must pay close attention and follow the instructions precisely. There is no room for error. Consider yourselves confined to your quarters until departure."

Cathardi officers escorted them back to their quarters and stationed guards outside their doors.

At breakfast, the crew sat in a conference room. "What is going on?" Jason asked.

"Do they think we are their enemies?" added Steve.

"I don't know," Josh said. "I heard the freighter crews talk about how the Cathardi are extremely careful with who they allow into their home world. It is unusual for us to be allowed to travel there. Let's relax until the jump and then we may learn more."

"What is Liria's involvement? Didn't the Commander say the only reason he allowed us to proceed was she ordered it?" Kim said.

"I don't think she 'ordered' it," Carla said. "But he said she vouched for us. I think she's more influential than we realize."

"They're not honest with us," Josh said. "They are hiding more than just the location of their home world. The longer this mission takes, the less I trust them."

"Now, who is being paranoid?" Sean said. "We can talk with the Cathardi crew members once we are on the shuttles. Since we will already go into their space, they may tell us more."

I would like to know more about Liria. Why does she have so much pull? How does the sisterhood fit into the Cathardi culture and government? Can she take over my mind? How come I never noticed how beautiful she is? I hope we learn more.

Chapter 7

As he had done at each stop during the mission, Josh greeted Liria and her entourage as they boarded the shuttle early the next morning. A Cathardi officer followed them and handed him a packet.

"These are the final jump coordinates. Do not open them until you receive authorization," she said. "Lieutenant Taral has instructions to ensure you follow these instructions."

After they cleared the station and the surrounding traffic, they received a communication from the Melal station with the jump start location and an order that all crew members had to remain at their stations for the two-hour cruise to the starting point.

After the jump into the Cathardi system, the scout ships requested a special clearance code, which the shuttles transmitted, before they led them to the Cathardi light cruiser. This ship was like the one that had brought their forces to Earth.

On board, the ship commander welcomed them aboard. "Lieutenant Oina will escort you to the observation lounge, where you must remain until we arrive at Cathardi."

The lieutenant smiled. "Please come with me." She led them to a transport tube that took them to the observation lounge, which contained a dozen white oval tables, each surrounded by four sky-blue chairs. A refreshment bar along the inner bulkhead held a large variety of fresh fruits and vegetables, as well as bottles of beverages and urns of the Cathardi tea. The passengers and shuttle crews sampled the refreshments and settled into groups of three to four and talked. Josh and his crew sat at one table next to the table where Carla's crew sat.

Liria walked up to their table. "May I join you?"

"Sure," Josh answered and stood to get an empty chair from the table behind him. Josh struggled to keep the erotic images out of his mind, but they cleared when he felt the vessel speeding up. "We're moving now."

Large doors opened on the outer bulkhead to reveal windows with a magnificent view of the stars streaming by them.

Liria explained what each of the fruits and vegetables were and where they originated on Cathardi. She also told them what she liked about each and explained the spiritual significance of the bottled juices and the tea to the Cathardi. Her eyes sparkled and Josh heard the excitement in her voice as she told of her home culture. Outwardly, she seemed happy to be going home, but he could sense an undercurrent of sadness. *Why do I sense her sadness?*

"Will your family be there to meet you when we arrive?" Kim asked.

Liria was silent for a moment, then replied, "Thank you for asking, but no. I have no family as you refer to it. I am an orphan. My parents died when I was only a child. The Sisterhood became my family. The Creator is my father, and he never leaves me. But I am happy to return after so many years. I like your world, but its customs and people are still strange to me. It will be nice to be back in the familiar culture, even if only for a short time."

"I am sorry, I did not know." Kim's smile left.

"I did not expect you to know, and I appreciate your concern. That is one thing I have learned about your people on this trip. You have concern for others. Thank you."

It took a moment before the conversation resumed and the awkwardness waned. An hour later, Liria pointed to the windows. "Look. The Cathardi solar system is coming into view. You can just see the six planets. Cathardi is the moderate size one-fourth from our sun." Josh watched as the system became clear. The two inner planets were smaller, and the third was almost identical in size to Cathardi. The fifth planet was slightly smaller, and the sixth was a red gas giant with a magnificent series of rings. He felt the vibrations as the vessel decelerated. They passed through the ring system of the gas giant and slowed more noticeably when they reached the smaller fifth planet. Josh could see artificial satellites orbiting the planet.

"Are the satellites inhabited? Josh asked Liria.

"Yes, we have satellites orbiting all four of the outer planets, and we inhabit all of them. The third planet also sustains life with some accommodations as well," she told them.

Even before they could clearly distinguish Cathardi's features, they saw its beauty. Only a few clouds were covering the surface, so they could see the blue water that covered over eighty percent of the planet. Expanses of ocean separated the two large, very green continents. Both continents were in the temperate zone, one in the Northern hemisphere and the other in the Southern hemisphere. He also saw chains of large islands dotting the oceans. The planet looked very inviting to life. As they approached, they circled to the dark side of the planet and the lights of the cities were clear, scattered over the surface on the continents and islands like those on Earth. Josh heard 'oohs' from the Earth delegation. Just as they were about to enter the day side of the planet, a large orbiting station similar in design to the one above Melal came into view.

"We will dock there," Liria told them.

Minutes later, the doors closed over the viewing windows. Josh felt the maneuvering thrusters position the ship for docking. After the ship was secure, the commander entered with several officers to escort them to the station. At the end of the main transport tube, guards stopped them. After they announced the Earth delegates in both Cathardi and English, the guards let them pass, though Josh, Carla, and the other crew members went through unannounced.

In the main passageway, several dignitaries met them. One, a much older Cathardi sister greeted each of them personally and, like Liria, she held onto Josh's hand. He sensed her probing his thoughts, and he did not resist. When she released him, she said, "Welcome to Cathardi, welcome. May the Creator's peace be upon you and all you have left behind. I am Moira, a member of the ruling council, and I will be your liaison during your stay here."

As she was speaking, they announced the passengers from Josh's shuttle. The crowd of Cathardi filling the station immediately went silent. Liria stepped out into the passageway and the entire crowd kneeled and bowed their heads. As she walked by, many gently touched her robe. Even the old sister who had greeted them bowed as she walked by.

"Who is she?" Josh asked her.

"Liria? Many believe she is a prophetess, and that the Creator speaks through her. They revere her. No seer in their lifetimes had predicted the existence of another world. Her gift has increased the Sisterhood's influence on the council, which some of the other factions resent. She will not find normalcy on Cathardi. That is a major reason she stays on Earth. She does not believe she deserves this adulation and will return with you to Earth after the conference."

***

Liria looked at all the people assembled, waiting. *Maybe they have forgotten me. I hope they are here for the other delegates and not me.* Her stomach churned while she waited for her name to be called. When it was, the entire crowd dropped to their knees. She wanted to run through them to get out as soon as possible, but she had to allow them to see her. She sensed their adoration, often feeling them touch her as she passed. *They should not worship me. I am only a tool, an imperfect tool. I need to talk with Moira and the other elders about this misplaced adoration and the uncomfortable feelings aroused by the encounter with Josh. Men's feelings scare me. They are often carnal or violent and remind me of my father. But with Josh, it is different. Though often carnal, his thoughts do not frighten me, and the feelings that he arouses are exciting. I need help. I need clarity.*

A station officer led her through the main hall to a side passage, guarded by two other officers, to her quarters. Another guard stood outside the door to her room. "The Elder Moira requested we keep people from interrupting you," her escort said. "You are free to move about the station if you desire. One of us will follow and be available if you need help with the crowd."

"Thank you, though I will most likely remain in my quarters until the shuttle leaves for the planet." She went into her room and closed the door.

He said I could move about the station, yet I feel like a prisoner here. Guards at my door and people clamoring to get to me. I need Moira's wisdom.

She washed her face and sat on a mat to meditate. Moira would be by soon, and they could talk. Her mind turned to Josh and the encounter on the ship. She replayed the images in her mind. His fingers were on her cheek, his lips touching her lips. *Stop! I cannot allow my mind to go there. I must remain clear-headed and prepare for my meeting with the Council.*

She got up and poured herself a cup of tea and sat at the small table to write out her presentation when there was a knock on the door. "You may enter."

Moira came through and sat across the table from her. "Ompresti, it is good to have you back. Though I sensed the greeting from the people upset you."

"Thank you, Reverend Elder."

"Enough of the formalities. Liria, you look troubled. How can I help?" She leaned on the table to be closer to Liria.

"The greeting upset me. I do not deserve such adoration." Liria sat back in her chair. "I have been away for so long and still the prophecy is unfulfilled. Was I wrong?"

"My child, did you expect it to be that easy?" Moira reached her hand across the table. "What do the sacred texts tell us about the prophets?"

Liria took her hand. "They all suffered not only doubt and unbelief but also rejection and even torture. Their lives were hard."

"The Creator works in ways that are beyond our comprehension. The prophecy has yet to be fulfilled because Cathardi is not in danger and does not yet need a savior." She smiled at

Liria and met her steady gaze. "I doubt you will be tortured, but the populace is fickle. Though they adore you currently, their adoration could turn to scorn quickly. You are wise to stay on Earth for now."

"Thank you. I intend to return to Earth with the shuttles." She paused and her lips puckered. "There is a personal matter that troubles me as well. I need your wisdom to guide me."

The older woman nodded, then listened as Liria recounted the incident with Josh on the voyage. She included other times when the erotic thoughts returned. "Even today, just before you arrived. I was meditating on my thoughts for the conference and my mind went to the visions. I am confused. How can I be so connected to someone not of our race?"

"I met the pilot earlier. He is quite receptive to our thoughts and feelings. I sensed there was more to him than there appears. His sensitivity is rare, but not unique. There have been instances recorded in the ancient texts of aliens with similar attributes." Pausing, she let their minds connect so she could get an accurate sense of Liria's struggle. "You are young, and you have no experience in sexual matters. These can be exciting and tempting, but you need to maintain your focus. You cannot allow them to cloud your judgment. Do you think he is the one to fulfill the prophecy?"

"I do." Liria stood and paced. "Since I first read the report about his efforts on a training exercise, I have wondered. Then when I met him, I sensed there was something special about him. I think he is the one, but I am confused by my feelings."

"What does he think?"

"I do not know. He does not trust us. I think if I tell him about the prophecy, he will reject it." Liria sat back down.

"You must tell him," Moira said. "Even if he rejects it. The creator will prepare his heart when it is time. If he is the one. If not, He will prepare your heart. You must remain true to your calling." She stood. "I will have him brought to you so you can tell him."

"Wait—" It was too late. Moira was already outside the door. *Now what do I do? Will he understand? Can I control my urges?* Her mind raced. She tried to slow her heart rate and clear her head. *The Creator will prepare his heart or mine. He is in control. I am just a messenger.*

This time, she got up and opened the door herself when she heard the knock. "Captain, come in." She gestured for him to go to the table, sensing her own suppressed urges. "I know this is as uncomfortable for you as it is for me."

"Ompresti, why did you want to see me?" He sat with his arms crossed at his chest.

Here goes. "I need to tell you why I led the Cathardi forces to Earth. You may already know some of the story, but not all of it. Please relax and allow me to explain it to you." Liria then told him the story of the prophecy and all that went into the expedition to find the planet that she now knew as Earth. "You saw the reaction of the people when we arrived. They believe I have returned with the one who will save our planet even though our planet does not currently need saving. It is hard for me to be here and tell them I may have failed." She stopped.

"What does that have to do with me? You know I don't believe in your religious mumbo-jumbo."

"I am getting to that. I said I *may* have failed. But I believe the Creator has chosen you to save my people."

"Ha! You must be kidding. I don't know your people. You are out of your mind. What makes you think I could ever be this messiah?" She didn't need to see the smirk on his face to know how he felt.

"There is something special about you," she said. "I felt it the first time we met. Your ability to sense my pheromones the night you came down the stairs while I prayed also points to your uniqueness. I know you do not believe me, but I am asking you to be open to the leadings of the Creator."

"Your Creator doesn't need me. I don't want to be your savior. But, thanks to your pheromones or whatever, I want you physically. You have invaded my mind, and I feel you want to control my thoughts and actions. I will be glad when this mission is over. I had hoped you would remain here. But Moira said you would be returning with us."

"Captain, I am sorry. I knew this was a bad idea. I will not trouble you further. Please forgive me." *He cannot know my desires are as strong as his.*

"Is that all?"

"Yes." He got up and left without another word. *That was worse than I expected. I must remember that I am not in control.*

Only the Creator can reveal His plans, even to those who do not believe.

***

Though they allowed the Earth crews to venture to the Cathardi home world, they required them to remain aboard the station, not allowing them to go to the surface of the planet. Unlike the Melal station, the Cathardi station was quiet, with limited recreational opportunities. They found little aboard the station to relieve the boredom. Josh was glad when the conference ended. Now, they could finally leave. He sat alone at the viewing windows in the station's lounge. He overheard the conversations of the delegates from Earth. Many discussed the similarities between the Cathardi and Earth belief systems, while others talked about the beauty of the Cathardi home world.

One of the older Cathardi sisters came to his table. "May I join you, Captain?" Moira paused, waiting for his response. He pointed to the chair at the table. "I understand you had a conversation with Liria before the conference."

"Yes," he said. *Let me guess. She is just as crazy as the Ompresti.*

"You must think her belief that you are the answer to a prophecy is strange. I would like to tell you a little about her history if you are willing?" Moira said. Josh didn't answer. "I met Liria when she was very young, after an extremely traumatic event in her life. Her father piloted a freighter from the frontier to the Melal station. Her mother worked in traffic control at the station. They had a volatile relationship involving substance abuse and rumors of infidelity. One day he returned, and they fought. Her father struck her mother, knocking her down. According to the report, she struck her head on the counter and died. The father was so distraught, he threw himself over the railing above the loading dock, killing himself."

Josh still didn't say anything. But she had aroused his interest. *No wonder the Ompresti is strange. I know how hard it is to lose a parent.*

"You should know violence among the Cathardi is so rare that her father's actions caused a huge stir among the officials and the civilian population on the station," she said. "Though Liria did not physically witness the events, she sensed everything that happened. Her connection with them was strong. Even stronger than her connection with you."

She looked into Josh's eyes, apparently trying to read his feelings before she continued. "Her presence on the station was a reminder to the Cathardi authorities of those terrible events. Nobody knew what to do with her. Neither her mother nor her father had any known living family. There was no place at the station for her. They contacted the Sisterhood on Cathardi. The station officials thought she might have a chance at our school, though I don't think they believed it. Even then, she was strange, detached.

"As head of the school, I went to get her from the station. On the way, I went through the information the station authorities had provided before the shuttle docked. I wanted to be prepared when we met, given the horrific circumstances of her parents' deaths. Her reaction surprised me. She was expecting me and was ready to leave the station. When I looked closely at her for the first time, I could not recall ever seeing such blue eyes. Except for her eyes, she had typically fine features, a thin straight nose, a small mouth, high cheekbones, and sandy blond hair."

"I visualize her being as skinny as a post," Josh said. "On earth. Young girls are often very thin."

"That is true, she was," the elder said, then continued. "During our trip, Liria spent every available free minute of the voyage in the observation lounge. When we finally entered the Cathardi system, she watched as each of the planets passed. After we arrived at the school, I sensed it was everything Liria had hoped it would be. It was warm, near the tropics, lush, with white beaches and crystal-clear water. The primary facility was on a hill overlooking the large lagoon. The manicured grounds, with cut green grass, covered the hill down to the semicircular white sand beach.

"Liria tried to fit in, but the girls at the school did not differ from the girls at the station. Liria was an outsider. Most of the girls were from wealthy families getting a religious education to prepare them for marriage. They laughed at Liria's naivety about the home world and Cathardi culture. They teased her about her 'lunatic' father. Her tactless honesty isolated her. She confronted them with the truth about their feelings, regardless of the circumstances or others. Despite this, she seemed at peace. She was used to isolation.

"She worked hard at her chores and in the classes. It did not take the sisters long to realize she had a special gift. The ability to sense the truth in others was a skill the sisters tried to develop in those who would pursue a place within the order. Liria had this ability naturally. She had a faith that was beyond her years. She believed the Creator spoke to her, which caused some consternation among the elders at the school."

"On Earth when someone says, 'God told them something.' We think they are lying or delusional. That's how I felt after talking with Liria," Josh said. "I don't mean to be disrespectful, but that is how I feel."

"We can feel the same way," Moira said. "But one day, she predicted a tidal wave would strike the beach at our school. We thought she was disturbed. The earthquake and tidal wave killed forty-three students and teachers. Liria spent two days in her room. She blamed herself for not being able to save them.

"In the months that followed, we met weekly, and I instructed her in the lives of the ancient prophets. Their persecution amazed her. Still, she continued to have visions. She predicted the sudden illness and death of a popular young teacher the day before it happened. She revealed the misconduct of the groundskeeper, who was secretly skimming funds from the school. Younger students sought her out for advice on not only studies but also relationships. She always took the time to listen. Her physical differences enhanced her spiritual aura. Though not beautiful by Cathardi's standards, she was at least two inches taller than most, and she was too heavy. Her stature made her appear superior. She became the youngest student ever to achieve Sisterhood.

"We assigned her to the capital, where she advised the Elders on the council concerning various matters. She continued to have dreams and visions, which she shared with them. In every case, her predictions proved accurate. Then one day she came to see me at the school with a disturbing dream about a prophecy. *Doom. Doom. The choice is yours. You worship me with your tongue, but in your hearts, you say, 'We are safe. We are secure.' Your pride will defeat you. You must humble yourself and find the one not of your people: the one I have chosen, the one who will deliver you from the Doom you have seen. Listen to the one you will not hear, for your doom is near.*

"The prophecy disturbed me, so I sought help from other elders. It turned out to be an ancient prophecy that was forgotten by most of us. But we found it in a one-thousand-year-old document that Liria could not have known. The people do not know of the prophecy, but they know she predicted the existence and location of your planet. So, they call her a prophet."

"So, you're telling me that Liria is a prophet, and she believes I am the *one not of your people.*" Josh shook his head.

"Yes. Though your connection, and her feelings for you, may have influenced her thinking," the elder sister said. "She has been waiting for over six years to find the one, and whether it is you or not, I cannot say. But she will find the one when it is time. I ask that you not judge her harshly. I sense your feelings for her are confusing to you. You will need to give them time to subside." She stood and prepared to leave. "Remember this, Captain. She trusts you with her life. I do not know why, but she does. Hopefully, you are worthy of that trust."

"I will try." Josh didn't know what else to say. Moira walked away.

It just gets more confusing. Now I have to deal with the possibility that Liria isn't crazy. But the one thing I know is that I am not their savior!

CHAPTER 8

The trip home from Cathardi had been, so far, uneventful. They spent a night at the Melal station before they retraced their steps. When they returned to the Cathardi heavy cruiser, their reception was less formal. Liria spoke with Josh. "Captain, I have not talked with you since we spoke at the Cathardi station. May we talk now?"

"Yes, Ompresti." She took the seat next to him and the other sisters stood a short distance away. They appeared to Josh to be acting as a fence to keep Liria from being disturbed.

"I ask you to forgive me," she said. "I am not known to be very tactful., and I often speak my mind before thinking."

"I have been told that." Josh had to smile.

"I am not sure you are the one since I have received no confirmation from the Creator. I may just be hoping." Her deep blue eyes seemed to penetrate his mind. "I spent time with the elders of my order while on Cathardi. They confirmed the connection we have could cloud my judgment. I hope that once we return, we can become friends. You can teach me a lot about your people."

"I would be open to that, Ompresti. I would like to get to know you better as well." He blushed as he thought of his visions of her.

"I will have someone contact you after we return. Thank you, Captain." He sensed her unease. *That wasn't very cool. I probably scared her.*

Now, as they prepared for their last jump, Josh smiled at the thought of returning home. "I can't wait to get to the mountains where I can spend some time fishing the Gunnison River. What about you guys?"

"Me, I'm going to go sailing along the coast," said Steve.

Jason piped in, "I want to take a long road trip. Maybe I'll drive the old Route 66 across the country."

"I just want to go home," Kim said. "I miss the warm sunshine and the wheat fields. But most of all, I miss my family, especially my mom."

"I know we are all eager to get home and enjoy ourselves, but we will be celebrities," Steve said. "They will probably have us scheduled for a lot of public appearances."

Josh began entering the numbers for the next jump, listening to the surrounding conversations. *Eventually, I will have time. I can see the sun reflecting off the river as I watch the line drifting in the current. I can feel the trout fight as I set the hook. It seems like ages since I've been on the river.*

"Hey Jason," Steve called out. "I bet you want to get back to that Melal sweetie. You spent the whole layover with her when we got back there."

Before Jason could answer, he heard a blood-curdling scream come from the lower level. Terror and anguish flooded Josh's mind with images of bodies lying everywhere; the ground stained with blood. There were screams and gunshots all around. He shook his head to clear it, then flew down the stairs with Steve right behind him.

Liria stood in the chapel looking at her hands, weeping. When Josh reached the bottom of the stairs, she collapsed.

"Get one of the other sisters!" he told Steve as he picked Liria up off the floor. She was lighter than he expected. He carried her and laid her on a padded bench in the galley. Then he went to the first aid kit for the smelling salts. Bending over her, he broke the capsule near her nose and lightly waved it. Liria came to and jerked up to a seated position. Her eyes were wide, staring past him, and he sensed the fear she felt as she turned her gaze to Josh.

"Something terrible has happened!" she sobbed.

Josh held her hand. "What was it?"

"I... I don't know." She turned her face to the wall. "Many people are dead. I do not know where or when, but I am afraid. A sense of dread overwhelmed me as I was praying. I felt the weight of thousands of hurting and dying individuals. But unlike most of my dreams, there were no specifics, just a general feeling. I am afraid something terrible has just happened or is about to happen. I do not think we should make the next jump."

"There was nothing specific?" Josh asked as he continued to hold her hand, thinking back to the conversation he had had with Moira.

"No."

"I'm not sure I can stop our return without more than a vague feeling. Can you be more specific?" *Maybe I should get Taral's advice?*

"No, but I am afraid," she said. "Perhaps I am overreacting." She squeezed his hand. "I am not so frightened now. Your presence is reassuring. I will be fine."

Josh stayed with her, holding her hand until she seemed completely relaxed and was ready to go to her quarters. He walked with her up the stairs to her berth. *It's odd. I am touching her, and I hold her, but there isn't any arousal. Yet I can sense her feelings as if they were my own. She is very frightened and confused.*

After leaving her at her door, he went to the bridge to complete the jump calculations. The Cathardi crewmen had manned their station ready for the jump.

"Can I speak with you, Taral?" Josh said and led him out of the bridge. Once in the passageway, he told Taral of Liria's vision. "What do you think?"

"Based on what you have told me and my limited knowledge of the Ompresti's history, I believe you made the correct decision," the lieutenant said. "She is known for the accuracy and precision of her prophecies, so the uncertainty of the vision's timing leaves you little choice."

"Thank you, Taral. Let's get back to our stations and make this jump. I'm sure the other shuttle is wondering about the delay."

***

Josh remained conscious and felt only a slight disorientation during the jump. He was alert as they entered normal space. He could see Carla's shuttle ahead of him. *What the heck is that?* Directly in front of her shuttle were two barely visible large, black, ominous-looking shapes. The first changed course to intercept Carla's shuttle.

"Carla. Carla. Come in Carla." Josh called into the radio, as he watched the second shape start toward his shuttle. Josh reached over and shook his copilot. "Taral, wake up."

He awoke just as the first of the black ships fired some kind of laser at Carla's shuttle. With no shields or defenses, the shuttle disintegrated in a burst of flames and debris. Next to him, Kim screamed. He used the maneuvering thrusters, altering their course, and rapidly keyed jump coordinates into the console, setting off the jump alarms. The jump was almost instantaneous, taking them out of visual range of the black ships, but Josh knew that if they had any sensors, they would be on them momentarily. Taral and Kim were just regaining consciousness, but he couldn't wait for everyone to recover. He made a second jump, knowing the quick jump would increase the crew's disorientation and other jump effects.

As they left normal space, Josh saw a singularity form, showing that at least one black ship followed them. He made four more jumps in quick succession, each one a little farther than the one before, and each one in a different direction. After the fourth jump, he stopped to allow the crew and passengers time to recover.

"Everyone, passengers and crew assemble in the galley," Josh announced over the intercom. Then he helped Kim, who seemed in shock, down the stairs to the galley. Everyone was moving, pacing, shaking their arms, or twisting to help relieve the jump effects. All the sisters gathered around one table rubbing their arms and looking puzzled.

"What's going on?" Steve asked when the bridge crew entered the galley.

"That is what I would like to know," Josh answered, looking directly at Liria.

"They killed Carla and the others!" Kim yelled through her sobs.

"Who killed them? How?" Liria took a step toward Josh.

"I thought you might know," Josh said, still staring at her intensely. *You know more than you have told us.*

"Tell me what happened," Liria said, turning away from his gaze.

"When we came out of the jump, there were two alien ships already there. They were larger than our shuttles, but not as big as the Cathardi cruiser we visited. Black or very dark with no markings, they appeared very ominous and changed course to come toward us. Then, without warning, they fired on Carla disintegrating her shuttle," Josh finished.

Everyone was stunned. Steve plopped down onto a bench. "What?"

"The black ships attacked and killed our friends." Josh sat and stared at his hands.

Jason paced. They were all silent for a few minutes.

Liria broke the silence. "Can you give me more details about the ship's appearance?"

"Though hard to see, they seemed to have three round tapered sections. The center section was longer than the outer sections. All the tapers appeared to end in weapons systems with additional weapons on the flanks and in the stern." Josh visualized the vessels and opened his mind to Liria.

"I have never seen the vessels you described. Lieutenant Taral, can you give more details?" she said.

"No Ompresti. It is as the captain described. I was barely conscious when the attack happened," Taral said. "I am not familiar with the vessels, but they sound like Urlak vessels. I know little about them. It has been decades since we first encountered them, and we have avoided contact with them. They are very warlike."

"If the Urlak are in the Earth system, we need to return to Cathardi-controlled space, immediately. They should not be near Earth! The Urlak will slaughter all the inhabitants of your planet. This may be what I sensed before the jump," Liria said.

Josh jumped up. "Why didn't any of you warn us about them? Will the Cathardi help my people?"

"We must return to Melal. I will use my influence to convince them to help," Liria said, but Josh sensed her panic.

She's afraid they won't help. They are afraid of the Urlak. "Okay, everyone, back to your post. We are going back to the Melal station," Josh ordered. He stayed with Kim and Jason, sending Taral and Wyn to the bridge. Liria joined him to help Kim. The other sisters remained in the galley. Their nervous conversations had become more animated at the mention of the Urlak.

"I can't believe they just killed them for no reason!" Kim said through her sobs.

With his arm around her shoulder, he said, "We are safe. We will get to the Cathardi. They can help us."

When he got to her room, he gave her a mild sedative he had grabbed from the medical cabinet in the galley. "Take this. It will help you relax." Then he stayed with her, waiting for her to calm down before leaving her with Liria and going to the bridge.

The Cathardi knew about the Urlak but said nothing. My friends are dead, and Liria is still holding something back.

Once at his station, he checked Taral's calculations to take them back to the Cathardi warship. He didn't want to spend any more time than necessary cruising in normal space, because he was uncertain about the Urlak ability to follow. They still needed thirty minutes before reaching a safe jump point. With

Taral taking care of things on the bridge, he went down the passageway to Liria.

"I was expecting you," she said as she stepped out of Kim's quarters. "We can go to my quarters." When they got there, she pointed to the bunk where he could sit. "You have a lot of questions I cannot answer. But I will tell you all I know." She related the history of the Urlak-Cathardi meeting and the surprise attacks by the Urlak on the Cathardi ships in the months that followed.

"Captain," Josh heard Taral call over the intercom. "Jump point in five minutes."

"I'll be right there," Josh answered through the com unit and got up to leave, but Liria took his hand.

"I am afraid! The Urlak should not be there!" she said and released his hand.

Josh returned to the bridge and prepared for the jump.

When the shuttle arrived, the Cathardi scouts were less than cordial at the unexpected appearance of the lone shuttle, and the mention of the Urlak only heightened their wariness. It was several hours after additional scouts arrived before they finally escorted the shuttle to the warship. Josh and his crew sat in a guarded briefing room before being questioned by the Commander. Kim broke down sobbing during the questioning, digging her nails into his hand as he answered the questions. Unfortunately, only Josh had any clear memories of the event because the others didn't recover from the jump in time. When he finished, the Cathardi commander looked at him in disbelief.

"Why are you the only one that remembers all the events? How did an unarmed, unshielded shuttle escape two Urlak warships? I need to confirm your story with the Ompresti. Remain here." He ordered and went to speak to Liria, leaving them alone.

Why are they treating me like a criminal? All they need to do is send ships to check on the Urlak vessels. How come, every time there is a controversy, they have to check with Liria?

An hour later, the commander returned, and said, "We are sending scouts to the location you gave us, as well as other locations in the system. We will find out the extent of the Urlak presence. The Ompresti verified your story, though, like the rest of your crew, she did not know the details. You may consider yourselves guests, but you must remain in your quarters or the recreation area at the end of the passageway." He turned and left the room.

Steve looked at Josh. "So, we are prisoners. What are they going to do to help Earth?"

"I don't think they will send any help to Earth. They are afraid of the Urlak," Josh answered. "And, given our current situation, there's not much we can do but follow orders."

CHAPTER 9

Garond sat on the bridge in the command seat, poised one step above the main deck of the Urlak cruiser's bridge. A dimly lit, circular compartment, the bridge had eight stations around the perimeter, with the command seat in the center. Two of his guards stood at attention just inside the door. His surly mood infected the crew. Most feared the commander, though all were the product of the Urlak Military training, and genetically engineered to be soldiers. Garond's aggression and deviousness gave him an unpredictability his crew feared. Powerfully built, like all Urlak, his short stature, barely two meters, belied a ruthless ambition and determination he used to rise quickly through the ranks. His compact build made him a formidable opponent in the challenge arena, and his dogged determination helped him to persist in the fight, even when the physical abilities of his opponent exceeded his.

He commanded one of four battle groups assigned to locate the cowardly Cathardi home world. Since first encountering the Cathardi forty years ago, the Urlak concentrated their efforts on finding the Cathardi home world. They were the only race to defeat the Urlak in a battle. But, after that battle, the Cathardi disappeared and had proved very elusive since.

Even when the Urlak conquered a world with a Cathardi presence, the inhabitants were no help. Garond continued to search the far reaches of the universe to find them. His orders were simple. Find the Cathardi homeworld at any cost. Use any method. The Urlak fleet awaits word to launch an assault to destroy the Cathardi forever.

Garond was a corporal on an outlying planet when the first encounter with the Cathardi occurred. He remembered the first contact. The advanced technology of the Cathardi allowed them to enter their system undetected by Urlak sensors. The ships seemed to appear out of a brief spatial anomaly. Surprised by the sudden appearance, they accepted the Cathardi professions of friendship, but within months, the Urlak scientists duplicated their drive systems and copied much of their technology.

The Cathardi were too naïve or too trusting to realize that Urlak had developed weapons capable of penetrating their defenses. Before the end of the first year, they had destroyed the Cathardi expeditionary fleet. The new drives, copied from the Cathardi, provided his people with an unlimited number of planets and races suitable for conquest. But, when the Urlak ventured into a Cathardi-controlled system, the Cathardi easily defeated them.

Now, the Urlak used caution when venturing into new systems. However, with their improved weapons, shields, and drives, the Urlak high command believed it was time to hunt and destroy the soft pale race. They must not fail. They must conquer.

"Commander." The communications officer interrupted his thoughts. "We have intercepted Cathardi communications from a nearby system."

"Alert sub-commander Morforn and have him report to the bridge." He hoped it was the break they needed. But his instincts told him it was not the Cathardi home world but another outpost on the edge of their territory.

"Commander." Sub-commander Morforn crossed his arms on his chest and bowed his head. "You sent for me."

Morforn's orange-tinged head reflected the dim light. Over time, Urlak scientists discovered the orange pigmentation increased the fear of the blandly colored populations they encountered and engineered it into their DNA along with the almost complete lack of body hair. Though taller than Garond at two and a third meters, Morforn had never challenged for leadership. He feared Garond, and he was loyal, an excellent second in command.

"Send scouts to determine the nature of the Cathardi presence. Have communication silence maintained until they return. We will hold our position."

"As you wish, commander." Morforn left the bridge.

When the scouts returned, Morforn reported. "The planet is relatively primitive, with only a minimal Cathardi military presence. We detected only one Cathardi cruiser and one smaller warship within the system. There is a small orbital station, but it appears unarmed."

"Send out additional scouts. I want to know the exact location of each of the Cathardi military vessels." He turned to the communications officer. "Have the command staff report, so we can plan the attack."

Though his instincts proved correct, the news disappointed him. Still, if they could surprise the Cathardi, they might capture an officer with enough rank to be of value. Their interrogation methods often proved successful even on stubborn subjects. With the seven ships in his command, one heavy cruiser, four light cruisers, and two planetary assault transports, Garond believed they could quickly overwhelm the Cathardi forces.

"Sub-commander Morforn," he began the officer's meeting. "You will lead the attack on the Cathardi cruiser. Take your two light cruisers and disable them as quickly as possible. Your approach must be undetected until it is too late." He highlighted the Cathardi positions in the target system projection. "Sub-commander Talor, you will command the other two light cruisers. Once the attack begins, you will put your ships between the other Cathardi warship and their cruiser. Do not let them escape. I will take our heavy cruiser and attack the orbital station. Remember, if they surrender, you are to allow it.

We want senior Cathardi officers for interrogation. After their surrender, kill the rest. Sub-commander Gaut, you will hold the planetary assault ships here until we eliminate the orbital defenses, and then you will bring them in to subdue the surface. You have your orders."

"Yes, Commander," they replied in unison.

The scouts reported no new military presence, as Garond ordered Morforn's light cruisers to begin the attack. He would attack in two. He hungered for battle. But settled for listening to the communications as the attack proceeded. The wait would prime his crew and assault troops for blood.

He visualized the Cathardi cruiser as it orbited the largest gas giant in the planetary system. Morforn's vessels planned to jump on the opposite side of the planet as close to the planet as possible. They reported their approach was undetected and moved behind one of the larger moons to wait for the heavy cruiser. The unsuspecting cruiser did not even have its shields up. Morforn attacked from below and the other light cruiser attacked from above. Within an hour, the heavy cruiser exploded when its gravity field generator took a direct hit. Morforn reported his light cruiser narrowly escaped being hit by debris. All but a few of the Cathardi fighters were aboard the cruiser, and the overpowering numbers of the Urlak fighters found and destroyed the others. No one escaped. *The Cathardi are so soft. No wonder they hid.*

Garond ordered the jump to begin the attack on the space station as soon as he heard the initial reports from Talor's ships.

They had intercepted the light cruiser and disabled it in minutes, destroying its engines and navigation and capturing its officers.

The only defenses his ship encountered were fighters, but their numbers were too few. His fighters held them away from the cruiser. He opened fire on the station, targeting the launch bays. The first two laser cannon shots breached the outer hull of the station ring, and the third shot hit the gravity generator in the center of the station. The explosion destroyed it, sending pieces into the atmosphere of the planet below.

"Commander," the officer on coms said. "Sensors show missile launches from the planet's surface."

He checked his tactical display. "Have laser weapons target the missiles and send additional fighters to destroy surface installations. Tell sub-commander Gaut to bring in the assault ships."

The lack of orbital defenses surprised Garond. *This must be a recent outpost. The Cathardi didn't deem it important enough to properly defend. We will get little information from the planet's inhabitants.*

"Have Gaut report as soon as his ships are in position," he said to the communication officer. "Are there any reports of bases on the planet's moon?"

"Reports from the fighters say there are only two small colonies that appear to be mining operations," the officer said.

Garond continued to monitor the tactical display even though it showed little action. When Gaut arrived with the planetary assault ships, they began the surface bombardment. Satisfied with their progress, he went to his quarters to wait for the Talor's prisoners. Morforn would set up defensive patrols just in case the Cathardi sent reinforcements.

***

"Commander," Morforn crossed his arms in salute. "Talor is here to report."

Garond stood as the sub-commander approached. "Report!"

Talor crossed his arms and went to one knee. "Commander, we were on patrol as ordered when two Cathardi shuttles appeared in our sector. We immediately changed course to attack before the jump effects wore off. I intercepted the first shuttle and destroyed it. But before we could get shots off, the second shuttle jumped. The other cruiser followed immediately, but by the time we followed, all we found was debris. The cruiser and the entire crew lost. We could not locate the Cathardi shuttle."

"How long after the shuttles appeared, did you first engage them?" Garond asked as he stepped down from the command station.

"It was less than two minutes, sir."

"Were the shuttles armed?" Garond walked behind the pilot.

"They did not appear to be armed, sir. If they were, they did not fire." Sweat beads glistened on Talor's forehead.

"How long did it take you to reach the shuttle's jump terminator?" Garond could not keep the growl out of his voice. *He is a coward and a liar.*

"Only five minutes, sir."

"You are telling me that two unarmed Cathardi shuttles jumped into a sector patrolled by two light cruisers, and one of them escaped, destroying one of our cruisers in the process?"

"Yes, sir, you can interview the crew if you doubt me."

"That won't be necessary." Garond reached behind his head and pulled his bytor. The short flat sword had a long cutting blade on one edge and an axe blade near the end or the other edge. A close combat weapon his race used to finish wounded enemies and to remove trophies from the dead bodies. He buried the axe blade into the pilot's skull. "Clear this trash from my bridge and execute his entire crew," He ordered Morforn as he wiped the blood from the weapon.

No Cathardi could recover from the jump effects that quickly. It was impossible. Even Urlak, with our genetic enhancements, required more time than that. I cannot have rumors spread that the Cathardi are immune to jump effects.

"What does sub-commander Gaut report from the surface?" He turned to the communications officer.

"Sir, sub-commander Gaut reports all assault forces have landed and the major population centers are under control. But the indigenous population has fled to the countryside and is fighting a guerrilla war. Progress has slowed and may take longer than expected. They are not as soft and helpless as their initial reaction led us to believe. They have formed small bands of resistance hiding in the demolished cities or countryside. Though primitive, their projectile weapons are effective against our shields. They ambush our forces and disappear. Our losses have been greater than expected."

This has been a disastrous campaign. No significant Cathardi prisoners. A cowardly sub-commander and a stalled invasion. This could occupy us for months. Maybe we should just move on. "Sub-commander Morforn, increase patrols in the system. The Cathardi will know we are here. I want no more surprises."

Three days since they entered the nearly defenseless system and not one piece of actionable intelligence. The Cathardi prisoners all died before they would divulge the location of the home world. He had watched the interrogation and seen them endure unimaginable pain. *I wonder if they even know its location. Surely some must, yet they all choose to die. Their indoctrination techniques must be effective. There must be another way.*

For now, they would stay and continue the assault, which provided some relief to the boredom for his troops. He needed to fight. He could get into the challenge ring, but who was ambitious enough to challenge him? Morforn and Gaut knew he could defeat them. He needed an ambitious junior officer. Maybe he should go to the surface. He had not collected a trophy in months. It might be the only way to keep from killing more junior officers.

CHAPTER 10

Two days after returning to the Cathardi cruiser, the commander called the shuttle crew into the briefing room. "We have confirmed that it was the Urlak who invaded your system. They were waiting for us at several jump points. Fortunately, we only lost one scout ship. We found debris that appears to be the remains of an Urlak light cruiser at the coordinates you gave us. The wreckage suggests a gravity field tore it apart. You left while they came through on their jump, and they were too close to you." The commander paced in front of the crew, staring at Josh. "We believe the combined gravity fields tore their ship apart. That was very lucky for you. However, the skill required to perform those jumps in such rapid succession is remarkable. We are sending you to the Melal space station for additional debriefing, while we prepare for the Urlak to move into this section."

"What about Earth?" Steve interrupted.

"We do not know the status of your planet, since we could not get close enough, but the Urlak had two planetary assault vessels in orbit along with a heavy cruiser. They destroyed the space station, and we know the Urlak do not take prisoners. They use other races for genetic materials only. There is not much hope for your planet." The commander continued to pace. "We believe by the time we assemble a sufficient force for a counterattack, the planet will be a total loss. I am sorry we will not be attempting. That is the high command's decision." The commander stopped, allowing the crew to absorb the decision. "I am told that once the debriefing is done, you are free to move about the station. And... if you want the opportunity to fight the Urlak, we are offering each of you a chance to join us in the Cathardi military."

The crew sat in silence. Josh was stunned. *They will not help us.*

"In other words," Jason finally broke the silence. "Everything and everyone we know is gone."

"That is most likely correct," the commander answered and shrugged his shoulders.

"If we don't join your military, what happens to us?" Josh hoped his anger didn't show in his voice. *They betrayed us, treating us like an early warning system when they knew about the threat.*

"You will be free on the station, having the same rights as any other citizen of the station. The Sisterhood continues to vouch for your trustworthiness concerning the information you possess. I will be in my ready room if you need anything before your shuttle departs." He finished and left the room.

"What are we going to do?" Steve asked.

"Join them, of course," Jason replied. "I want a chance to get back at those cowards for what they did to Carla."

"Sounds good to me," Steve said. "What about you two? Are you ready to sign on?"

"Not me," Josh said. "They betrayed us. They knew about the Urlak and said nothing. I don't want any part of them. You guys do what you want. Joining up is probably the best chance to get back at the Urlak. But it's not for me."

They all looked at Kim. "I can't." Tears streamed down her cheeks. "I... I don't think I could face seeing someone else I know disintegrated. I can't fight."

Later that day, the Cathardi put the Earth crew on a shuttle to the Melal station. Kim held onto Josh's arm. He realized she didn't feel safe in space. So, he let her hold on to him. *She's still in shock. It will take a while for her to recover once we get to the station.* During the jumps, they went to the galley and strapped into adjoining seats.

When they disembarked at the Melal station, the station commander and a Cathardi sister met them. "Welcome back. I know you will have questions," the commander started. "We are trying to monitor the situation around your home world and will keep you updated. Meanwhile, we have arranged for quarters for each of you. Your first debriefing session will be later this afternoon."

The sister took them to their quarters in the Cathardi ring. "These are only temporary until the debriefing is complete. I or another sister are available should you need anything."

"We should be fine," Josh said. "The sooner this is over the better."

"Very well, I will return to get you when it is time," she said and left them in the passageway.

"I'm going to go sack out while we wait," Jason said and went to his room.

"Me too." Steve also went into his quarters.

"Can you stay with me?" Kim took Josh's hand. "I know I'm being a baby, but I just keep seeing Carla's shuttle explode in front of us."

"Sure, your room?" He squeezed her hand. She nodded, and they went into her quarters.

Not as nice as the rooms they stayed in on their first visit to the station, it contained a bunk on the far wall, a communications terminal on the desk to their left, a seating area in the center, and a door Josh assumed led to the head in the right wall. The chairs in the seating area were more comfortable than they looked. Josh sat and looked into her blue eyes. "This will be over soon. Then we can start a new life away from the Cathardi."

"I don't want a new life. I want to go back to my family and the farm. How could God let this happen?" She covered her face with her hands, wiping the tears from her eyes. "I thought the Cathardi were great. They healed my mom's cancer. Kel was my friend and helped me through the Academy. But now, they act like everyone on Earth is dead. I've lost everything."

"That's true. I've lost everything too," he said. "It will take a long time for this to get better, but eventually it will."

They sat and talked about their time at the Academy, recounting the good times and bad, remembering their lost friends. He learned a lot about Carla who had been Kim's roommate. "Remember that creep we played soccer against who kept fouling me?" she said.

"The one who said he enjoyed playing against girls."

"Yes. Then you tackled him and said the same thing to him." Kim laughed for the first time since the tragedy.

"Didn't you kick his butt in self-defense class? You broke his nose if I remember right."

"Thanks to Ray and Carla. They kept telling me I was faster and smarter than him. That I shouldn't be afraid. So, I watched Carla who regularly beat the guys in class, then Ray took some time and showed me a couple of moves, so the next time I faced a guy, I had some confidence."

"You looked confident out there. The instructor had to pull you away from him." Josh shook his head. "I don't think I want to get in the ring with you when you're that confident."

"I thought they might suspend me," she said. "Ray and I went to the infirmary later that day. The guy was a good sport, and we eventually became friends."

A rap on the door interrupted them. "Come in," Kim said.

"It is time for the debriefing," the Cathardi sister said.

"We will be there in a moment." Kim stood and kissed Josh on the cheek when he stood. "Thank you for helping me remember some of the good times."

***

Josh and Kim met Steve and Jason in the passageway outside of the briefing room. "Hey, guys," Steve said. "Are you ready for the bad news?"

"What bad news?" Kim looked puzzled.

"You don't think they are just going to let us go, do you? Remember what the cruiser commander said?"

"Steve is right," Josh said. "The Cathardi have no intention of helping Earth or letting us move about the galaxy freely. They don't trust us."

"But the Ompresti will vouch for us. She has done it before," Kim said.

A Cathardi officer stepped out of the room. "The commander is ready for you now." He motioned for them to enter the room. Then followed them in before closing the door.

The station commander and several officers were already in the room along with the Ompresti, two sisters, and two Melal officials. Liria was whispering to the commander who frowned and shook his head. Josh sensed Liria was unhappy. *Steve was right about this being bad news.*

"Captain, Lieutenants, take a seat," the commander said to the Earth crew. "Thank you for your efforts in safely bringing the Ompresti and her companions back here after the tragic incident on your voyage back to Earth. The Cathardi High Council expresses its deep appreciation for your skill and courage. Since the incident, our forces have continued to monitor the Urlak presence around Earth. Though the Urlak have been vigilant, we know they have sent forces to the planet's surface and are establishing defenses around the system. I am afraid Earth is lost. The council believes and the top military commanders agree, we cannot mount any counterattack. I know this is not what you want to hear, but that is the council's decision."

He walked to the end of the table. "Here." He pointed to a stack of data pads. "Are the enlistment forms for any of you who would like to join the Cathardi in our fight against the Urlak. I believe the commander of the cruiser made the offer to you before you came to the station. If you decide to join, we will send you to a training station. The shuttle departs tomorrow, so I need your decision in the next two hours." Another Cathardi officer handed a data pad to each of them.

"If you do not wish to join, you will remain as our guests at the station." The commander pointed to the Melal officials. "You will be as free as any other resident on the station except you cannot leave the station." The commander left them there not waiting for a response.

Liria came up to them. "I am sorry," she said. "I tried to convince them to send our forces to Earth. But they would not listen even when I told them I believed it was critical to fulfilling the prophecy. The council is afraid of the Urlak. They did not expect them to be so close and did not want their forces any closer. They will sacrifice your world hoping to protect ours."

"If it doesn't cost you anything, it is not a sacrifice! My dad was right when he said you would desert us." Josh slammed his fist on the table. "You said you came as friends, but friends don't turn their back on friends when they need help. You used us!"

"I know you feel that way. I will continue to talk with the leaders on Cathardi to change their minds. But even if they do, it may be too late."

Josh sensed she was telling the truth. She would do everything she could to help, but she didn't feel confident. He shouldn't have been so angry at her. She might be their only friend in the Cathardi leadership.

The four of them left and went to Steve's quarters, where they talked a little longer. Jason and Steve used their data pads to send word to the commander that they wanted to join. The next day, they left for a training base. Josh and Kim met them at the shuttle. Kim hugged and kissed both and cried.

"Good luck, you two." Josh hugged them. "I hope you get the chance to kick some Urlak butt."

"You take care of yourself," Steve told him. "And look after Kim. I am worried about her."

Josh held Kim to his side at the viewport while their friends flew out into the darkness of space. When the shuttle was out of sight, Josh moved his hand from her shoulder and clasped her hand.

Kim turned to face him. "You are all I have left. I have lost everything and everyone else. Stay with me." She squeezed his hand so hard it hurt.

"I will stay with you." He put his free arm around her and held her to his chest. "You are all I have, and I won't give up hope."

When they returned to their quarters, a Cathardi sister met them. "The Ompresti asked me to arrange more permanent quarters for you. If you follow me, I will show you to your quarters."

They followed her to the Melal habitat area, barely noticing the surrounding activity. Their quarters reminded Josh of the academy. There was a central living area with a food storage and preparation area in one corner, an island separating it from the living area, and an entertainment area in the opposite corner. Sleeping and lavatory facilities were off each of the other two corners.

"I hope these are adequate." The sister said. "These were the best available and are hopefully only temporary. The Ompresti thought you would not mind sharing the accommodation. She thought it was like your quarters on Earth."

"They will do," Josh answered. "Thank you."

When she left, Josh looked over at Kim, who slouched in a chair. "Are you okay?"

"No. I want to go home and see my mom and dad. I don't know how long I can take this."

Josh kneeled in front of her chair and took her hands. "Remember what the sister said. This is only temporary. We will get through this together. Come on. You need to pick out which room you want." He stood and helped her out of the chair.

While they put their few belongings away, a Cathardi officer came to their door. "The commander thought you might be interested in this." He handed Josh a data pad. "Since your stay here may be long, you may find employment while we resolve your status. There are many opportunities listed on the pad for those with your skill sets, especially in the transport area. They are always looking for engineers to keep the freighters space-worthy."

"You mean we can't leave and should prepare to stay permanently?" Josh asked, not knowing where they would go.

"I am afraid that is correct. You must remain at the station. There is some concern on the council, despite the Ompresti's assurances, that you might try something foolish and endanger the entire Cathardi population."

"Then we are prisoners." Josh could barely contain his anger.

"Not prisoners. You are free to take part in the activities of the station. But you may not leave the station."

He turned and walked away, ending the conversation.

After several days, Josh took a job repairing gravity drives for an ex-freighter captain who couldn't hide his dislike for the Cathardi. Kim worked assigning destinations to the various freighter crews. They spent their free time together in the quarters they shared. Kim seemed to sink deeper into depression as the weeks passed. Josh tried to book a passage off the station. But each time the Cathardi authorities denied them travel papers. One night, he returned to their quarters and found Kim collapsed on the floor. He quickly knelt beside her and took her hand, feeling her pulse.

"Kim," he said as he gently shook her. "Kim, wake up. I need you to wake up." She opened her eyes and saw Josh. She threw her arms around his neck and sobbed.

"I can't take it anymore!" she cried. "I need to see the sky and trees. I need something normal. All I can think about is Carla's shuttle disintegrating in front of us."

"It wasn't our fault. We couldn't know. The Cathardi weren't honest with us. Be patient. I'm working on a way to get us off this station and as far away from the Cathardi as possible. Are you willing to wait for me to arrange it?"

"Yes! Can you do it?"

"We're being watched, but I think if we're careful, I can get us off this station and to a planet far away from here."

***

After the debriefing on the Melal station, Liria left to return to Cathardi. She stared out at the cold emptiness of space through the viewports of the ship. Since their return to the Melal station, she felt empty inside. *Everything is wrong. The Urlak presence is wrong. Josh's rejection of me and the Cathardi is wrong. The emptiness is wrong. God, where are you? Help me.*

She went back to her quarters and contacted Moira on a private com channel. "I was so sure the human was the prophesied one. Yet, the Urlak are destroying his planet and he wants nothing to do with me or the Cathardi. How could I have been so wrong? Was my judgment clouded by the intense connection and the physical desires he aroused? Am I being punished?"

"It is not unusual to have doubts when the Creator does not respond the way we think He should," Moira answered. "Especially when our personal feelings intervene. Your intense connection with an alien is unusual, but it is not unique. Our historical writings contain several documented cases of similar connections. You must realize you are inexperienced in the ways of the world outside our close-knit community. You lack clarity. I will arrange for you to spend some time at the convent in the Carsas Cliffs after you meet with the council. I suggest you be less forthcoming about your feelings for the human and only relate the facts of the incident during the debriefing."

"Thank you. I need clarity. Hopefully, the council will help Earth."

"We can meet when you arrive. I look forward to seeing you," Moira said.

"And I you." Liria switched off the com system. Then returned to the lounge to watch the approach to Cathardi. *Why don't I hear you, Lord?*

Moira met her at the terminal, and they went directly to the room that would act as her quarters during the debriefing. There, Moira began explaining some of the current political changes. "The Council is more divided now than it has been for years. Marlon has become chair and has solidified the support of the other civilian members. He also has consistent support from General Sinola. He objects to the Sisterhood's influence and wants to use the Urlak presence and the destruction of the planet you predicted as a lever to discredit us. Be very careful about what you reveal to the Council."

The next morning, Liria entered the nearly empty council chamber alone. She sensed the tension and division among the Council members. Marlon and the other two civilian members huddled together, whispering. The three generals looked bored with only two seated and General Ao pacing behind the chairs. Moira and the other two sisters sat straight and nodded at her, occasionally smiling. *At least I have allies in the sisterhood.*

Marlon stood and faced Liria. "Welcome Ompresti. We will begin this informal debriefing with your description of the events that led to your unexpected return to Cathardi, and the now confirmed presence of Urlak forces on the planet called Earth." He glared at her, then turned his back on her and strode to his chair, not waiting for her to start.

"Mister Chairman and honored Council members, I have provided a full report of the events, the video recordings, and the ship logs which contain all the details of the incident. I have limited memories of the specific details since I was not conscious during most of what transpired. But in summary, before the last jump to take us back into the Earth system, I saw a vision of death and destruction on a large scale." Liria paused as the images flooded back to her. She took two deep breaths, then continued. "The vision disturbed and frightened me, so I asked the captain of the vessel to not make the jump. He felt he could not abort the jump based on my vague feelings and a non-specific vision. Because of the jump effects, I remember nothing else until after most of the events took place. When I was finally alert, the captain summoned all of us to the galley and asked if anyone could identify the vessels that attacked our shuttles. Though I did not recognize the vessels shown in the video recordings, they appeared like the Urlak ships described in our historical records. This is what I and Lieutenant Taral told the captain. Then we insisted we return to Cathardi space."

"Ompresti," said General Sinola. "I have gone over the video evidence provided and find it to be unbelievable. The unarmed shuttle you were on destroyed an Urlak cruiser and moved out of their sensor range in a matter of minutes with no downtime between jumps. This is unheard of. You are certain the videos are accurate and not altered."

"I believe the videos are accurate, but you can have them analyzed to determine their authenticity. The captain is an exceptional individual and does not require downtime between jumps."

"Sister Liria," Marlon said, not using her title. "He may be an exceptional pilot, but he is now a threat to the security of our world and all the Cathardi people. Yet, you have suggested he remain free despite the incredible circumstances of the events you do not remember."

"I trust the captain, Mister Chairman." Liria squared her shoulders. "He is not a threat to the Cathardi, and I cannot condone punishing him for saving my life and the lives of the sisters who were with me. I also believe we must send forces to his planet to defeat the Urlak there."

Marlon stood, but before he could speak, Moira said, "Mister Chairman, perhaps now would be a good time to recess the proceedings so we can deliberate what we have heard. We can also take the time necessary to examine the physical evidence and the follow-up reports concerning the military's investigation. The Ompresti has always been open and honest with this Council and her predictions and judgments consistently prove accurate."

"I agree with Elder Sister Moira." General Ao said. "We have a lot to look into and discuss."

"Very well," Marlon said. "I recess the meeting until further notification. Ompresti, you will remain available here in the capital until further notice."

The council members, except for Moira, left the chamber. "You did well. The Council will take the time required to go through the evidence now. You should relax while you are here, though I know it will be more difficult here than it will be at Carsas."

During the nine days, Liria waited for the council to reconvene. She prayed and talked to Moira. She felt like the Creator did not hear her prayers, and she sensed Josh's increasing resentment against the Cathardi. When she mentioned she could still sense his feelings, it surprised Moira, who continued to support her even though it was unusual for such a strong connection to exist, especially with an alien.

Their conversations turned to the council as it became clear they would meet soon. Moira told her that Marlon was building consensus with the generals to keep Josh and Kim at the Melal station until they could incarcerate them. His knowledge of Cathardi's location represented a danger to all of Cathardi.

Moira said, "I believe Marlon will try to blame the Sisterhood and especially you for the Urlak presence. Rumors already circulated that if the Ompresti hadn't taken the Cathardi to the planet, the Urlak presence there would not be an imminent threat."

The morning, Liria met Moira before the meeting. Moira said, "Remember, do not disclose too much to the council. Be honest and tell them only what you know. I fear their decision will disappoint you." She squeezed Liria's hand and left to take her seat.

When Liria entered, Marlon was standing and talking with General Ao and General Stanko. General Sinola walked with Councilman Bakar as they came to their seats. When the council members took their places, Marlon opened the meeting.

"Sister Liria, thank you for your patience while we completed our investigation. General Ao will present the results, then I will give the Council's recommendations. General Ao."

The general stood. "Thank you, Mister Chairman. After a thorough analysis of the audio and video evidence, as well as the electronic data from the shuttle, we have determined the account of the shuttle incident is accurate. The pilot's actions made the return to Melal possible and provided us with a warning concerning the Urlak. We find no fault in the evidence or actions taken and recommend the investigation be closed."

Marlon stood and sneered at Liria. "Sister Liria, the Council unanimously agrees with General Ao. We will take no further action in this matter. You may leave the capital and return to your duties. I adjourn the Council." He turned and immediately left the room.

General Ao came down to her. "This alien pilot of yours, did an incredible job escaping the Urlak, though it was only luck that he destroyed the cruiser. If he were Cathardi, he would be a hero."

"He is a hero," Liria answered. "He saved us all."

When the General left, Moira put her hand on Liria's shoulder. "Now that this is over, when do you want to leave for Carsas?"

"Tomorrow. I sense Chairman Marlon is planning something else, and it scares me. "

"I know," Moira answered. "He has a deep distrust of the Sisterhood and wants to see our influence eliminated. He is always scheming, and with the power he now wields, he poses a genuine threat. But we are aware of him and will do what we can to maintain the balance of power. You do not need to fret. I will arrange for your trip and meet you for breakfast."

"What about Josh and the other humans?"

"Two of them have joined the Cathardi military and are in training. The Cathardi authorities have restricted the captain and the young woman to the Melal station. The military watches them and prevents them from leaving, but for now, they are free to move about the station. We will continue to monitor them as well. In time, this will all pass."

Liria left the next day for the convent.

Chapter 11

Over the next few months, Josh worked in secret to arrange passage for both Kim and him on a freighter. The freighter captain, Faili, who had become a good friend, flew to the outer planets but would be back on the station in thirty-three days. When Josh told Kim that they would leave the station, she regained some of her vitality as the depression waned.

After finalizing the arrangements with Faili, Josh began taking a few of their belongings to the hangar, where he worked every day. He and Kim started going out regularly and meeting with friends who had no love for the Cathardi. Josh watched for places that presented opportunities to catch their chaperones off guard. The best chances came when they attended the dinner theaters. The crowds and bawdy content often made the Cathardi so uncomfortable, that they simply watched the exits and didn't bother following them inside. This was perfect for

Josh since Cali, the serving girl they had met on their first night at the station, worked in one theater. With her help and the help of a couple of her friends on staff, they developed a plan.

The night of the freighter's scheduled departure, Josh and Kim went to the opening night of a new comedy sure to embarrass the Cathardi. They sat in the first row of tables near the stage and far from the main entrance.

During the most risqué portion of the program, the lights went out, and the audience stood. Josh grabbed Kim's hand and pulled her under the table. They crawled on their hands and knees along the stage to the kitchen entrance. A transfer cart with dirty laundry bags sat outside the kitchen door. They climbed into the cart hidden by the bags and a cloth draped over the sides. When the lights came back on, a kitchen worker placed refuse bags on top and wheeled the cart through the kitchen to a storage area near the central axis.

The Cathardi guarding the kitchen entrance didn't even check the cart. A few minutes after the worker left the cart, Josh lifted the draping cloth just enough to look out and determine if it was clear. He put his finger to his lips, signaling Kim to stay quiet. "We'll get out now, but be careful and stay quiet," he whispered. "Stay low and follow me. We're going to the storage area on the left."

They left the cart and hurried through the storage area door. Once inside, they stood near a maintenance duct. Josh opened the duct. "I taped the latch earlier this week. We'll use this duct to take us to the central shaft."

He helped Kim up into the duct and then climbed in after her. He removed the tape so the cover would latch shut. The duct was only about four feet square, so they crawled on their hands and knees, with Josh leading, until they reached the central maintenance shaft. They climbed out of the duct into the circular chamber that ran from the lowest levels to the highest. There was a constant hum of machinery and a current of air that rushed through from bottom to top.

Josh pointed to their left, to a ladder that went down to the next level. "We must climb down a couple of levels from here. I will go first and help keep you on the ladder. Remember, only move one hand or one foot at a time."

Halfway down their long descent, they stopped on a landing. "How are you holding up?" he asked Kim.

"Okay, but I need a rest. My hands are hurting."

"Let me see." He looked at her hands and cringed at the blisters forming on her palms. "Ouch. I can see why. You're getting blisters. We still have a little farther to go." He tore strips from his shirttail and wrapped them around her hands. "This should help."

"I'll be okay." She smiled. "Ready?"

"I'll keep my arms around you, and we'll go down together in case your hand slips. Take your time."

Josh got on the ladder and went down a few rungs, where he waited for Kim. When she was on, he let her descend until his arms held the ladder rails on each side of her waist. It took a little while to get the coordination of going down together, but it worked.

When they reached the hangar deck level, they went through another duct to the hangar where Josh had stashed their belongings. Then they climbed to the catwalk high above the passageways and walked toward the freighter's gate.

"Stay out of sight," Josh pointed to the Cathardi guards checking the IDs of the crew entering the freighter.

"How are we going to get past them?"

"We'll wait for an opportunity. My friends have something planned."

They watched the entrance to the freighter, but nothing happened. Finally, the freighter captain came out to the gate and talked to the guards. He handed them the roster for the crew.

Josh was nervous. *Don't leave without us. We may never have another chance. What happened to the distraction?*

Thirty yards down the passageway below, a fight broke out. People screamed and crowded around. The Cathardi guards ran down to break it up.

"Let's go." Josh took Kim to a support pole. "Slide down. When you get to the deck, go to the gate as fast as you can."

They slid down to the passageway and ran into the gate that Faili held open. Once they were through, he let the gate close, and they hurried on board.

Faili, the freighter captain, took them to the engine control room. "This will serve as your sleeping quarters and also your duty station." He pointed to the bunks at the rear of the control room. "One of you must always remain on duty. The guards locked the gates before the fight, but I held it open. Now, we have clearance to leave, and with luck, we will get past the station security without issue."

"Thank you Faili, we are in your debt," Josh said while examining the console, which took up two walls of the room. The controls resembled those of the Cathardi shuttle, but he didn't recognize a couple of symbols.

"Can you handle it?" the captain asked.

"I think so, just minor issues with a few of the symbols, but I can work through them, providing you are not expecting any immediate trouble. You can help me with them after we depart if I need it," Josh said.

"Very well. I will be on the bridge." The captain left.

Josh looked around the compartment. A communications island occupied the center of the room. The entry, storage bins, and tool cabinets were on the third wall. And the fourth wall held the sleeping berths separated from the rest of the compartment by a curtain. The head and galley were down the passage to the left on the same level.

Josh called Kim over to the control panel and pointed to a read-out. "This is the field generator control indicator" But when he looked, Kim was sitting at the communications station with her head in her hands.

"I don't know if I can do this," Kim said. "All I can see is Carla's shuttle disintegrating in front of us."

Josh put his hand on her shoulder. "It's hard I know, but if you want to get away from this space station, you must work through it. I'll be here with you, but I can't do the job by myself. You need to help me." He held her for a few minutes.

Finally, Kim stood. "Okay, I can do it. I need to get away from this station." They went through the controls for the next few minutes until the captain called down to start the maneuvering engines. As the ship moved away from the station Josh tensed, waiting for the Cathardi to stop them at any minute, but they cleared the station and opened the thrusters to proceed to the jump point. They stayed busy during the first few hours after departure as they learned the controls and prepared the jump drive.

After the jump, they rendezvoused with another freighter. Josh and Kim would change places with the engineering team on the other ship. They hoped to throw the Cathardi off their trail by changing ships a couple of times on their way to Bapto. There would be no record of their arrival or departure until they finally reached their destination. Before they left for the other ship, Faili came down to the control room.

"When you get to Bapto, look up my friend Taibon. He runs a pleasure house near the spaceport. He is an odd character, but he will help you if he can. Here is a letter of introduction to help get you in to see him." He handed Josh a folded piece of paper. "Good luck."

"Thank you. I don't know how we would have left that station without you. You have been a good friend."

Josh and Kim boarded the small shuttle that would ferry them to the other ship and prayed their plan would work.

***

The rest of the trip to Bapto was uneventful. Kim settled into the routine and concentrated on the tasks assigned during her duty cycles. When they got to the planet, Josh looked out of the viewports as the freighter's shuttle made its approach. The planet was beautifully rugged and sparsely populated. Their destination, the only large settlement on the southern continent, sat in the jungle near the southern coast. From above, the town was smaller than he expected and resembled a Colorado resort town. It lay in a narrow valley, where a swiftly running stream divided the town. Shops and condominium-like structures dominated the East, while saloons and pleasure houses dominated the West bank.

Once the shuttle landed, Josh and Kim grabbed their belongings. "When we get on the ground, stay close to me and pay attention," Josh said. "We don't know what we will find, and we don't want to stumble into a Cathardi security check."

Erinda, the freighter captain, had said the security at the spaceport was lax, especially for the freighter crews that arrived regularly. He would help them get through if any problems arose. But Josh was cautious. They were fugitives, and he believed the Cathardi would search for them. He had not shaved since before they left the station and Kim had cut her long blond hair short on the shuttle. Erinda had helped them forge documents with their new appearance and identities.

Heat mirages danced across the open tarmac of the landing field that stretched out in front of them as they walked down the ramp from the ship. Heavy humidity weighed on them in contrast to the controlled conditions of the freighter and the smell of fuel and chemicals hung in the air.

The passenger terminal appeared to be on his left with carts shuttling people between the building and the ships. Josh and Kim joined the other crew members and boarded the cart that stopped near the bottom of the ramp. They rode to the terminal, where they filed through a side door designated for crew members. To his surprise, the door opened into the main room with an uninterested Cathardi soldier standing at the door to prevent unauthorized personnel from going onto the tarmac. But no one checked the incoming crews. Inside, Erinda stopped and handed out payment vouchers.

"We're going to the west bank for some relaxation. You are welcome to join us. Otherwise, there is a hotel you can see from here just across the river." He pointed to an enormous structure. "It gets dark quickly here and you probably don't want to be caught out after dark."

"Thank you, but we need to find a friend of a friend. We will be fine." Josh said.

He and Kim walked to the hotel, only to find no rooms available because of the unusually large number of freighters in port.

"Can you tell where we might find a Melal named Taibon?" Josh asked the hotel clerk.

"Go across the river to the westside and you will see a very large pleasure establishment. Just look for the large screen with three dancing females. Taibon is the proprietor. He will be there with the crowds in port tonight, though I doubt he has any rooms. But if you want to sell the woman, the Melal will find her a place for a cut."

Kim and Josh looked at each other in unbelief for a few minutes before Kim said, "If it's the only room available, we should try. But you are not pimping me."

They entered the pleasure house through a narrow corridor beneath the gigantic screen. A tall alien at the door stopped them. "How can I help you?"

"We need to talk to Taibon. I have a letter for him" Josh held the letter up but would not give it to the doorkeeper.

The alien looked at them for a moment, then said. "Follow me." He escorted them to a small table along the wall of the large, crowded room, dominated by a round platform in the center.

"I'll let Taibon know you are here. Shall I have a girl bring you some refreshments?"

"Not yet," Josh said. "We will sit here and wait."

Mostly, male patrons occupied the crowded room. They stood around gaming tables or the central platform, ogling the nearly naked dancers performing there. After a few minutes, three of the men from the next table came over to their table, leering. Sturdily built, they stood about as tall as Josh, with long muscular arms. Their unkempt dark hair fell in curls over their foreheads above the broad noses and wide mouths of their unwashed faces.

"How much for an hour with the girl?" one asked.

"I am not that kind of girl!" Kim said.

The speaker ignored her and asked again as the three aliens crowded closer. "How much?"

"She is not for sale," Josh said. "We are just here to see Taibon."

One alien leaned over the table between Josh and Kim. His breath reeked of alcohol and a sweet scent he couldn't identify.

Josh stood, trying to look big. "I said she is not for sale."

"In that case, we will just take her." One grabbed Kim's arm, but she twisted free and hit him in the throat. The alien drew his arm back to hit her and Josh grabbed it. He stepped between Kim and them. "Keep your hands to yourself. She is my wife, and she is not for sale!" He had to raise his voice above the driving techno-beat music, which unfortunately stopped just as he yelled.

A short round Melal came up to them and laughed, then turned to the doorman standing next to him. "Show the gentlemen back to their table and let the server know their next drink is on the house." He stepped up to Josh. "I am Taibon. The drinks will hold them back, but only for a little while. Come with me."

He took them into a private office. "What can I do for you?"

"We need lodging for a few nights. The hotel is full and Faili told me to see you if I needed help." Josh handed him the letter.

"Well, ordinarily I would accommodate you. But, with all the freighters in port and the miners down from the mines, I am full as well. Unless we can work out an arrangement for your wife." He smiled.

"We can't," Josh said and stood up.

"Very well, I thought as much. I'm afraid you will have to go to the edge of town and find an empty shanty. You should hurry if you want a decent one. They fill up quickly as it gets dark. I assume you can defend yourself based on what I saw earlier." Taibon called for an assistant to escort them through the crowd of miners. "Your best chance is to go along the river. Be careful, there are a lot of unsavory characters there, but it's early enough you should be able to find something if you can keep it. I am sorry I cannot be more helpful. Faili is an excellent friend."

Outside, Josh and Kim walked up the street along the river to the shanties, looking for some shelter as night fell. Everything close to the town already had occupants. Just after full dark, they rounded a dimly lit corner where an elderly Cathardi was being accosted by a large, angry man. The assailant wore coarse, ragged clothing and had an unruly mop of long black hair. His nose was broad and flat. He stood nearly seven feet tall and probably weighed over three hundred pounds, dwarfing the frail Cathardi in front of him. Kim let out a startled yelp.

"Mind your own business and keep walking!" the assailant spat and looked over at them. "Unless you want me to gut both you and that pretty thing on your arm." He flashed a large curved-bladed knife.

Don't back down. Josh heard a soft internal voice. He stared at the giant alien, his stomach knotting up. *Help the old man.* The voice said again.

Josh swallowed the lump in his throat. "I'm afraid that won't happen. Come with us old man." Josh said calmly to the Cathardi.

The large man growled and ran at Josh. Josh dove to his left, avoiding the knife, but the assailant swung his other hand and struck a glancing blow on Josh's shoulder. On the ground, he rolled to evade the second lunge, which caused the attacker to stumble. Josh regained his feet and crouched in a defensive position, facing the alien. When the attacker swung wildly, Josh ducked under the blade. Pivoting, he side-kicked with all his force at the outside of the attacker's knee. The leg cracked loudly as it broke, and the big man fell. Josh followed with a front kick squarely to the broad flat nose, crushing it. The big alien moaned and lay motionless, blood streaming from his nose. Though the fight was over in minutes, Josh felt like everything had happened in slow motion, like a dream.

"I am in your debt, Nakir." The old man bowed, using the Cathardi term for a warrior.

"I am not a Cathardi warrior," Josh said.

"Maybe not, but I know the training," the old man said. "You are not Cathardi, but someone trained you in the Cathardi way. Thank you. He would have killed me."

"What do we do now?" Josh looked at the assailant who stirred.

"We wait for the authorities. The Cathardi military will be here soon on their rounds." The old man bowed again.

While they waited for the authorities, the figure on the ground stirred and moaned. Josh stepped over to him, picked up the knife, and said, "Help will be here soon."

Just then, two uniformed Cathardi rounded the corner. They drew their weapons. "Drop the knife. "

Josh dropped the knife and raised his hands.

"What happened here?" asked the first officer.

"The big man would have killed me if not for this young couple," said the old man.

The other officer looked closely at the man on the ground. "It's Hulolo. How did you take him?" They looked at the old Cathardi who they seemed to know.

"This young stranger stepped in to help me."

"We have been looking for Hulolo since he killed two men last week up at the Joli Boi Mine. He is one tough character. " The officer turned to Josh. "What are you two doing out in this part of town?"

"We just arrived on a freighter and were looking for shelter for the night, but we couldn't find any available rooms," Josh said.

"That happens. We will need to get statements from all of you. Though I don't think we will need to detain you."

One officer interviewed each of them to determine what happened. The other put restraints on Hulolo and then put him into the ambulance which had arrived during the interviews. After the questioning, Kim and Josh stood in the dark and cold with the old man waiting for the authorities to let them leave.

"What do we do now?" Kim held tightly to Josh.

"Stick with the plan. Try to find an empty shelter for the night," he said.

"If you need shelter, I will gladly share my home with you. It is not all that big, but there is a warm loft you could use. It is the least I can do to repay part of my debt to you. Let me check with the officers. They may provide us with transportation." The grateful old man went over to the two Cathardi officers.

"Why did you help him?" Kim asked. "He could have killed us."

"I don't know. I just had a feeling I should help. Almost like someone was telling me to do it. I still don't believe what happened," he said.

The old man returned. "Come with me."

A few minutes later, a police vehicle pulled up. The three newfound friends got in for the ride out of town.

CHAPTER 12

The Cathardi police took the three newfound friends north, several miles out of town, into the jungle. During the drive, Josh sat in silence. Kim leaned on his shoulder, dozing. It had been a long and eventful day.

As they pulled up to his farm, the old man said, "Forgive me, my name is Loral. This is my farm, where I also run a repair shop for mining equipment and an occasional freighter. But since I no longer move as well as I used to, and my technician left, business has slowed."

The vehicle turned into a natural clearing on the northern road. In the lights, Josh saw a wooden structure with a pitched roof sitting a hundred yards away. In the light of the twin moons, he could make out several outbuildings. East of the house, closer to the road was a large rectangular structure. Judging by its bay doors and several pieces of machinery sat lit by dim security lamps, it was a workshop. The sign on the front of the building read "Equipment Repair" in Cathardi. Farther away from the road, west of the house, was a wooden corral and a small barn with a coop attached. Several odd-looking animals wandered around the enclosure. North of the barn was a smaller structure, possibly a cabin.

Once inside the house, Loral started a small stove. "The nights up here get colder than down in the town because of the higher altitude. Let me fix you something to eat while you tell me what brings you to Bapto."

Josh sensed a connection like, but weaker than, the one he had the first night he met Liria. The old man's gentle manner and generosity, along with that connection, led Josh to lower some of his barriers. He felt he could trust the old man and gave him an abbreviated account of their experiences since leaving Earth, skirting his distrust of the Cathardi authorities and their fugitive status. He provided more detail when relating their experiences, since arriving on Bapto, that led up to the encounter with Loral's assailant.

Loral served them steaming bowls of spicy stew and warm bread. "Please eat. It is quite good. I raised most of it here."

"I didn't realize how hungry I was. This smells so good. It reminds me of home and the chili my mom made." Josh's stomach growled when Loral put the bowl in front of him. "We have told our story. What are you doing here so far from the Cathardi home world?"

"Ah, good question, young man. I came here many years ago as the commander of the local forces before all the alien miners arrived. In those days, most of the miners were Cathardi. It was much different before the lure of wealth and freedom from the restrictions of the civilized planets brought so many other races here, especially the greedy, licentious Melal. After years as the commander, I retired from the military but stayed as a priest for the Cathardi population. However, over time, the need for a Cathardi priest became less necessary, so I retired again. The military and other Cathardi officials have a younger priest and a small chapel on the east bank in town. I help occasionally, but mostly I spend my time working on the farm and in my repair shop. I enjoy this wonderfully wild planet." He took a bite of stew and sighed.

They sat quietly for a few minutes. "There is something else I need to tell you," Loral said. "When you told the patrons of the pleasure house that your companion was your wife, she did not object to this?" He looked at Kim, who shook her head, staring into her empty bowl. "According to Cathardi frontier law, there is no need for a ceremony or legal document for couples to be married. Witnesses to the confession of marriage are the only requirement. Is she your wife?"

"No!" Josh answered quickly.

"Well, according to the law, now she is." He looked at Kim again. "Kim, do you object to being his wife?"

Kim stared at Josh, then quickly to the Cathardi. "I don't object." She said as she looked back into her bowl to avoid eye contact with Josh.

"Good," Loral said. "Josh, you may feel trapped in this, but it will make your stay here much safer for Kim. This can be a lawless place for young women, but the aliens respect the marriage arrangement. They are less likely to force themselves on a married female. You know it is a marriage of convenience, and it does not require the physical or emotional intimacy you associate with marriage. That is your choice." He gave them a minute to think. "Josh, can you accept that?"

"I... I suppose I can," Josh said. *This is crazy. I like Kim, but how do I tell her about Liria? Do I tell her? Is this just another Cathardi prison?*

"Good, good." Loral smiled. "Now finish eating and I will get blankets for you to take to the loft. Unfortunately, there is only one bed up there, but it is big enough for both of you. Tomorrow, we can start cleaning out the cabin across from the barn. It will give you more room and provide some privacy."

Josh and Kim spent an uneasy night as they slept in their clothes, sharing the mattress on the loft floor above the kitchen. When Josh got up early the next morning, he climbed down the steep stairs to the kitchen. Loral had brewed a pot of strong tea and left it sitting on the stove. He poured himself a cup and wandered out to the corral. Where he leaned against the rail fence, sipped the bitter tea, and took in the agricultural odors of manure and cut grass. One animal in the corral came right up to him and nuzzled his arm. The curly-coated beast looked like a cross between a horse and a llama. Nearly six feet tall at the shoulders, it had a long, slender neck and a small head. It was chestnut brown with lighter stripes across its neck and back, with a short, dark mane down its neck and a horse-like tail. Josh turned and scratched the thick, curly coat behind its upright ears as it leaned into him.

"Maci likes you." Loral came out of the barn with a bucket of grain. "She doesn't normally accept strangers like that. Do you want to feed her?" He handed Josh the bucket, not waiting for an answer, and pointed to a box on the corral fence several feet away. "There is more grain in the bin in the barn. You can scatter some around the pen over there." He pointed to the coop. "I will see to our breakfast." He turned and went into the house.

Josh dumped the grain in the box, scratched the animal's ears again, and then went into the barn, where more strange animals stood in stalls already eating. Josh partially filled the bucket and went to the coop to feed the fowl, though some looked more like reptiles than birds. When he returned to the house, Loral had breakfast on the table, and he and Kim were talking. Kim was radiant. She was smiling. He hadn't seen her look this happy since before the destruction of Carla's shuttle. When he sat next to her, she reached out, took his hand, and squeezed gently. *This is the Kim I remember.*

After breakfast, Kim and Josh did the dishes. Loral straightened up, and before he went out, said, "I will be in the cabin if you need me. You two should talk in private. If you leave the farm, stay on the road, and do not go into the clearing north of here. The vines are dangerous."

When they finished the dishes, Kim took his arm. "Do you want to walk?"

"Sure." Josh went out the door with her and they walked to the road together.

"Did you mean what you said last night?" she said after they had walked a short distance. "Will you take me as your wife?"

"Yes...Yes, I will. It will be good for us. Even at the academy, I thought we might be more than friends, and now we need each other more than ever." He took her hand. Kim stopped put her arms around his neck and kissed him passionately. He held her tightly and returned her kiss. Though images of Liria flashed in his mind, he pushed them aside and concentrated on Kim. The feel of her body pressed against his, the scent of her hair, her warm breath on his cheek.

"Thank you," she said. "I will do my best to please you and be a good wife. I know the circumstances are not what we would like, and we didn't plan on any of this. But you are the only human male around. And, you make me happy."

She kissed him again before he could say anything. Then she laughed and skipped up the road ahead of him. Josh hurried to catch her. They walked for a while and talked about the good times they had shared. On the return walk, they stopped beside the clearing Loral had warned them about. It was full of pumpkin-like plants with bright orange blooms and large yellow fruit. Small animals with long, black, snake-like necks and pointed snouts poked their heads above the leaves and made chortling noises, which reminded Josh of the geese that wintered on his uncle's ranch in Colorado. With their necks stretched above the plants, they would look around, then duck down and move under the leaves, making it difficult to determine if there were ten or a hundred of them in the patch. They watched the intriguing creatures for several minutes while they talked about the future.

When Josh and Kim returned to the farm, Loral was busy carrying containers out of the cabin and into the shop.

"Would you like some help?" Josh asked.

"Certainly," the Cathardi said and pointed to several more containers inside the cabin.

They took most of the morning to clear the containers from the cabin. Once cleared, the small building surprised Josh with how roomy it seemed inside. It reminded him of the cabins his family would vacation in near Twin Lakes. The main room was a combined living, dining, and kitchen area with a fireplace along the short wall and two stuffed bean-bag-like chairs with a small table in front of the hearth. The kitchen was on the opposite wall, and along the long wall under the large window sat a square table with benches. Down the short hall, left of the kitchen, was a bedroom with a good-sized bed that didn't look like much but was very comfortable when he tried it. A window looked out onto the mountains. The bathroom was across the hall and further down was a study with a table and a stool.

"I know the place smells a little musty, but once it's cleaned and aired out, it will smell better. This was my secretary's house before I retired. He was a young priest and too ambitious to stay here after the miners flocked into the area. He could not endure the threat of physical and moral injury they brought," Loral said.

"It is very nice, very comfortable," Kim said, looking around the main room.

"It is yours. You can have some privacy. Newlyweds need privacy, especially reluctant newlyweds."

"Speaking of being newlyweds," Josh said. "I know the law says she is my wife. But we would both like to know if there is a proper ceremony to make it more official?"

"Oh, yes!" he said. "I would be glad to perform the ceremony."

That night they shared the cabin and the bed, with Kim curled up next to Josh. They had talked that afternoon and agreed to wait for additional physical intimacy until after their wedding ceremony. Still, Josh felt the urge and relived the visions of Liria from the shuttle. He wondered if he would ever be free of her.

The morning after their first night in the cabin, Josh went to the kitchen, where he brewed a pot of tea wishing it was coffee. *What was that drink they had at the Melal station? I could ask Loral.*

He poured himself a cup of tea and went out to the barn and began feeding the stock. He scattered grain on the ground for the fowl and heard the snorts from Maci, the Bonogo. She wanted to be fed, but she also wanted her ears scratched. She liked Josh and called to him with snorts whenever he was near.

"Just a minute, girl." He turned and went back into the barn, then he returned with the full bucket of grain and dumped it into Maci's feed box. She waited for him to put the bucket down before nuzzling his arm. He scratched behind her ears, and she laid her head on his shoulder.

Loral came out of the shop. "Good morning, Josh. I am amazed at how quickly she took to you."

"I like her too. When I was young, my family always had a dog. They give you unconditional love with no judgment. Maci reminds me of an enormous dog, especially because she enjoys having her ears scratched." The bonogo lifted her head off Josh's shoulder and shook it, her ears slapping against his head.

Loral laughed. "How was your first night in the cabin? Did you sleep well?"

"Kim did. She was still asleep when I came out this morning. I was restless and I think we are going to have to adjust the sleeping arrangements. Being so close to her was hard for me." His face reddened.

"You have already legally married her." Loral shook his head and chuckled. "It is unnecessary for you to control your natural urges."

"That's true, but we agreed to not have physical relations until after the ceremony. I want to honor that commitment." Josh reached down for the bucket. "Do you need any help in the shop?"

"No. But later, you can take Maci into town and pick up some supplies. In the meantime, I will find a cot. You can put it in the office. Are you sure you don't need to talk about some-thing else? You still look troubled."

"I'm okay," Josh said. *How do I explain the feelings and images of Liria? It would break Kim's heart if she knew I often think of Liria when we are close.* "The cot will help. Let me put the bucket away and I will see if Kim is up."

***

Josh went into the cabin after feeding the animals. When he opened the door, the aroma of freshly baked bread made his stomach growl. "That smells wonderful."

"Thanks," Kim grinned. "Are you hungry? I'm frying sausages to go with the rolls. It will be just a couple more min-utes."

"I'm starving." Josh smiled at her and refilled his cup of tea before he sat at the table. "Did you sleep well?"

"I slept great. What about you?"

"I slept well but having you so close is a problem. If we are to wait for our ceremony before becoming more physically intimate, I'm going to need a little distance. I have asked Loral to find a cot I can put in the office until after the wedding."

Kim's smile faded, and she stared at Josh. "We're married. We don't have to wait. I enjoy having you near me."

"Being close to you is great. I like it. I like it too much, but we talked about it, and we wanted to make our wedding night special. It's just a few more nights. I think we can wait, and it will be good for us."

She stood at the pan of sausage for a minute before answering. "You're right. We talked, and it was important. I can wait if you can." Her smile returned. "How many sausages do you want?"

"I'll take three, thanks."

Kim dished up his plate with the three sausages and two of the still-warm fruit-filled rolls and brought it to the table. After fixing her plate, she sat across the table from Josh and reached across for his hand.

"These taste even better than they smelled. You're going to make me fat, Mrs. Albertson." Josh said after his first bite. "Do you have any plans for the day?"

"I would like to go into town. Loral gave me the name and address of a girl who could help me with a dress for the ceremony. I would like to go see her."

"We can walk into town together. Loral asked me to take Maci and pick up some supplies this morning."

"You mean I'm going to have to compete against that tall brunette for your affections?"

"She is pretty demanding, but I can share my affections."

When they got into town, Josh took Kim into a shop run by a tall, dark-complexioned woman. "Welcome, I am Oreo. I don't recognize you two, but I assume you are Kim," she said, nodding toward Kim.

Josh laughed when she said her name and quickly apologized. "Forgive me. Where we come from, Oreo is the name of a cookie, a sweet treat."

Oreo laughed when Josh explained it, then said to Kim, "I hope our time this morning is a treat worthy of my name. Shall we go into the back and talk? I have a fresh pot of tea ready. I would like to get to know you before we get to work." Then turning to Josh, "Will you be joining us?"

"No. I have other errands to run. I will come by to get Kim for the walk home."

"This will take two or three hours. Can you wait that long?"

"I will be back in three hours. You two enjoy yourselves."

Josh continued down the street toward the spaceport, where he would pick up the supplies. As he was passing Taibon's pleasure house, he heard someone call his name. "Josh, can I talk to you?" It was Taibon who was standing at the entrance to his establishment.

"Sure. What can I do for you?"

"Please forgive my inhospitality on your arrival. Faili is a good friend, and I hated having to turn you away. Hopefully, we can be friends." He bowed and Josh returned his gesture. "Do you have time to join me for a midday meal?"

"I don't know. I have several things to pick up at the spaceport for Loral. And my experience with Melal meals is they are quite long."

Taibon laughed. "Your experience is correct. But I will have one of my men pick up your supplies while we eat. Do you have a list of instructions?"

Josh pulled his datapad out and scrolled through the receipts, showing them to Taibon.

Taibon took out another pad and gave Josh the I.D. code. "Transfer them over and I will have them brought here."

Josh did the transfer, and they went inside, where a long table near the bar held an assortment of food. They served themselves and went to a table near Taibon's office. While they were eating, The Melal asked, "Can you tell me how you became acquainted with Faili?"

Josh told him about meeting Faili at the Melal station and how their friendship developed while he worked on the docks. But he left out the part about leaving without the permission of the authorities.

When they finished the meal, they continued to sit and talk. Finally, Taibon said, "The Cathardi call you Nakir. You are famous for your exploits on that first night. You should be careful. Fame has its advantages, but also its disadvantages. Here, most of the Cathardi will treat you with respect, but a few of the officers may wonder where you learned your techniques. My intuition tells me you don't want that kind of interest because you are hiding something. I don't need to know what it is, but I will keep my ears open and let you know if suspicions arise. It is the least I can do for a friend of Faili."

"Thank you for the offer, but it isn't necessary," Josh said. "I need to head back. The meal and conversation were great. Thank you again." *What does he suspect? Can I trust him? Faili said I could.*

When they got outside, Maci was standing near the door, tied to a rail with packs full of supplies on her back. He untied the lead rope and started up the street.

"Remember, Nakir, I will let you know if I hear anything," Taibon called after him.

Josh waved and continued walking. *I hope his suspicions are baseless. It would be very hard for us to leave now. We are both looking forward to a new beginning.*

***

The morning of the wedding ceremony began just like any other day, with Josh feeding the stock. Maci waited at the fence, wanting her ears scratched. "You know, girl, I like our little routine," he told her as she laid her head on his shoulder. She couldn't purr, but she made a soft 'mmmm' sound like a long sigh of pure pleasure.

He heard Loral call from the shop door. "You spoil her. I don't know what she will do if you ever leave."

"Yeah. I think she has spoiled me as well." They both laughed.

"When you finish, can you give me a hand in the shop? The lorry does not want to start, and I need to go into town and pick up some things for the ceremony today."

"I'll be right there as soon as I put the bucket away."

When he got into the shop, Loral was lying under the electric vehicle that looked like a tractor with a flatbed trailer attached.

"Try the power switch for me," Loral asked.

Josh turned the switch, but nothing happened. Loral crawled out from under the lorry. "I charged the batteries last night and checked them this morning. It ran fine the last time I needed it."

"When was that?" Josh asked.

"Days before your arrival."

"Well," Josh said. "You have a short somewhere. Do you have a meter I can use to check the wiring?"

"Yes, it is over on the bench under the window."

Josh went to the bench and found the meter in a jumble of tools and took it to the lorry. After opening the battery compartment, he checked the terminals and the connections before checking the voltage in the battery. Then he crawled under the lorry to check each of the wires leading from the battery to the motors mounted on the rear tractor wheels. The connections to the motors looked good, but there was no conductivity from the anode to either motor.

Using his hand, he traced the wires from the motors to the junction box. The conductivity checked okay there. That left the wire from the battery to the junction box. The wires snaked through the frame and the battery compartment wall. Still using his hand, he followed the wire to the frame and, reaching into the channel on top of the frame, found a handful of grass and hair. As he pulled it out, he touched the wire and received a shock. When he looked at the hair, it was the dead body of a small animal.

"I think I found the problem. There is a rodent nest in the frame channel. I think they gnawed through the wire. Can you get me some tools so I can disconnect the wire from the junction box?"

Loral handed Josh a multi-tool, wire cutters, fusion tool, shrink insulation, and ultraviolet light to use on the insulation. Josh removed both wires from the junction and threaded them back out past the frame. The broken anode wire had a twenty-five-millimeter section of insulation missing. He cut the ends of the wire and slipped the insulation over one of them. Using the fusion tool, he joined the ends together. He slid the insulation over the bare wire and shrank it using the UV light. After reconnecting the wires to the junction box, he crawled out and asked Loral to try it. The whine of the motors let them know it worked.

"Thank you, Josh. I am not sure I would have found it so quickly. You are good with equipment."

"Yes, my father owned and operated a machine shop. I know how things work. With a little instruction, I'm sure I can operate everything in the shop. My guess is the unit in the corner is a laser sintering machine for polymers, and the big unit between the bay doors is a metal fusion machine."

"Very good." Loral cocked his head and looked at Josh. "Would you like to work with me in the repair shop? I will split the profits with you, and maybe we can rebuild the business. There is a lot of demand, especially from the mines."

"Sure, why not?" Josh took the tools back to the bench.

"Great, we can talk more in a few days, after you and Kim settle into your new relationship. Now, I need to get into town." Loral got into the lorry and drove out.

Josh spent several minutes straightening up the shop, putting tools away, and checking out the machinery before heading in to eat. Maci snorted at him when he walked out of the shop, wanting her ears scratched again.

In the house, Kim was dancing around, setting the table. Her blonde ponytail swung with each step. The delicious aroma of hot bread and cooked meat filled the room.

"You are just in time. Wash up. I'm taking the pie out of the oven," Kim said.

"It smells wonderful," Josh answered and walked to the sink.

Josh sat at the table while Kim spooned out plates of the aromatic meat pie. It tasted even better than it smelled. The meat was tender with just a tinge of wild game flavor that Josh remembered from Colorado. He couldn't identify the vegetables, but they had the consistency and sweetness of yams.

"This is Loral's recipe. He sure knows how to cook," Kim said. "I hope my cooking won't disappoint you."

"I'm sure you will do great, especially if this is any indication. This pie is delicious." Josh shoveled another spoonful into his mouth. "You were an excellent cook at the academy, unlike some of us guys." They had all shared in the cooking, taking turns on weekends. "Fortunately, my mom taught me how to cook at least the basics."

"Yeah, I remember your broiled salmon fillet and oven-fried sweet potatoes." They sat and finished their plates before Kim asked. "Are you excited about today?"

"I am, and I know you are. You have been beaming since we got to the farm." Josh took both of their plates to the dishwashing unit and poured another cup of tea.

"I am happy. This feels so real. Ever since the incident, it's been one long nightmare. Now, the nightmare is over. We may never return to Earth, but I think we can live a relatively normal life here with each other."

Josh stood and moved behind her chair. He put his hands on her shoulders and bent down to whisper in her ear. "I'm looking forward to it." He kissed her neck. "I need to finish a few more chores before Loral gets back." He heard Kim singing as he went out the door, smiling.

Loral pulled the lorry into the yard just as Josh finished running the mower over the grass and weeds in front of the main house. Two brightly clad Melal rode in the back of the lorry along with stacks of benches and several poles. "Why so many benches?" Josh asked. "I don't think we will have many guests."

"You are in for a surprise." Loral laughed. "You've been a bit of a celebrity since that first night. People want to meet the new Nakir."

Another vehicle pulled into the farm and parked in front of the shop. Two women got out and waved at Loral. Josh didn't know who or what race they were, but he thought one was a dancer he remembered from Taibon's. "You will find the best flowers over on the western edge of the jungle." Loral pointed down the hill. "Be careful of the wildlife, especially down by the river."

The two Melal worked on erecting a four-post arbor in front of the house, while Josh and Loral set the benches in front of the arbor. After setting the posts, workers took one bench to stand on while placing the top beams onto the posts. Before they finished, the two females carried armloads of flowering vines and laid them near the arbor.

Three Melal females arrived in the next vehicle and carried packages into the house. Vehicles began arriving every few minutes after that. The only other people Josh recognized were Oreo and Taibon. He came up to Josh and Loral bowed and looking at Josh said, "Congratulations Nakir, I hope your life here brings happiness and many children."

"I think it will work out. I'm going to be helping Loral get the repair shop going again." *Why did he call me Nakir? I am not Cathardi. I'm not a warrior, or the savior Liria wants. And why can't I get her out of my head?*

As they talked, they heard a scream from the river, followed by a piercing screech.

"Josh, hurry, that was a gwenna!" Loral ran into the house and came out with two rifles. He threw one to Josh. "Come with me." They both ran toward the river, where the two females were still screaming. Just before reaching the girls, Loral signaled Josh to move off to the right.

When he got to the river, the girls were in a small tree with three of the carnivorous reptiles circling and leaping for them, snapping their large, sharp-toothed, reptilian jaws and screeching. Josh fired at the closest gwenna. It fell with a loud cry. The two remaining gwennas turned in Josh's direction, but before they could move, Loral shot, killing another. The third leaped toward Josh, covering fifteen meters in one bound. Josh fell to his right, firing into the gwenna's mouth as it flew past him, swiping at him with its sharp clawed hands.

Loral ran to Josh. "Are you okay?"

Josh took a few seconds to assess. "Yeah, I'm fine. Just this scratch on my chest. Why were they here?"

"I don't know. But we need to take care of you and remove the carcasses, so they don't attract more." He went to the tree. "Are you two okay?" he asked the girls.

"Yes. Just scared," one of them answered.

"You can come down. It is safe now."

They climbed down and started gathering the flowers they dropped when the gwenna appeared.

"If you still need to pick more flowers, I can give you a gun or provide an armed guard," Loral said.

"The guard would be better," the other girl answered. "I don't know how to use a rifle."

"Let's head back to the house." Loral led them up the path and left the girls with Taibon. Then asked a Melal to act as a guard for the girls, and to oversee the removal of the gwenna.

He took Josh into the shop. "Take your shirt off so I can see the scratch," he said once they were inside.

The scratch was not too deep but was six inches long. Loral cleaned it and bandaged it before giving Josh an antibiotic. "This will prevent infection. The gwenna claws are full of nasty bacteria that can infect quickly. The wound is not deep and should heal nicely now, though you will be sore for the next few days."

When they got back out to the yard, the two females had returned with more flowering vines that they threaded around the arbor. The vines had large dark green heart-shaped leaves with light blue veins running out from the central stem. The trumpet-shaped flowers were red on some and orange on others. They also interspersed white and red flowers resembling daisies. When they finished, the entire arbor provided a colorful canopy.

In the meantime, the two Melal joined by others set up long tables behind the benches. When new vehicles arrived, the occupants brought dishes of food and placed them on the tables.

Loral put his hand on Josh's shoulder. "Come with me." He led Josh into the cabin. Taibon was there with a Cathardi who greeted Josh. "Good day Nakir, I am honored." Josh recognized him as an officer he met on his first night on Bapto.

"The honor is mine," Josh replied.

"We have several tunics for you to try before the ceremony," Taibon said and pointed to several laid out on the table. One was the dull gray traditional Cathardi robe, but the others were more colorful. Josh guessed they were Melal. "The bride is wearing blue; may I suggest dark blue for you? It is not as colorful as I would like, but I think it will suit you."

Josh tried on the dark blue, the gray, and a couple of wildly ornate robes, but settled on the dark blue. It was a solid color except for gold embroidery around the neck, sleeves, and hem. It fit loosely over his clothes and fell to his ankle. He held out his arms with a wince. "What do you think? I hope I don't bleed through and ruin it."

"It suits you," Taibon answered. "And it is yours, so don't worry about the blood." Loral nodded in agreement, then picked up his gray tunic and slipped it on.

Josh and Loral stood under the flower-covered arbor looking at the crowd of nearly fifty people. Consisting mostly of brightly dressed Melal and gray-clad Cathardi with a few other races spattered through, the crowd buzzed with conversation. Josh didn't even know most of them, though he recognized a few. Some were business acquaintances he had met while working with Loral, others he had seen but didn't know: employees at Taibon's, military police, and shopkeepers. He couldn't help staring at all of them.

Loral leaned closer to Josh. "I told you. You are a celebrity. Besides, this is the first actual wedding we have held in over four years. Everyone wants to be a part of it."

The crowd, cheering and rising to its feet, interrupted Loral. Josh's jaw dropped when he saw Kim at the door of the house. She was radiant in a knee-length royal blue off-the-shoulder gown. Her blonde hair was in thin braids, forming a crown on her head. Her entire face glowed. She was stunningly beautiful. The short round Melal females made the petite Kim appear tall and elegant as they walked down to the arbor to join Josh. He stared into her moist blue eyes.

She is amazing. Will I ever be able to tell her I still get flashbacks to the mission and Liria? Am I being honest with her?

The actual ceremony was a blur for Josh. The joy on Kim's face enraptured him, blocking out everything else. When the ceremony ended with a passionate kiss, the crowd cheered, and Loral led them to a table. Loral joined them along with Commander Caran, head of the local Cathardi forces, whom Josh had only met once, and Taibon. They ate the meat from a local beast Loral had cooked in a pit overnight, a variety of cooked vegetables, fresh fruits, and a strong, cold beer. After the first cup, Josh just sipped the beer, nursing the second cup until the end of the feast.

The conversation at the table centered on the state of the mines and the town itself. Taibon and Commander Caran disagreed on many things, making the conversation interesting without descending into an argument. They knew each other well.

During a lull in their debate, the commander turned to Kim. "How do you two like Bapto so far?"

"I feel like I have found a home," Kim said. "A place where I can settle in, maybe raise a family. I love the farm, the warmth, and the sunlight."

"I am glad to hear that. We need more settlers like you who want to make this their home. So many of the miners and others come looking only to make a fortune with little regard for the community."

"Are you referring to me?" Taibon said.

"No, I am not, and you know it. Unlike others, you came to settle. You do a lot for the community, and even though I do not approve of every part of your business, I know it helps keep the miners and others from more destructive behavior."

Taibon turned to Josh. "Don't mind us. The commander and I are quite good friends. We eat together monthly and enjoy arguing about current events."

Josh took a sip of beer and laughed. "It is good to have friends, and I look forward to making more here without being referred to as Nakir."

"Speaking of that," the commander said. "Where did you learn to fight like that?"

"On my homeworld, at the school where I learned about space travel. But honestly, I just got lucky. The big guy was slow and lost his balance." Josh turned to Kim, not wanting to go further into the conversation.

After the meal, Kim and Josh circulated among the attendees, introducing themselves and enjoying meeting new people. The sun was getting higher, and the increasing midday heat and humidity made it uncomfortably warm, so people began to leave.

Loral and his helpers loaded the lorry for the trip back into town, but before leaving, he escorted them into the cabin. Then said, "May the Creator give you joy and peace as you become one in His eyes. Enjoy each other. There is food in the kitchen. I will be away for a couple of days, so all you need to worry about is feeding the stock."

In the cabin, Kim went into the bedroom to change out of her wedding gown. Josh took off the tunic he wore and laid it across the back of a chair. It hurt when he lifted his arm to remove the tunic.

When Kim came out of the bedroom in a short sleeveless dress and looked at him, she said, "What happened? There's blood on your shirt."

She hurried over and helped him take off the torn, bloody garment. "How did you get this?" she asked with her hands on her hips.

Josh told about the incident with the gwenna. "Loral said it would heal, but that I would be sore for a few days. I am all right if I don't lift my arm too high. I think the pain meds have worn off and I need to take more."

"What about tonight?" Kim's lower lip protruded slightly. "I have been waiting to get close to you."

"Tonight will be wonderful. We will just need to take our time. I am really fine." Josh smiled. "I can't wait to get off that cot and into your arms."

CHAPTER 13

J osh had just finished loading the titanium powder into the electron beam printer when Loral came into the shop. "Good morning, Josh. What are you working on today?"

"This is the yoke for the Norfac Mine. It will be ready in three days if the power stays steady. I hope the upgrades we made to the backup generator will prevent any losses. I also have the new polymer gears in the laser sintering machine for Taibon's gaming table. They will finish today."

"I still find it hard to believe how much work you put out. Even with three people working for me, we never produced this much."

"I just know the equipment." Josh shrugged. "It's not much different from the machines I ran at my father's shop, plus we have organized things a little better."

"You cleaned this place up." Loral pointed to the once cluttered work benches. "It looks like a Cathardi factory, clean, and organized, with everything labeled."

"Yeah, on Earth there is an expression: A place for everything, and everything in its place." Josh closed the e-beam machine door.

"I am going into town. Do we need anything?" Loral asked.

"No, I don't expect the freighter engine part until next week, and we can evaluate it once it is here."

Loral walked out, and Josh turned to the e-beam control and input the program and parameters. He enjoyed working in Loral's shop. It reminded him of home and kept his mind busy. He smiled and thought about the change in Kim since their arrival. She seemed happy. He often found her singing and dancing around the cabin or the farm. Several of the ladies who attended the wedding spent time with her, including a couple of Taibon's girls, which surprised him. He had never thought of Kim as someone who would associate with exotic dancers. But they are just young women trying to survive in this wild place. Many other couples they knew met at a pleasure house.

He heard a vehicle drive into the yard just as he started the e-beam cycle. A short black-haired alien in the dirty clothes of a miner ran into the shop. "Where is Loral?" he said, his wide eyes scanning the shop. "We've had a cave-in, and our extractor broke. It trapped several miners."

"Loral went into town and may not be back until tomorrow," Josh answered.

"Can you help? The extractor auger does not work, and the miners will run out of air before morning if we don't do something."

"I can try. I'll look at the extractor, but if it needs any major repairs, I won't be able to fix it in time. Can you get an extractor from another mine?"

"We are trying. Please come. We need help?"

"Give me a few minutes. I must gather some tools." Josh grabbed a bag and quickly gathered various tools to take with him.

He followed the miner out the door and hollered to Kim, who had stepped out of the cabin door. "There is an emergency at a mine. I'm going to see if I can help." He kissed her, then climbed into the miner's vehicle.

It took over an hour for them to reach the mine near the timberline. When they got there, the shift foreman and another miner took Josh down four levels deep into the mountain. The brightly lit shaft they entered sloped down for a quarter of a mile before leveling out and continuing. Josh saw the extractor partially buried in a dark rubble pile. The cave-in had knocked out the power for the section of lights near the working face. The shift foreman handed Josh a headlamp. As they got closer, he saw the front third of the dimly lit extractor buried in the darker rubble pile. He took a few minutes and walked around the extractor. He heard the whine of the conveyor motor and saw the indicator lights on the dash, but the auger was not turning.

"Who was operating the unit when it stopped?" Josh asked.

A miner stepped toward Josh. "I was. It worked fine until it got here. Then it growled and stopped with a clunk. The maintenance guy checked the circuits and hydraulic lines, but everything was good."

Josh crawled under the front of the extractor to the auger drive. He called to the driver, "Shut off the power. Do you have a bucket? I need to open this gearbox, and I need my tool bag."

The driver slid both the tool bag and bucket under the machine to him. He moved the bucket under the gearbox and removed the drain plug to let the fluid out. Once the oil had finished draining, he removed the lower cover and looked inside. The main gear was missing a tooth and had several chipped teeth, as did the secondary gear. Looking closer, he saw the missing tooth wedged between the two gears. He took his handheld laser cutter and goggles out of the bag.

It took several minutes to cut the missing tooth free, but it finally fell out from between the gears. After that, with the auger disengaged, he tried to turn the gears by hand, but they wouldn't turn. He smoothed out the chipped teeth with his micro-grinder until the gears meshed easily, and he could turn them by hand. He put the cover back on and screwed in the drain plugged, and he slid the bucket out. "Put new fluid in the gearbox and then slowly try the auger."

He stayed under the machine to make sure no fluid leaked.

The operator restarted the extractor but had the auger speed set too fast. When he engaged it, the extractor lunged forward, dislodging the rubble pile around the auger. Josh couldn't move fast enough. A boulder rolled under the extractor and onto his chest, cutting off his yell.

Everything went black...

***

Consciousness came slowly. He looked through bleary eyes at the stark white ceiling. Pain shot through his chest when he tried to move. His throat felt parched, and he had a tube in his nose. Kim's face appeared above him. "Don't move. The doctor is on his way." There were tears in her blue eyes. "I thought I'd lost you — you've been out for three days."

Another face joined Kim's. "I am Doctor Arlo. Please remain still. Your injuries are quite severe and not yet sufficiently healed. You are lucky to be alive," the Cathardi doctor said. "The mine medic did a good job stabilizing you before the evacuation shuttle could get there to fly you down from the mountain. You have a punctured lung, and you suffered significant internal bleeding. Fortunately, we were able to synthesize plasma to replace the fluid you lost. Fortunately, none of your other major organs sustained any damage. I am going to give you some pain medication. It will put you back to sleep and keep you from moving too much."

When Josh awoke the following day, Kim and Loral were both in the room. The tube was missing from his nose, but his throat still hurt, and the pain in his chest made it hard to breathe.

"I will get the doctor," Loral said and left.

"The doctors say you are recovering well. They expect you to come home in a day or two." Kim sounded happy, but the creases in her forehead showed her worry.

The doctor came in and was examining Josh when he heard someone knock. "May I speak to the patient in private?" He turned his head at the familiar voice. It was Commander Caran, the Cathardi military commander.

"Give me a minute to finish. You can wait outside, and I will call you in," the doctor said. When he finished, he left with Kim and Loral, while the commander entered the room.

"Josh, my friend, you have put me in a difficult situation," he said. "My superiors consider you an enemy of the Cathardi people, and every unit is on alert to find you and your companion. But your time here on Bapto makes me doubt you are an enemy of the state. Loral and I did some discreet checking. They held you against the recommendation of the sisterhood, and other than the unauthorized departure from the station orbiting Melal, you have committed no crime. Can you tell me why they have labeled you such a threat?"

"I piloted a shuttle into the Cathardi system on a diplomatic mission," Josh admitted, knowing it might mean deportation.

"You know the location of the Cathardi home world?" The commander's eyebrows rose.

"I do. Are you going to send us back?" Josh tried to sit. "If they confine us to that station again, it could kill Kim."

"I don't plan to send you back, at least not yet. You require more time to heal, and Loral believes you are just as secure if we restrict you to Bapto. He and others here do not want you sent away. They say you saved twenty miners the day of the accident. I will investigate further, and we will talk again after you have recovered. I won't contact my superiors until we talk."

After he left, Kim and Loral came back into the room. "What did the commander want?" Kim took his hand.

Did she know? She looks troubled. "He just had a couple of questions regarding the accident. He'll be by to talk more after I recover."

"Once again, you are a hero," Loral said. "The miners you rescued want you to get an award."

"They want to give me an award for getting my chest caved in?" Josh tried to laugh but only coughed. "I wasn't a hero. I was a mechanic."

"An excellent mechanic." Loral stood. "I will leave you two alone. I'm sure there are things you need to talk about."

Kim stayed with him, but they talked very little. Josh felt she was worried, but he couldn't concentrate long enough to ask her what troubled her. They would be home soon. They could talk then.

***

Josh had been back at the cabin for a couple of days before he finally felt able to step outside. When he did, Maci started whistling and stomping her feet, looking at him. He walked over to the corral, and she pushed her head into his chest. He winced. "Glad to see you too, girl," he said as he scratched behind her ears. "It is good to be home, at least for a little while."

His conversation with the commander still worried him. He and Kim might have to flee the area if not the planet. Kim wouldn't be happy, but he didn't think she would go back to the Melal station. He needed to talk to her. Besides, something was bothering her. They had barely talked since he got home from the hospital.

"You finally made it out of the house. Are you ready to get to work?" Loral's voice startled him.

He turned and faced his friend. "I'm ready, but I'm not sure how much I can do."

"You can work into it slowly. I have hired a couple of technicians to help with the physical tasks, but I am not as proficient with the programming as you are." Loral came over and put his hand on Josh's shoulder. "How is Kim holding up?"

"Okay, I think. But she seems stressed. She doesn't talk as much or laugh as easily as I remember. I think the accident scared her and worried her."

"You need to talk to her. She needs to know about Commander Caran's dilemma. Only you and I know he is aware of your identity," Loral said, before turning to return to the shop.

"Hey beautiful," Josh said later when he returned to their cabin. Kim was at the sink rinsing vegetables for lunch. "Would you like to go for a walk before it gets too hot?"

"Sure, let me finish these." She rinsed the last few and dried her hands.

They went outside and Josh took her hand. "You will need to take it slow. I'm not fully fit yet." They strolled up to and along the road, then stopped at the clearing they went by on their first day at Loral's. Josh pointed to a fallen tree on the edge of the kavi vines. "Let's sit."

They watched the mandili's snake-like heads pop up and down among the vines for a few minutes before Josh asked, "What's troubling you? You seem worried and distracted since I got out of the hospital."

"Do you love me?" Tears were forming in her eyes. "Don't I please you?"

"Of course, I love you—I married you. You make me happy." *Where did that come from?*

"You married me out of necessity." She pulled her hand away from his. "You didn't want to."

Something is wrong. What did I do? "Kim, I know the circumstances were strange, but I wanted to marry you. I'm glad I married you. I need you, and I want to spend my life with you."

"What about Liria?"

"Liria, what does the Ompresti have to do with this?"

She turned her back to him. "You called her name while you were unconscious in the hospital."

They sat in silence for several minutes. *How do I explain this to her? Will she understand what happened? Do I tell her I still see Liria in my mind, even when I'm with her? I'm dead.*

Then Josh told her everything that had happened since the night on the shuttle when he came down while Liria prayed. "I don't know how, but I can still feel her in my mind. It wasn't my choice, and I didn't ask for it, but it's there." He reached for her hand. "I didn't choose her. I chose you!"

Kim turned to face him again. "I don't know if I believe you, but thank you for telling me."

"When we get back, maybe you can talk to Loral. He understands and can explain my connection with Liria better than I can."

They sat in silence, and then Kim took his hand. "Do you really choose me?"

"Yes, I really choose you."

"Good, because I am going to have your baby."

"You're pregnant? When?"

"I'm a little over two months along. I found out the day of your accident."

"This is great. Is it a boy or a girl?"

"I don't know yet. Does it matter?"

"No, I can't wait to be a dad." Josh grinned and pulled her close. The sparkle in her eyes told him she was happy.

They talked about planning for the baby; what to name it, where it would sleep, and who it would look like. They held hands as they walked home. Kim was smiling again.

When they got close to the farm, Josh stopped and pulled Kim back. "What's wrong?" She asked.

"Commander Caran is there. He knows who we are and where we came from, though he seemed reluctant to send us back." They moved behind some trees where they couldn't be seen from the farm. "The Cathardi consider us enemies of the state and want us returned to the Melal station. I planned on telling you while we walked, but I got too excited about the baby and forgot. Let's step into the forest and wait for him to leave."

They watched in silence for a while.

"I will not let them take us back to that station. If they come for us, we can go into the forest and find a safe place away from the authorities," Josh said.

"But what about our baby? We will need to be close to medical care in case of an emergency. It's not just you and me now." She pulled him around, so he faced her. "We must think about what is best for our child. I'm willing to go back if we must. Besides, you said he was reluctant to send us back. Let's go down there and find out."

"Are you sure?"

Kim nodded and stepped out of the foliage. Josh followed, just as the commander and Loral came out of the house. Loral waved at them and stood with Commander Caran, waiting for them. *Maybe that's a good sign.*

"I am glad to see you two," the Commander said when they were closer. "I have decided not to arrest you, though I am prohibiting you from leaving Bapto. Loral has assured me you are trustworthy. But I know, based on your previous actions, that if you wanted to escape, you would find a way. I hope you will not make me look like a fool. If my superiors knew, it would ruin my career."

"We don't want to escape," Kim said. "This is our home. We're going to raise our family here." She stood erect, looking confident and determined.

Maybe things will finally work out for us. "I'm thirsty," Josh said. "Would you like to come in with us?"

"No, thank you. I just wanted to tell you personally. I'm needed in town." The commander got into his vehicle and left them there.

"Let's go into the house," Loral said. "It looks like you two have worked through some of your issues since the accident."

"I want to talk to you," Kim said. "You can enlighten me on this connection between Josh and Liria."

"Good, He told you. Let's go inside and talk."

***

Josh parked the lorry in front of Taibon's pleasure house and walked to the door. In the months since the accident at the mine, he and Taibon had become friends. The doorman opened it as he approached. "Taibon is in his office. He is expecting you, so go right in."

The main gaming room was almost empty this early in the day, with only a few customers sitting around the stage where the girls danced while the music echoed in the cavernous room. Josh saw Taibon, who looked up, as he entered through the already opened office door. "Hello, my friend, did you bring the new capo wheel?"

"Yes, it's on the back of the lorry out front. I also upgraded the programming slightly to make it more random."

"Great, I'll have it brought in." He called to the girl who was serving drinks just outside his door. "Go find Lial and tell him to get enough help to bring the new capo wheel in off the lorry. He knows where it goes. Then, please bring us some cold tea." Turning back to Josh, he continued. "Sit. Have some tea with me. You look like you're recovering well since the accident."

"Yes, quite well, I'm nearly back to full strength and I've been very busy in the shop."

"Rumor has it the Cathardi hierarchy wants you deported."

"Commander Caran has restricted us to Bapto. We're not allowed to go off-world. He thinks the threat is overblown. For now, he hasn't reported us to his superiors." Josh looked at the Melal to see if he could read his motives. *He is a friend, but he is also Melal. Were the Cathardi offering a reward?*

"If I were you, I would keep my options open," Taibon said. "Commander Caran is pragmatic, but the Cathardi regularly reassigns military personnel. There is no guarantee the next commander will be as accommodating. Fortunately for me, Loral was the Commander when I first arrived, and by the time they replaced him, I had enough time to establish my business here."

"Loral was Commander here? I thought he was a priest."

"He was both. Did you know he was a hero?" Josh shook his head. "He destroyed an Urlak ship after it attacked several Cathardi outposts. Then they ambushed the vessel he was on when it arrived to investigate. The story I heard was the Urlak killed everyone on the bridge. Loral was second in command in the engine room. I don't know all the details, but he performed a jump maneuver with the enemy vessel near some wreckage. It was destroyed in the wake. Afterward, they offered him any position he wanted. He wanted to go away from the war. They say his mate was on the bridge at the time of the attack. So, he came here as the Commander."

The girl came back into the office, interrupting Taibon. "Lial says the table is ready to test. Do you want to watch?"

"No, tell him to go ahead. I'll check it later. I still need to talk with my friend," Taibon answered before continuing. "Later, when they wanted to reassign him, Loral resigned his commission and became the post priest, because he wanted to stay on Bapto. Since that time, many commanders have come and gone, and they each make changes, but the colony survives, because the Cathardi don't have enough troops or miners to turn Bapto into an entirely Cathardi colony. All they can do is maintain a semblance of order. They allow me to operate because I provide an outlet for the miners that rarely results in violence."

Taibon picked up a data pad from his desk and handed it to Josh. "It's an invitation to a birthday dinner I am hosting. I would like you, Kim, and Loral to attend. It is informal, just for friends, and will be at my home. Talk it over with Kim and let me know if you can be there."

He looked at the information on the data pad and transferred it to his own. "Thank you. I will let you know after I talk to her. My guess is we will attend, but some days she does not feel well enough."

"Oh yes, the baby is coming soon. Give her my regards."

Josh left the meeting troubled by the thought of a new commander. He would investigate his options. Though Kim had said she would return, he didn't want to leave. Bapto was home now.

CHAPTER 14

It was Liria's first visit to the convent, though she had heard much about it from the other sisters. Built directly into the cliffs high in the Carsas Mountains, the highest on Cathardi, it overlooked the Capricic River Gorge several hundred feet below. Cut into the solid rock of the cliffs, the passages and chambers formed an underground complex. Colorful tapestries depicting natural scenes from the planet and floral-patterned drapes lined the stone walls to dampen the natural reverberations. Sleeping chambers, all of them along the cliff face, had balconies overlooking the gorge. Each contained simple furnishings: a single bed, a desk, a lamp, and a small wardrobe.

For the first few weeks of her stay, she felt as though God had closed his ears. Her prayers and pleas echoed off the stone ceiling. Nothing seemed to get through. *Is God real? Did I imagine hearing his voice? Does he really care about me?*

She spent days fasting and praying. The evening of her twenty-fourth day while fasting, she collapsed in a trance on her balcony.

Lying there on the floor, she heard a voice calling to her, "Liria, my child." The voice grew louder and clearer. "Liria, my child." She tried to get up but could not.

The figure of a man surrounded by brilliant light stood over her. It was his voice she heard.

"Yes Lord," she answered, still unable to move her arms or legs.

"Be patient," the voice said. "I have not forgotten you. I have heard your cries, and I am with you. Be patient, it is not yet time. Soon I will reveal your task."

The light faded to darkness, and the voice silenced. She stayed in the silent darkness for a long time until she heard another voice calling her, "Liria, Liria, wake up! Are you all right?"

She opened her eyes and saw Lenara, the tall elder sister of the convent, kneeling over her. Her long gray braids, hanging down over Liria's face. "It worried me that you missed prayer this morning."

"I am well. I dreamed," she said. "God spoke to me. He has not forsaken me."

"Let me help you up." Lenara took Liria's hand and helped her to stand. "Are you sure you are feeling well?" she asked again. The softness in the elder sister's eyes belied the harsh features of her angular face.

"I am cold, but I think I am fine," Liria answered.

Lenara took the blanket from the bed, and put it around Liria's shoulders, then helped her stand before taking her back inside.

"Since you first arrived here, I have sensed feelings of loss and doubt in you," the soft-spoken administrator said, leading her out into the passageway toward the kitchen. "Now, I sense the powerful presence of God's peace surrounding you. Have you received the answers you sought?"

They sat at a table near the wall, away from the main preparation areas. The cook brought Liria a bowl of hot cereal and a cup of strong tea. Lenara sipped her own tea as Liria told her of her dream between spoons of hot grain. "I thought God had deserted me, but he just wanted me to wait. He is still with me. I did not receive all my answers, but I am sure God will reveal them to me in time." Liria smiled for the first time since her arrival at the convent.

After that, Liria settled into life at the convent. She taught the acolytes, whose silliness amused her, reminding her of the girls at the order's school. They all wanted to hear stories of Earth and how its religious beliefs intertwined with the sacred texts of Cathardi. Retelling her experiences on Earth often saddened her, but the constant reassuring presence of God always comforted her.

One evening, months later, she sat on the balcony of her room watching the birds soar, swooping in and out among the cliffs. Their hypnotic motion caused her to slip into another trance. Again, she heard a voice calling her name. The voice was oddly familiar, not the same as the voice from her previous vision, but a voice she knew.

"Liria, Liria, Liria forgive me," it said. The figure came closer.

She knew the figure. "Father?" she asked.

"Yes Liria, you must forgive me," he pleaded.

"I have forgiven you, father!" she exclaimed.

"No, not for leaving you; not for killing your mother. Liria, I have destroyed us all! You must forgive me!"

"Forgive what, father? How have you destroyed us?"

She awoke quite agitated. Trembling, she got up and staggered down the passageway to Lenara's chambers. The elder listened patiently as Liria recounted her dream. "I am so confused!" she said. "My dreams have always been so clear. Now, they leave me with more questions. Questions I cannot answer." She sank back into her chair.

"Since you arrived," Lenara said. "You have had doubts about God, about his speaking to you, and the truth of what he has shown you. I think you still need to be patient." Lenara reached across the table and took her hand. "He is rebuilding your faith slowly. Allowing you to realize your timing is not his timing. Just because you want to know the answer now does not mean he will reveal it now. It may be later, much later, before he reveals it. Now, be patient. Why don't we plan on talking regularly, especially when you dream? Maybe we can discern the answers together. God will give you the answers you seek when you are ready."

"Thank you. It will help to talk. I have felt very alone since I returned to Cathardi."

***

Liria went to the crowded kitchen, where the sisters busily cleaned up after the morning meal. She made her way to the table beside the large fireplace, where Lenara sat with a cup of hot tea waiting for her. They had met weekly since Liria's dream. They talked about everything from Liria's dreams to her experiences at the convent. This morning, after the cook brought her a cup of tea, he left to join the bustle in the main part of the kitchen, allowing the noise to cover her and Lenara's conversation.

"Good morning, Ompresti. I would ask if you slept well, but I can see by your face, you did not. Are you still dreaming of the invasion?"

"Yes. I continue to dream of the Urlak ships appearing over Cathardi. But I still do not have any clarity other than knowing it is an invasion. I know it is coming, but nothing more."

Lenara held her teacup and looked into Liria's eyes. "You have dreamed this for several weeks, but it has not disturbed you this much since the first week. What has brought about this change?"

"It is a new dream that does not seem to fit within the prophecy. I am on a strange planet where Urlak soldiers are chasing me through the jungle. They capture me and one Urlak glares at me, threatening me with his weapon. 'Can your God save you now?' he taunts. Then I wake up."

"How frightening. No wonder it disturbed you." Lenara sipped her tea. "We have talked regularly for months now, and one thing is very clear. God gives you the answers you need when it is time."

Liria smiled at the older woman. "That is true. You always reassure me of that when we talk."

The two women sat and drank their tea in silence for a few minutes, then Lenara said. "Something else is troubling you. Something you are not telling me."

Do I tell her about my dreams of Josh? "There are other dreams, but they are personal." Liria's cheeks reddened.

"Sometimes, just talking about the things that disturb us is enough to help us sort them out. It can help to bring clarity." Lenara signaled the cook to bring more tea.

Liria waited until the cook set the pot down on the table. "The dreams are embarrassing. They involve the shuttle pilot Josh and one of his crew."

"He is the one you had the unusually deep connection with during the trip. The one you believed was to fulfill the prophe cy.?"

"Yes." *Why is this so hard to talk about? I can trust Lenara.*

"Tell me about the dreams. You do not have to go into detail. You know I was young once."

"Ever since that night on the shuttle, I have felt different about him." Liria could not look into Lenara's eyes even knowing the older woman could sense her feelings. "The visions we had were exciting and brought out feelings I never felt before. Now I dream about him and intimate physical contact. Sometimes he is with me. Sometimes he is with the crewman Kim. When he is with me, I feel pleasure and even joy. When he is with her, I am angry and jealous. Last night's dream was about them, and it was very graphic. He seemed happy, and that confused me. I should be happy for him, but it hurt me."

"It sounds to me like you love the pilot. And now that circumstances have separated you from him, it is difficult to determine if your dream is just a dream associated with your memories of the voyage or if they are more real and the result of your connection with him. Your dreams are natural, and they should not be a source of shame or embarrassment. Your feelings are genuine, and your connection is real. God will sort out these dreams, just like He will sort out your prophetic dreams."

Liria's father still appeared as a recurring figure in her dreams. He always asked for forgiveness. Each time, it seemed more urgent, and each time he revealed slightly more. The usual images centered on a Melal, several alien females, and jula juice. Finally, one night, she slipped into a trance. Her father sat at a table in a dimly lit room with a Melal he addressed as Taibon. Her father drank blood-red jula juice from a cup.

"They treat me like I am an alien. They keep me on this God-forsaken run hauling ore. At the station, they belittle my wife and daughter. You, Taibon, are the only real friend I have," her father said.

"Listen, my friend, I think you have had enough of the jula juice for the evening. Let me get you a room so you can sleep it off. We can talk again in the morning."

"Wait, just one more round, then I will go. I need to talk to someone."

"One of my girls will gladly listen to you." He pressed a button on the table and a girl came into the room. "Bring us another round and then take my friend to room fourteen."

The girl left and Taibon stood to leave, but Liria's father grabbed his arm.

"They think I am stupid, but I know their secret just like all the other Cathardi pilots they train."

"What secret? It is the jula juice talking. You need to sleep it off."

"I know the secret they never tell an off-worlder."

Then Liria heard her father tell Taibon about the location of the Cathardi home world. Liria awoke, startled. Her heart raced. She ran to Lenara's chambers and knocked.

Lenara opened the door. "Liria, come in. What has brought you here? Are you okay?"

"I have had another dream, and it is important."

They sat in Lenara's chamber and Liria told her about the dream.

"It upset you. But are you sure he gave the correct location?" Lenara asked.

"I am certain, and I know the dream is a warning. We must let the council know of the danger."

"I will contact the elders on the council. They may want to meet with you. For now, you need to pray and ask for guidance."

Liria returned to her room and prayed. *Creator, help me understand. These dreams are confusing. Give me clarity to know your will.*

Lenara sat at the desk after she brought the evening meal to Liria's room. "I have contacted the elders. They have asked to meet with you. A transport will pick you up in the morning to take you to the capital. Moira will meet you when you land."

That night, Liria's dreams were more disturbing and confusing. They jumped between the Urlak invasion and Urlak soldiers chasing her and taunting her. *Something is wrong. Something is missing. Creator, help me see clearly.*

Moira met her when she arrived in the capital. "The council has agreed to meet with you immediately. From what Lenara has told us, you have very disturbing information."

She escorted her to the council chambers, where she repeated her dream.

"I believe God revealed to me a great danger to our people. I fear because of my personal confusion that I may be too late. It is my belief we should prepare for an invasion of the Cathardi system. I also believe someone must go to Bapto and find the Melal Taibon before he can reveal the location of our planet if we are to have any hope of avoiding disaster," she said. Though her stomach churned, and she could not keep her hands still, she stood erect with her chin up. The certainty and confidence in her voice surprised her.

"Thank you, Ompresti," Marlon said. "Give the council time to deliberate on what you have told us. We will convene again when we have a consensus." He stood, signaling an end to the meeting.

***

"Commander." the communications officer approached Garond. "There is a distress call from an unidentified ship that just entered the system."

"Call Sub-commander Morforn to the bridge," Garond ordered, pulling up the details of the report on his monitor.

He hoped they might get information on how to find the Cathardi homeworld. If he could find it, he could skip this worthless rock. Though he doubted the freighter would provide any meaningful information, the interrogation would provide a brief distraction now that the assault on the planet below had bogged down.

"Commander." Morforn crossed his arms. "You sent for me."

"Sub-commander," Garond said and stood. "Have you seen the report on the distress beacon we are receiving?"

"Not yet, sir."

"Review it quickly, Sub-commander. You must bring the vessel and its crew here intact." Garond looked down on his second in command from the raised platform of the command station. "I will not tolerate another failure. We must interrogate the crew and analyze their ship's data. Do you understand?"

"Yes, sir!"

***

When Morforn returned with the captured freighter, Garond ordered the immediate interrogation of the crew. Garond went to watch and listen. He leaned on the railing of the observation platform above the interrogation chamber where they held the captured crew. The smell of urine, sweat, and fear rose from the chamber. The crew's fear showed in their wide-eyed stares and shaking. *This will not take long. They are weak.*

The Melal crew, restrained to one wall, faced the center of the chamber, where the first crewman lay strapped to the table. The Urlak interrogator slowly skinned him alive. Garond smiled when the prisoner screamed. He enjoyed watching the patient and the very precise interrogator work, eliciting the maximum level of pain without causing death. When the prisoner lost consciousness, he simply stopped and waited until his assistant revived the victim. Then he began again. Without a single question, he skinned the helpless Melal from neck to ankle. The prisoner's voice, hoarse from screaming, was barely audible when the interrogator finished with him. The interrogator turned and looked at the remaining captives. He pointed to a second, turned back to the first and, with a quick slash, cut his throat.

Once they strapped the second captive to the table, the interrogator asked, "Where is the Cathardi home world?"

When the prisoner did not know, the interrogator began the process on him. Each time they revived the prisoner, he asked the same question, and each time the prisoner responded, that he didn't know.

After the interrogator finished with the second Melal crewman, Garond laughed. *The next one will talk.*

They strapped the third Melal to the table. The interrogator asked, "Where is the Cathardi home world?"

The prisoner screamed, "I don't know! None of us do! They keep it a secret. Only the captain might know something."

"Which one is the captain?" the interrogator asked.

"The one with the broken arm."

Erinda screamed curses at the crewman as the interrogator turned and pointed at him. But his curses were in vain as they strapped him to the table, and the interrogator asked, "Where is the Cathardi home world?"

Erinda cursed some more and yelled, "I don't know. They don't let us go there. Only the Cathardi know."

The interrogator smiled and began the process on the freighter captain. After reviving him for the second time, the interrogator asked again, "Where is the Cathardi home world?"

Erinda sobbed, "I don't know." Then he lifted his head and whispered, "Taibon knows."

"Which one is Taibon?" the interrogator asked.

"He is not part of the crew. He runs a pleasure house on Bapto. But he said he knew the location of Cathardi," Erinda said. "He let the secret out over dinner one evening. Taibon said it was his ace in the hole, his security blanket."

"Tell me more," the interrogator put the knife to Erinda's throat.

The Melal told him everything, including the location for Bapto, how to find Taibon and the Cathardi military presence on the planet's surface and in orbit.

Then the interrogator ended Erinda's pain and looked up at Garond, who nodded and left the chamber.

The interrogator could have fun with the remaining Melal. Garond needed to plan the mission to Bapto. If this Melal, Taibon, really knew the location of the Cathardi home world, they would need to take him alive and in secret. Their attack on Cathardi must be a surprise.

***

After the meeting, Marlon met with Bakar and Goian, the other two civilian council members, in his office. "How do you think we should respond?" he asked them.

"We need to find this Melal and bring him back. If word gets out to the people, there will be an uproar." Goian answered.

"Do we know anything about the location she gave?" Bakar asked.

Marlon signaled for the attendant standing at the door. "Go to the freighter routing office and see if they can tell you what is at this location." He entered the location on a data pad and gave it to the attendant. "Bring it back to me as soon as you have an answer."

He waited for the attendant to leave, and then he said to the councilmen, "Goian is correct. We need to keep this quiet. We must do everything in secret. If it turns out to be a false alarm, we can put the blame on the sisterhood and their upstart Ompresti. If it is true, we can take credit for acting in the best interests of the Cathardi people. Goian, you will filter everything that is released for public information. Bakar, you will interface with the generals and work to keep them on our side."

They discussed their options until the attendant returned with a name for the location provided by Liria. Marlon read the data pad. "Bapto, do we know anything about Bapto?"

"If I may," the attendant said. "Bapto is a frontier mining planet. If you will continue reading the information, it says that, before his untimely death, the Ompresti's father piloted a freighter bringing ore from Bapto to the Melal station."

"Thank you. You may leave." Maron said, smiling. "Now we have the Ompresti right where we want her. The Ompresti's father bears the responsibility for this crisis, and possibly the Ompresti herself."

"May I suggest we send her with a small detachment to Bapto? Then, if she fails, it really is her fault." Bakar said.

"Good idea. I will call the council together and present our plan. I think even the Sisterhood will approve. While we wait for the council to assemble, Bakar, you will go through the plan outline with the generals. We must have their support."

Two days later, at dawn, Marlon and the other council members watched as Liria and two acolytes, accompanied by a government liaison and a company of soldiers, boarded a shuttle. The secret departure was arranged to prevent the arousal of public speculation due to Liria's notoriety.

No one except Liria, not even the crew or the soldiers, would know their destination until she handed the jump coordinates to the pilot after their departure.

Chapter 15

Josh was in a hangar on the landing field where he had just finished returning a repaired drive component for one of the field's vehicles. Earlier that morning, he had thought about Liria for the first time in months. Now, there was no mistake. She was close. He sensed her call for help. He finished his instructions to the mechanic on duty and went outside. The customs center was visible from the hangar door. Liria was there, and she was asking for help. *Why here? Why now?*

While he walked to the customs center, he saw Caran and the magistrate, along with other local officials, hurry into the building. This confirmed what he already knew. Liria was in there. The guards stopped him at the door before he could enter the building. But a Cathardi officer stepped out. "He is not to be detained. The Ompresti is expecting him."

The officer pointed to the ramp leading to the upper level. "If you will come with me, Captain."

"I'm not a captain anymore," Josh said. "What's going on here?"

"The Ompresti will explain," the officer said as they walked up.

Josh saw Liria standing in the center of the room, surrounded by local dignitaries. When they stepped into the room, the Cathardi officer forced his way through the crowd to Liria. He appeared to say something to her. She turned and made eye contact with Josh, then gave a hand signal to her escorts, who moved in to show the dignitaries out.

"I apologize, gentlemen," she said. "I must be leaving. It has been my pleasure to meet all of you, but my mission is very urgent."

After the soldiers escorted the officials out, Liria hugged Josh. "It is so good and unexpected to see you. I need your help. Do you know a Melal called Taibon?"

"I do," Josh answered. "Kim and Loral are with him now. I am due to join them for a celebration."

"Will you take me to him?" she asked. "It is urgent that we find him."

"If you wish, Ompresti."

She signaled the officer in charge of her escort. "The captain will take us to Taibon." She turned to Josh. "How far is it?"

"It is just at the edge of town," he said. "But you probably don't want to walk."

"I have arranged for vehicles with the local commander," the escort said. "They will deliver them soon."

Something was wrong. Josh sensed Liria's agitation. She wouldn't normally get so impatient. She couldn't stay still, pacing to the balcony and looking for the vehicles, then back to Josh, not saying anything. On her third trip from the balcony, she said, "The vehicles are here. We must go."

Josh directed Liria's party through the town, and then to Taibon's. *Kim will not be happy to see Liria. She still worries about the connection I have with her. Liria's agitation won't help.*

But before they reached the house, Liria said, "Stop the vehicles! Something is wrong. The Urlak are already here. We are too late."

"The Urlak!" the commander said. "We don't have any reports of the Urlak in this sector. Are you sure?"

"Yes, I can feel them." The color had drained from her face as she stared up the road. "Deploy your men. They are still in the house."

The escort commander spread his troops out before proceeding to the house. Then Josh and the commander went to the door. Liria refused to stay behind and joined them. The door stood wide open and the body of a young Melal female lay just inside. The commander signaled his men to move in ahead of them. As they moved down the hall, they encountered Urlak warriors and fighting erupted. Josh started down the hall, but the commander grabbed him. "Let my men do their job."

"But Kim is in there." Josh broke free and grabbed a weapon from a fallen Cathardi, then ran ahead of the Cathardi troops, through the weapons fire, straight to the parlor. He burst through the door only to find Kim in the grasp of an Urlak warrior who held a blade to her throat. Loral lay on the floor, dead or unconscious. Two additional Urlak warriors flanked the one holding Kim.

"Humans!" hissed the Urlak in Cathardi. "You are so weak. No wonder your world fell so easily."

The Urlak's communicator beeped, and the ground shook from the explosions from the other side of town. "Now you are too late," the Urlak said, drawing his blade across Kim's throat. Blood spewed as she sank to the floor.

"Noooo!" Josh screamed and fired, killing the warrior. Then he dove to the floor. He rolled left behind a chair that provided some cover from the fire of the remaining two Urlak.

He swallowed the bile in his throat. *They killed her! I've lost everything.* Josh fired again, killing another warrior. But the remaining Urlak kept him pinned down. He couldn't get a clear shot without exposing himself. He was about to move again when Cathardi troops finally entered and killed the last of the Urlak in the room.

Josh rushed to Kim's body. Falling to his knees, he picked up her bloodied head and held it in his lap. He stroked her forehead with tears streaming down his face. "Kim, beautiful Kim. Why?"

Liria came to him and put her hand on his shoulder. He looked up at her but couldn't see that she also had tears running down her face. His entire world was a blur. He kissed Kim's lips, smearing blood on his face.

"Commander Faras," he heard a soldier call. "The old man is alive, but the other Melal are all dead."

"Get the medic in here immediately!" the commander ordered. "I am sorry, Ompresti, they have taken the Melal. Our mission has failed."

What are they talking about? Why? Josh sensed Liria trying to comfort him, but he didn't want to be comforted. He wanted Kim and the baby.

He heard another soldier whispering something to the commander.

"My Lady," the commander said. "The Urlak have destroyed the landing field. All the ships report severe damage, including our shuttle. They have also knocked down the communications tower. They have cut us off. Reports from the garrison say the Urlak forces are fighting their way in this direction. We don't know how many are coming, so we must get you out of here."

Liria knelt beside Josh, trying to comfort him physically and reaching out to him mentally.

"Ompresti," the escort commander said. "We must get you out of here now. A larger Urlak force is just minutes away, and I do not think we can protect you."

"Where would I go? The Urlak are between us and the town. They destroyed our ship, and everywhere else is jungle."

"The medics revived the old man, Loral. He says the alien can guide you through the jungle."

Josh continued to stroke Kim's forehead and weep. He felt her hand leave his shoulder as she stood. She was trying to get through his grief with her thoughts.

"Get out of my head!" he said.

"I know you loved her deeply," she said, putting her hand back on his shoulder. "But the Urlak are coming, and I must leave now. Will you help me?"

He kissed Kim's forehead, then stood. His clothes were soaked with her blood. His face was smeared with blood and fists clenched at his sides. "Why should I help? Your people did not help my planet. You didn't help Kim. You're the reason I've lost everything."

Liria looked into his teary eyes. "Because I asked. And because you are a good man who cares about others. Even the Cathardi."

She kept eye contact with him for several seconds in silence. His shoulders slumped and his hands relaxed. "What do you need?"

"I must warn my people that the Urlak took Taibon. He can lead them to the Cathardi home world. If I do not warn them, the Urlak could overwhelm my world, just as they did your world. Can you take me someplace where I can communicate with our ships or find me another way off the planet?" she asked.

The commander interrupted them, "We must get you out of here now, Ompresti. The Urlak will be here in minutes. They have already reached our vehicles and they must not capture you."

Liria looked imploringly at Josh. He looked down at Kim, then back at her. "There is a small two-man shuttle in a mine west of town," Josh said. "It is several day's trek by foot, less if we can ride."

"Take a squad of men with you," the commander ordered a subordinate. "Go with the Ompresti. The rest of us will stay and hold them here as long as we can."

Loral came to him. "I will take care of her."

He took one last look at Kim, then picked up a weapon, grabbed Liria's arm, and pulled her through the kitchen, past the bodies of the servants, and out the back door. They ran across the open field to the rail fence Taibon put up to mark his property line. Beyond the fence was the jungle.

When they reached the cover of the jungle, they paused. Josh said, "The mine is northwest through the jungle. There is a road we can take about five kilometers north. It will take us to a farm just beyond the road that leads to the mine. If we are lucky, we can get supplies and pack animals there. Since the Urlak have the vehicles, the roads will not be safe. We will go through the jungle. Listen and do exactly as I say. The jungle is full of hidden dangers and unexpected hazards. I will lead. Liria will stay between the two of you." He pointed to the squad leader and another soldier. "We travel in single file."

As Josh finished, the sounds of fighting erupted behind them, near Taibon's house. He led them through the jungle. No air moved in the dense foliage. The hot air weighed on them as they pushed through the undergrowth; climbed over fallen trees; and avoided clearings. An hour into the trek, the soldier behind Josh said, "The Ompresti cannot keep up at this pace. We must rest."

Josh looked back at Liria. Her sweat-soaked robes clung to her, making it difficult for her to move. Josh signaled a rest. He went a few paces off the trail to a large bush where he picked grapefruit-sized red fruit and gave each of them one. After he handed them out, he cut the stem end from the one remaining in his hand and showed them how to drink the sweet juice. He bent down to Liria, who sat on a fallen tree.

"You will need to remove your outer robes." He whispered. She looked at him questioningly. "The rest of the trip is even more difficult. You will need to take off those heavy outer robes so you can move freely and not have to carry the extra weight."

She nodded and started removing her robes. The soldiers stood to protest, but Liria waved them back to their seats. She stripped to a light knee-length frock and the light leggings she wore under her robes. When she finished, Josh nodded his approval and started them through the jungle again. The fruit nectar had helped to restore their energy levels and Liria kept up the pace more easily without the heavy robes. Two hours later, Josh signaled another stop.

"Rest here while I check the road," he said and left them. He hurried to the edge of the jungle along the road. The way was clear, so he decided they should risk taking the road. They would make better progress and they could reach the farm before sunset.

After he returned, he told them, "When we get to the road, stay in single file, we'll walk along the shoulder. If I signal, move immediately back into the jungle. I want to make the farm before nightfall because the jungle is unsafe at night, especially with no supplies."

***

Josh led Liria and the soldiers up the road until they neared the fork, where he stopped and moved them off the road and into the jungle. He went ahead, where he checked both roads to ensure the way remained clear. When he returned, he told them, "The way is still clear. I'll take Liria across the fork first, then the rest of you will wait out of sight and follow individually every two to three minutes, checking the road before you cross."

After everyone was across, Josh left one soldier at the fork with orders to stay for thirty minutes before following. He took the others an additional two kilometers further up the left fork to a farm.

As they approached the farm, a man came down toward the road with a rifle in his hands. When he recognized Josh, he waved. "Hi Josh, what happened to you? You look terrible."

"Thanks, Mattu. I look better than I feel. I need your help."

"Sure, what can I do? Would you like some water or something to eat?"

"Yes, thank you." Josh knew Mattu wanted to know more, but he wasn't sure he could talk about it. "You are a good friend, but you may be in big trouble if you help us." He struggled to maintain his composure. "The Urlak have attacked. They killed Kim and may want to capture the Ompresti." He pointed to Liria, who stood a few feet away, watching them.

"Kim is dead? No wonder you look so bad. Come up to the house where there is shade." They followed him up to the farmhouse, where Mattu had them sit on the large porch that encircled the house. He brought food and cool water to the group.

Then Josh explained their situation to him, "We need enough supplies for at least two more days: food, water, shelter. If you have them? We are trying to get to the old mine above the cliffs. They used to have a small shuttle there."

"I have all of that and a sonic fence if you want it. You can even take the bonogos. But that is a dangerous section of the jungle. Why not take the road?"

"Thank you, the bonogos will help. I'm afraid the Urlak have vehicles, so I don't want to use the road just yet. If they're not following, maybe we can avoid the worst of the jungle and move to the road after the first day. Either way, the Ompresti can ride one bonogo if you have a saddle."

"I'll take care of that for you. Do you want to change out of those bloody clothes? I think I can find something you can wear." Mattu went to the door.

"Thank you, I do. Do you have anything more appropriate for the Ompresti?"

"Let's go look." Mattu took Liria and Josh inside, where he dug through some old clothes and found enough for both to change into. While they were changing, he went to show the soldiers where the supplies were and saddled the bonogos. When Josh finished dressing, they had loaded the supplies on the packsaddle on one bonogo. The other had a riding saddle for Liria.

Josh helped Liria onto the bonogo, then turned to Mattu. "Thank you, my friend. Take care of yourself. You should get away from here for at least a few days. The Urlak may follow us, and they are merciless."

"Don't worry about me." Mattu clasped his hand. "I will be gone, and I may leave a surprise or two for them. Good luck."

Josh led his party North, back into the jungle. They moved along game trails for a couple of hours until they came to a small clearing as the sun sank below the mountains, turning the sky a brilliant orange.

"We'll camp here tonight," Josh said. "Set the shelters up in a circle with the bonogos in the center. Then put the sonic fence another two meters out. That will discourage most of the wildlife from intruding on us. Put the infrared scope looking back down the trail." He pointed to a spot near a large rock with a good view of the trail. "We will maintain a watch with two-hour shifts. I will take the last shift."

One soldier helped Liria off the bonogo. Josh fettered both beasts, while the other soldiers set up the shelters, defenses, and a portable latrine. They ate a cold meal of dried meat and fruit.

Josh didn't allow a fire since they were still too close to the farm and the road. Everyone was exhausted, so there was little conversation as darkness fell.

"It sounds like the battle is over," one soldier said.

"Yes, but we don't know who won, so we will proceed with the original plan until we're sure the Urlak aren't following." Josh stood. "Get some rest. We break camp at first light. Who has the watch?" One soldier raised his hand. "Who is his relief?" The soldier on his right raised his hand.

"Good. The rest of you try to sleep. As hot as it was today, it will get quite cool tonight, so the sentry will want to keep moving to stay warm."

As they finished their meals, the group moved individually to their shelters. Josh checked the bonogos' fetters and the infrared scope before going to Liria's shelter.

"Ompresti, you did well today. Tomorrow will be more difficult as we go deeper into the jungle and climb toward the mountains. We'll not be resting as often unless you cannot keep up."

"I will tell you if I cannot keep up. Thank you for helping me." Josh saw her reach her hand out, but she stopped before touching him and looked down. He sensed her concern and her reluctance.

Since the sonic fence signaled the sentries through an earpiece, each time a creature approached, Josh figured it would keep them alert during their watch. The ultrasonic vibrations from the fence discouraged the animals from entering the perimeter. But for the others, the darkness and quiet meant they could all get a welcome rest, despite the tensions of the day.

Josh took the last watch, and even though he had not slept well, the fence alarms prevented him from dozing. The events of the day replayed in his mind. The sight of Kim's pregnant blood-soaked body sinking to the floor woke him several times. *God, why am I here? Why did Kim have to die? She was so happy and looking forward to the baby's arrival. What did we do to deserve this punishment?* He wept silently.

He thought back to the conversation he had with Mattu before leaving the farm. Hopefully, Mattu left before nightfall and had arranged a few surprises to keep the Urlak from "messing with his stuff".

The scream of a gwenna interrupted his melancholy. Though they still had an hour before sunrise, he roused the party so they could eat a quick meal and break camp. They moved into the jungle as the sun rose. If the Urlak followed, the next two days would be the hardest part of the journey.

That morning, they climbed steadily as they moved through the thicker jungle of the foothills. Josh led them, cutting a path through the undergrowth until they came to a game trail they could follow. Two hours later, he signaled a brief rest.

Sitting on a fallen tree trunk, he surveyed the rest of the party. Their clothing stuck to their bodies as they plopped onto any convenient rock or tree. Liria appeared to be in better shape, though sweat ran down her face from her matted hair, and she moved like her hips were stiff. *Bonogos are not the most comfort-*

able ride. If the Urlak aren't following, we can go to the road, making the trip to the mine easier.

A loud explosion behind them interrupted Josh's thoughts. "I'm certain the explosion was Mattu's fuel supply," he said to the squad leader. "That means the Urlak wanted it for their vehicles, so we will need to stay away from the road and in the jungle. Let's get moving. If they pick up our trail, we cannot stay ahead of them for long."

The well-used game trail and the pack animals helped their progress. Still, the Cathardi were not used to the heat and humidity, so their progress slowed as the morning waned. At midday, they stopped beside a fast-running stream.

"Stay here," Josh said. "I'm going to look behind us for any signs of Urlak pursuers. I'll be back in twenty minutes. Be ready to leave once I return."

He moved back down their trail until he found a large bango tree he climbed. Near the top of the tree, he had a view of the jungle below. In the distance, he saw the smoke, and using a Cathardi binocular, he could make out Mattu's place in the distance. Looking further up the hill from the farm, he saw the orange figures of the Urlak as they approached the field where his party had spent the night. At least eight Urlak warriors pursued. They were four or five hours behind but moving quickly. Josh needed to slow them down somehow. He returned to the stream and found the soldiers waiting.

"Where is Liria?" he demanded.

"She went to the stream," one answered and pointed downstream to a large boulder.

"Get ready to leave," Josh ordered. "The Urlak are not far behind. I will get her."

Josh went downstream to find Liria. He stepped around the boulder and stopped. "We must hurry, Ompresti." He blushed and turned around.

Liria did not face him because her pants were on the bank near where he stood. She was standing in knee-deep water with a rag in her hand. "It is the time for my cycle, and I needed to refresh."

He heard her wade to the shore. "I understand," he said, clenching his fists, trying to keep his mind clear as he waited for her to dress. "It is dangerous out here. You must not go off alone where a predator could attack, and the Urlak are following us. We need to move to stay ahead of them."

They returned to find the others were ready to leave. Josh helped Liria into her saddle. "Where I come from, predators can smell a female during her cycle. They are attracted to the scent and become aggressive. It is likely that the local predators like the gwenna may behave in the same way. You must not go anywhere alone."

They continued up the trail and across the stream until they came to a very large clearing full of kavi vines. "Wait here, while I find a way around, and stay away from the vines," Josh said.

He circled the vines to the left of the group and climbed onto a large fallen tree trunk. He walked along the tree and then disappeared into the jungle. A short time later, he reemerged on the tree trunk.

"It will be difficult at first, but we should be able to slow the Urlak down," Josh said when he returned. "Unload the bonogos and let them go. They will find their way home. We will proceed on foot."

"What about the Urlak?" the squad leader said.

"Don't worry about them yet. We need to get to the other side," Josh said, throwing a pack over his shoulder and taking Liria's hand. "Bring only the food, shelter, and any explosives you have. We'll spend the night on the other side of the clearing."

They unloaded the bonogos. Josh had them all walk to the edge of the vines and then carefully walk backward in their tracks to where they started. He tied a rope to a tree limb. He tossed the limb into the vines and dragged it back, making it look like they walked through the kavi vines. He took them to the tree trunk and had them wait while he covered their tracks. The short hike around the clearing was arduous. They climbed over a lot of deadfalls and around boulders before they reached the other side. Again, Josh had them leave tracks to the edge of the vines, before leading them a short distance into the jungle.

"We'll camp here tonight. Gather some dry wood for a fire. We will need it to keep us warm and to ward off any predators," he said.

The soldiers put up their shelters and gathered dry wood. Liria found kindling while Josh dug to make a small fire pit and started the fire before he disappeared into the jungle. He returned with two chicken-sized birds which they cleaned and put on spits.

"Why did we have to go around the clearing?" Liria asked as they ate the birds.

"Watch." Josh tossed a few of the bigger bones into the vines. They began moving and small black heads on long necks popped up over the leaves.

"The kavi vines and the animals, the mandili, share a symbiotic relationship. Kavi vines entangle the feet and legs of anything that tries to go through, tripping them. Then the mandili swarm around the victim, tearing off its flesh with their razor-sharp teeth. The blood and scraps feed the vine. The mandili can strip a bonogo down to its bones in minutes. Tomorrow, we will leave the jungle and begin the climb up the open mountain slope. Hopefully, our tracks will lead the Urlak into the vines."

The shrill scream of a gwenna pierced the night, followed by more distant answering screams. "We need to keep the fire going tonight and the guards need to be alert. I don't believe the gwennas are close enough to attack, but we need to be ready if I'm wrong," he said.

"What is a gwenna?" a soldier asked.

"It is a large carnivore, taller than me, and weighs 150 to 200 kilograms. It is like a cross between a bird and a reptile that runs on two legs with a one-meter-long neck and a long snout, a mouth full of sharp teeth, and three-fingered hands having 15cm claws. On Earth, we would have called it a dinosaur, a raptor. Though normally solitary, when they sense blood, they will swarm to the source." He used a stick to draw a representation of the creature in the dirt at his feet.

The gwenna's screams grew louder and closer as the night progressed, making sleep difficult. As the sun rose the next morning, Josh roused the party. Though there was no frost, it was cold enough that they could see their breath. He heated water over the fire and poured hot tea for everyone to help them warm up.

"We will need to move fast this morning. It is just a few kilometers to the jungle's edge, then we have a long, strenuous climb up the mountain. Everyone needs to keep their weapon ready. The gwennas are close and could attack."

While the soldiers packed up their gear, Liria came to Josh. "I must wash. Is there a place I can wash?"

"Yes, but not alone. I'll accompany you."

She nodded. "I will be discreet."

Josh gave a few instructions to the soldiers, then took a laser rifle and led Liria to the small stream. Liria waded into the ankle-deep water. She went behind a rock where only her head and shoulders were visible to Josh. She dropped her pants to her knees and cleaned herself.

Josh positioned behind the rock watched the jungle while she washed. *At least now I can be near her and block all the disturbing feelings or images.* A rustling in the brush interrupted his thoughts.

"Hold perfectly still." She reached out mentally to him. He responded with a mental picture of the gwenna.

He remained calm when the guttural growl came. His eyes focused on the blue feathered head of the gwenna across the stream. He held his aim steady on its large yellow eye. Just before the gwenna pounced, Josh fired. The gwenna shrieked and fell on the bank of the stream. Josh fired again into the fallen body, but the gwenna didn't move. He crossed the stream and took his knife out, cutting the creature's throat.

"We need to hurry. There may be others close by." He rinsed his hands in the stream and cleaned his knife. Liria finished quickly and took the hand Josh offered to help her out of the stream.

"What was that?" a soldier said when they returned to the campsite.

"A gwenna," Josh said. Then he led the party up through the jungle, which ended a short distance from the base of a steep escarpment.

"We will rest here awhile," Josh said when they were beyond the trees. "You will have a clear field of view if any more gwenna follow. Though they are reluctant to leave the cover of the trees. I need a volunteer to go back to the clearing. We need to slow the Urlak pursuit. We can't let them catch us here in the open or on the cliff face."

One soldier stepped forward. "I will go with you."

"Good, the rest of you take the Ompresti up the escarpment." Josh pointed to the vee-shaped gully in the cliff face.

"Stay on the scree, then climb the notch where the slide came down. When you make it to the top, set up camp there. It will be cold tonight, but don't light any fires, and watch the trail closely. Both moons are out tonight. They will provide enough light for you to see anything approaching. If we do not return, the mine is ten kilometers southwest along the plateau. The shuttle is in the maintenance building on the West end of the complex."

"Captain." Liria stood and came to Josh. "You must return. Nobody else can pilot the vessel."

"If we get to the clearing before the Urlak, we will be back. We won't take any unnecessary risks. But if we don't slow them down, they will catch us in the open on the cliff."

Chapter 16

Josh watched as Liria, and her escort, began the climb up the scree to the escarpment. A drizzle fell, and clouds hung along the cliff face. He turned to the soldier with him. "Let's move out. We need to hurry back to the edge of the clearing."

They retraced their path from the morning, sneaking through the jungle. When they got to the clearing, they hid behind the trunk of a fallen bango tree and waited silently. Josh eyed the clearing through a fork between the trunk and a branch. He didn't have long to wait. The first Urlak warrior approached the clearing through the trees.

Josh took careful aim. The warrior stepped warily out of the tree cover and followed their tracks to the edge of the clearing. When the warrior bent to study the tracks, Josh fired. The Urlak fell, and the others took cover returning fire. Josh and the soldier with him fired for several minutes at the Urlak, wounding at least one, before he signaled the soldier, and they got up and retreated several meters into the trees, allowing the Urlak to see them.

They took cover in the jungle. The Urlak didn't blindly follow them. But two of the Urlak warriors moved cautiously into the vines and started across the clearing. The rest stayed under cover. Five meters into the vines, the first Urlak became snagged by the vines and tripped. The vines erupted as the mandili swarmed over the fallen warrior. Their snake-like heads popping up and down among the vines. The second warrior turned to flee, but it was too late. Kavi vines snagged both of his legs, and he fell into the chirping mass of mandili. The Cathardi soldier with Josh turned away as the mandili tore the flesh from the still-living, screaming Urlak.

Josh tapped the Cathardi on the shoulder. "It is time for us to go. Stay low and don't let them see you."

When they cleared the trees, Josh saw Liria and the others, about halfway up the notch. He signaled the soldier with him to stop. Then they waited a few minutes, listening and watching the trail. Josh could still hear the Urlak shouting and an occasional shot from the clearing. "That should slow them down," Josh said. "Let's hurry and catch up with the others. We need to have our defenses set before nightfall."

When they finally reached the top of the crag, Liria and the other Cathardi soldiers were waiting for them.

One soldier came up to Josh. "Captain, there is a suitable campsite over there." He pointed to a large overhanging rock face. "It will provide some shelter and it has a clear view of the trail."

"Let's go look," Josh said and walked over to the spot with the soldier. "Excellent choice. Set a lookout over there on that point while the rest of us set up the camp."

It was dark when they finished. They sat in a tight circle around a small stove drinking hot tea and eating dried meat while one soldier a few yards away kept a lookout from the point.

The soldier who took part in the ambush recounted their actions to the others. "What were those things among the vines?" he asked Josh.

"They are the reason I had you go around the clearing. The mandili are insatiable. Their slender bodies and long necks allow them to move effortlessly through the vines without disturbing the tendrils. When other creatures move through, the vines wrap tendrils that ensnare their legs, the mandili flock to it and tear into its flesh with razor-sharp teeth." Josh took a sip of tea. "I thought I explained this earlier. As you saw, when the Urlak tried to cross the clearing, they didn't make it far."

"It was horrible." The soldier shook his head. "The sight of them tearing into the warriors and their screams was horrible."

"But it has slowed their pursuit. They probably will not attempt to follow us until daylight," Josh said.

"Is there another way up the escarpment?" asked another of the Cathardi.

"Nothing anywhere close," Josh said.

"Two of us could hold them off for a long time from here," the soldier continued. "One on each side would pin them down. We might kill them all before they reach the top."

During the night, shots and screams from the jungle below woke Josh and the others on the top of the escarpment. "It sounds like the gwenna have found the Urlak," he said. "It will not be light for a few hours. Try to get back to sleep. We'll need to prepare our defenses early. I'll take over the watch and rouse you when it is time."

Josh took his rifle and relieved the sentry on the point.

"I have never heard screams like that," the sentry said as he stood.

"Most of the screams are the cries of the gwenna, but some are the Urlak." Josh sat. "We made it out of the forest just in time. The scent of blood attracts them from kilometers away. They typically are solitary hunters, like the one I killed earlier beside the creek. I think it came after the Ompresti when we separated from the group. But when there is a large group of prey, they form packs before attacking. It sounded like a pack of six or more attacked the Urlak. Now, go get some rest. The gwenna will not leave the jungle. We are safe up here."

Just before sunrise, Liria came out to the point and sat next to Josh. "We never had the chance to talk after the conference while we were traveling back to Earth. Can we talk now?"

"Sure. What do you want to know?"

"I was on your planet for six years and studied the religious beliefs of the people there. But you have expressed no real religious views. Were you taught the Christian beliefs?" she asked.

"My parents were believers, and I went to Sunday school when I was young. But, like many, I did not find the practices necessary as I grew older. They seemed like a lot of superstitious rites."

"Do you believe in the existence of the God of Earth?"

"Do I what?" His brows knit as he stared at her.

"Are you a Christian?" she said. "You do not have to answer me now, but you must think about it. Do you believe in God? I dreamed that your answer to that question may determine the success or failure of our mission."

They sat quietly for a few minutes before Josh answered, "I think God has deserted me. If He was with me, my home would be safe, and Kim would be alive."

"Your people have an expression: God works in mysterious ways. I do not understand all that the Creator allows, but I believe He has our best interest at heart. Regardless, the question will need an answer."

Liria did not wait for his response but changed the subject and talked about her experiences on Earth until Josh said. "It is time to get ready."

Josh roused his team, and they prepared to leave, and the two Cathardi volunteers took their positions. They would try to prevent the Urlak from reaching the top, giving the others time to get to the mine.

Josh came to Liria as she packed her bedroll. "It is essential that you do not wander away from me today. We don't know what is ahead, and we won't have the protection of the jungle if we run into any Urlak."

"I will do exactly as you ask."

"Good, let's go."

As they moved that morning, Josh thought about Liria's question. *Do I believe in God?* He remembered praying with his mom when he was a child, going to church with his family, and marveling at the God who created the heavens. Even when he was older, he marveled whenever he stared into the clear Colorado night sky. *But where was God now? The Urlak destroyed Earth. My friends and family are dead. I left Kim and our unborn child lying in a pool of blood. Where is God?*

The party walked in silence until just after midday. When they neared the top of the ridge that overlooked the mine, Josh had them get down, and they crawled to the top. He peered down into a bowl at the mine complex, which had shut down several months ago. The buildings looked deserted, with boards over the windows, and the equipment parked in rows just south of the buildings. Everything looked quiet, so they went down. They moved stealthily, staying close to the limited cover available. They stopped behind a large boulder twenty meters from the primary structures.

"The Urlak are here," Liria whispered to Josh. "I can sense them waiting for us. Is there another way?"

"No, the shuttle is here. It will take days to find another way to get off this world," Josh answered.

"We will just have to make it then," she said.

Josh led them to the rear of the main building. They moved along the wall and sprinted across the open area between the main building and the machine shop. The air cracked with the first laser shot. The Cathardi soldier who came with them fell before reaching the cover of the shop. Josh ran back and helped him to cover. The Urlak shot had destroyed his knee; he could not continue.

"Leave me here," he said. "I will give you some cover."

"I can't do that," Josh said. He moved some empty metal drums to provide more cover.

"Leave me," the soldier said. "You must do everything possible to get the Ompresti to the home world."

Josh looked at Liria. She nodded, "We must warn the home world. Nothing else matters. Not even my life."

She kneeled beside the injured soldier and prayed. "You will have the courage you need for this sacrifice." She said, looking into his eyes.

"Thank you Ompresti, I will give you as much cover as I can."

She crawled to Josh. "Where do we go from here?"

Josh pointed to a smaller building with an open bay door. He signaled the wounded soldier, who fired continuously toward their attackers. Josh and Liria ran to the building, crouching as low as possible. Just as they got inside, the firing behind them stopped. Josh pointed to a door at the far side of the building.

They moved toward it when an Urlak warrior stepped through the door. They turned to run back the way they came, but two more Urlak were already there.

"You cannot flee," the first warrior said. "Throw down your weapon. She is more valuable to us alive than dead. The Cathardi will not attack us if we have the witch. She is important to them."

Josh stepped between Liria and the Urlak.

The Urlak laughed. "You cannot save her. You will die and we will take her."

"It is God you should fear, for He is my protector," Liria said.

"Will your god save you from me?" The Urlak twisted his mouth into a sneer. "I do not think so. I will kill this earthling just to show how impotent your god is."

"Now is the time," Liria whispered into Josh's ear. "Do you believe in the God of Earth?"

"God does not take mocking lightly," Josh said to the Urlak. He felt a rush of assurance fill his chest. "You may kill me, or God may save me. Either way, he is God, and my life is his to do with as he pleases. You have no power here."

Josh took a step toward the Urlak warrior, who tried to fire his weapon, but it didn't fire. He and the other Urlak continued trying to fire as Josh took another step toward the warrior, who threw his weapon down in frustration and unhooked his bytor. He rushed Josh but tripped over his own weapon and fell, landing with the bytor beneath him. The impact drove the point of the bytor through his heart. Josh picked up the rifle and turned to face the two remaining warriors approaching him with their bytors in hand. He fired. The weapon worked perfectly; he killed both Urlak.

He pointed to the door the first Urlak had occupied. "The shuttle is in there." He grabbed Liria's hand and led her through into a room with a locked metal door.

"Stand back. Watch the door and warn me if more Urlak follow." Josh used the Urlak laser rifle to cut through the bolt that locked the bunker door.

Once inside the bunker, Josh turned on the generator and opened the roof doors that provided the exit for the small two-person shuttle revealed by the light. The paint had faded, and it didn't look like much.

"That's our way off Bapto," Josh said and climbed the ladder that led to a platform near the cockpit of the shuttle. At the top, he opened a circular hatch. "Come on up."

Liria joined him on the platform, and he helped her through a small hatch. Then followed her inside and sealed the hatch behind them. He moved to the pilot's chair and directed Liria to the other seat. "Strap in."

Josh did a quick check of the propulsion, guidance, and life support systems. He didn't know how many Urlak remained outside, so he would check the remaining systems in flight.

"Are you ready?" He asked.

"I am. You may launch."

He started the conventional engines, knowing the roar would bring any remaining Urlak to the bunker. When the engines reached peak thrust, he released the mooring clamps, and the shuttle shot out of the bunker. As it cleared the buildings, he took a quick look at the ground. An additional half dozen Urlak converged on the now empty bunker while firing their weapons at the shuttle. They could have prevented the shuttle from leaving if it had launched any later.

Once they reached a low orbit over Bapto, he shut off the rocket engines to save fuel. Then he began checking the remaining shuttle systems. The jump drive was in order, and everything else looked good except the transmitter on the communications system. Sensors were operational and warned of several fast-moving ships approaching them. *Probably fighters from a Cathardi warship in orbit over Bapto.*

The shuttle could receive transmissions from the fighters. "Unknown shuttle craft, please transmit your identification." But without the transmitter, he couldn't reply.

"If you do not respond, we have authorization to fire," the fighters said over the com. Josh didn't wait. He did a quick jump while the fighters were still far enough away that he wouldn't catch them in the shuttle's singularity. It would give him time before the fighters could follow them. He executed a second jump immediately after returning to normal space. He hoped to gain enough time to work on a plan before they could track them. They were still within range of the warship's sensors, but it would take them a while to locate the small shuttle.

He turned to Liria and waited until she seemed to recover from the jump effects. "Do you have any suggestions?" he asked, and without waiting for a response. "Our radio is not working; we cannot talk to the Cathardi fighters or the warship. They should know about the attack by the Urlak on Bapto. We can wait and hope they don't fire while I try to repair the radio, or we can run and try to make it somewhere safe."

"If we try for Cathardi, how long will it take?" Liria asked.

"Fourteen standard days, give or take. It depends on how far I can push the jump engines. This is a short-range shuttle, not built for extended jumps. We have enough life support. The recycling unit should provide enough water, but we are short on food." He turned so he could look into her eyes. "If we wait for the Cathardi fighters, do you think they will destroy us?"

"If we cannot communicate with them, the Cathardi ships will attack because of the Urlak threat. We cannot wait," Liria said. "I believe you can get me to safety. I trust you. The fate of my world is now in your hands."

Josh turned and quickly made the calculations for the next jump, which would put them out of reach of the Cathardi sensors.

With enough distance between them and the warship, Josh removed the control console cover to look at the transmitter. Reaching back into the console, he pulled out a handful of fur and wire. *Oh man, what is this?* He reached in again and pulled out another handful. This time it included the singed body of a huldo.

"Liria, can you get me the handlight from the maintenance bin?"

"Did you find the problem?" she asked when she returned with the light.

"I think so." Josh used the light to scrutinize the damage caused by the rodent.

"There is no way I can get this working again. The rodents built a nest inside. They gnawed through several wires and shorted out one of the transmission control boards." He crawled out from under the console, shaking his head.

Liria was sitting in her chair. Her face looked drawn and paler than usual. She appeared very frail. The rigors of their escape must have taken a toll on her physically. "Why don't we get you to the bunk? You look like you could use the rest," he said.

She stood. "I could use the rest."

Josh went to the rear of the shuttle to the bunk and helped her with the restraints. He covered her with a blanket from the overhead stowage bin before returning to his seat. When he looked back, she was already asleep.

She slept for sixteen hours, and when she awoke, they were cruising between jumps. Josh was in the small galley, preparing to eat.

"Where are we?" she asked.

"Away from Bapto, and on our way to the Cathardi home-world," Josh answered. "Would you like some food?"

"Yes! I am famished. I feel like I haven't eaten in days."

"You haven't," Josh explained. "It has been almost a day since we left Bapto, and almost another full day since you ate the morning before we reached the mine."

He gave her a cup of tea and heated one of the prepared meals for her, then explained their situation with their communications. "I cannot fix the transmitter. I'm not sure what we will do once we arrive at the Cathardi system. I hope, when the Cathardi find us, they don't shoot first."

"I think we will be far enough away from Bapto. They will only see an unknown, unarmed shuttle. They will be cautious, but not aggressive," Liria said.

"If they take us aboard their vessel, you must convince them who you are and the importance of your mission. You don't have your robes and your appearance has changed."

They spent a few quiet minutes eating. "It may take us longer to get to Cathardi space than we thought. Without communications, I'll need to avoid heavily trafficked areas."

***

Liria sat in the copilot's chair, breathing deeply, and praying. "Creator, I ask you to forgive me for my doubts. I thought my desires interfered with your plan to rescue my people. But now, I know Josh was your choice from the beginning. Help us complete the trip to Cathardi so I can warn my people of the coming invasion."

Josh lay in the bunk, apparently trying to sleep for the first time since they left Bapto. His body jerked restlessly; sweat covered his creased forehead as he moaned. "Kim."

Liria went to the back and sat on the edge of the bunk. She still felt conflicted by her attraction to him. Her feelings made it difficult for her to prevent them from being transferred to him, and her physical desire had persisted ever since that first connection on the shuttle to Cathardi. She took his hand and thought of the ocean waves washing up on the beach at the sisterhood's school when she was young. It was her most relaxing memory, and she knew he would sense her serenity. She felt him relax and finally fall into a much-needed deep sleep.

She continued to sit with him and looked around the interior of the shuttle. The rear section with the single bunk where she sat also housed a small galley with a recycled water dispenser, a small microwave heating unit, and storage for emergency rations. Also in the rear, the head, separated by a thin curtain, contained the toilet. There was no shower or sink. *We will stink before we get to Cathardi.* The front section contained only the two seats with the shuttle controls on three sides.

When Josh awoke, he pulled his hand away from Liria. "Your sleep seemed troubled, and I thought I could help," she said.

"Thank you, I slept well. I was dreaming of the ocean, and it shocked me to see you there. How long did I sleep?"

"About four hours." She stood and moved to the galley. "Would you like some tea?"

"Yes, thank you. I need to work on the calculations for our next jump."

She fixed tea for them both then carried his cup to the pilot's seat and handed it to him. Then she sat in the other chair and watched as he worked at the console in front of him.

He sat back in his chair and looked at her. "Are you messing with my mind?"

"No, I cannot do that. Your mind is too strong. You can block me anytime, though I can allow you to sense my feelings. When you were trying to sleep, I could let you sense my calm. In the same way, I can sense your feelings. Your distress at Kim's death troubles you. I do not want to interfere with your grief. You loved her, and you need to grieve, but you also needed to rest."

"I don't understand all of this. How could I sense you across the galaxy when you were on Cathardi and I was on Bapto? Loral told me that was quite unusual but possible."

"It is extremely rare; I have only heard of two other instances from our legends. I sensed you as well and do not know how or why. But I know you can consciously stop it because you have done it before, but during sleep and other semi-conscious states, it is more difficult. We should not have any problems with it since we are aware of it and only one of us can sleep at a time."

They sat in silence, looking out at the icy darkness of space through the shuttle viewports. Finally, he stood. "I need to finish the supply inventory. I haven't checked all of the food or the condition of the water unit."

He walked back to the galley. *This will be a long trip and I may not have the strength to hide my true feelings.*

She watched as Josh looked in each of the storage bins, occasionally pulling packets out to get a more accurate count. When he finished, he shook his head slightly before getting on his hands and knees to look at the water recycling unit.

He returned to the forward section. "It looks like the recycler will provide us enough water, but we only have food for about half the trip, even rationing it to the minimum for survival. We need to stop someplace where we can get some supplies and maybe repair the communications system. I'll need to study the charts." He sat at the console, scrolling through the charts and data.

She sensed his frustration. "It will be okay. I do not need to eat. I can fast until we reach Cathardi. It is something I have done occasionally."

"That was different. You weren't in space subject to the rigors of the jumps. Your body will need to replenish."

"God will sustain me; you are the one who will require replenishment to keep your mind sharp enough to make the jumps. If only you eat, do we have enough?"

"Possibly, on reduced rations, but I cannot allow you to starve."

"You must. One of us has to warn my people and I cannot pilot us there."

He just stared at her. She looked into his eyes, knowing he would do what was right.

***

The shuttle had been traveling toward the Cathardi system for four days, and the voyage was taking a toll on Josh, both physically and mentally. He felt someone shaking his shoulder and vaguely heard someone call his name. "Josh…Josh. Wake up, Josh." He saw Liria bending over him. It was her hand he felt on his shoulder. He rolled over and rubbed his eyes to clear his vision. "Josh, you need to wake up. There is an alarm."

He rolled into a sitting position on the bunk. "I'll be there. Just let me get my bearings. How long have I been asleep?"

"Five hours. You were dreaming."

He stood and stretched, then went to the control console. The amber contact alarm was blinking, and when he queried the system, it showed: ***unknown signal detected - unauthorized sensor scan***. Checking his sensors, he found a distant object emitting electromagnetic pulses that did not match any of those from known sources. The object was heading toward the shuttle. "There is something out there and it is coming to us," he said. "The computer doesn't recognize the source and cannot identify it. Do we wait to see who or what it is, or do we jump out? If we wait, we can't communicate with them."

"Since the computer does not recognize it, we can assume it is not Cathardi. We should not wait," she said. "We cannot risk a delay and we cannot fight, so our only logical option is to flee."

"I agree and the sooner the better. Because the alien scans seemed quite sophisticated, they may track us through the jump, so I will need to do multiple jumps to be safe. Strap in."

He performed three consecutive jumps. After the third, he shut down the jump drive and allowed the shuttle to coast without engines or thrusters.

"That stressed the gravity drive. We need to let it cool, so we'll sit here and watch the sensors to see if there are any indications that they've found us. If we could jump farther, I would."

Her drawn face and the distinct dark circles under her eyes made her look very frail. She put her thin hand to her mouth to cover a yawn. "An unidentified signal troubles me," she said after yawning. "We have not encountered another race with new technology for twenty years. They could present an unknown threat; the council will need to know about this. How much longer until we reach Cathardi?"

"I am guessing three or four more days. I think you should eat something. There are two more rations in the galley."

"No, I am fine. You will need them."

Josh knew not to argue with her, no matter how weak she looked. "What about some tea?"

"That would be good. I would like that."

They sat in silence as they drank their tea. He monitored the sensors for a few hours.

When the gravity drive had cooled, he said, "The drive is ready and there isn't any sign of the aliens. Are you up for another jump?"

Liria fastened her safety harness. "Yes."

"I'm going to program a longer jump. All the short jumps since we left Bapto have stressed the gravity drive. Maybe longer jumps will help get us to Cathardi space sooner and only slightly increase the heat generated on each jump. Hopefully, they won't tax the drive as much as the shorter, more frequent jumps."

"It sounds like we may have trouble reaching Cathardi."

"We may," he said. "I still think we can, but the drive may fail." *I hope she doesn't sense my doubts. We could die floating in space with no one else around.*

Her shoulders slumped into the chair, and she stared out into space. "You will get us to Cathardi, I am sure of that. You are the captain; do as you think best."

After the jump, he slept again while the drive cooled. He dreamed of his wedding night, but when he gazed into Kim's face, he saw Liria. "*What are you doing here? Where's Kim?*"

"*Kim is dead. I am the one you need. God predestined us to be together. Don't you like me?*"

"*Get out of my bed! Get out of my head!*"

Josh woke up and saw Liria asleep in the chair. He got up and went to her chair. Her face was ashen, sweat beaded her forehead, and each raspy breath seemed labored. When he touched her face, he knew she was feverish. He lifted her out of the chair and carried her to the bunk, then went into the galley and got the medical kit. There wasn't much in it, but he found a general analgesic that might help her fever.

After he made some tea, he put the remaining sweetener into her cup. He tried to wake her. She finally responded to his shaking, and he held her up so she could drink and swallow the analgesic. After a couple of sips, she coughed and would not take any more tea. He let her back down. As he watched her sleep, he had to focus to keep the thoughts and images of the two of them from creeping back into his mind.

She is so sick she can't control her thoughts. I must get her someplace where she can get medical attention. He went to the controls and started running through jump scenarios to see how quickly they could get to Cathardi or another occupied area like Melal. Anywhere she could get help. None of the options were good, but he chose one that would get them to the edge of Cathardi-controlled space, near where the shuttles encountered the first Cathardi cruiser on their maiden voyage. He needed two jumps if the drive would hold up on the last one. He strapped Liria to the bunk and jumped.

Afterward, he sat on the edge of the bunk holding Liria's shoulders, trying to wake her up enough to get her to drink a little and take another pill. Since the jump, she seemed worse, tossing in the bunk and mumbling nonsense. It had become harder for Josh to keep her out of his mind. When he lifted her, he felt her bones just beneath her skin. Eventually, she woke up enough to sip the tea and swallow the pill, but he didn't think she was truly conscious.

After he laid her back down, he knelt beside the bunk. "Heavenly Father, I need your help. We must make one more jump and I don't know if we can make it. If we don't, Liria will die. I believe that is not your will. She says I am the one that was prophesied. I don't know if I am, but I know you spoke to her and have led us here. I saw your power at the mine on Bapto and believe you can deliver us in this time of need. You have been faithful to me even when I was unfaithful, and I am asking you to be faithful to Liria now. Father, help us make it to Cathardi in time to save Liria. In Jesus' name, amen."

Back in the pilot's seat, Josh stared at the control screen, shaking his head, and typed in a new set of coordinates and started the jump simulation. *Come on, something has to work.* He watched as the drive readouts on the simulation flashed red; it showed a failure to make the jump.

He looked back at Liria lying in the bunk. Her shallow breathing caused a barely perceptible rise and fall of her chest. *I don't know how long she can last in that condition. I need to get us somewhere we can find help.* He entered new coordinates and watched the simulation as the drive readouts went from green to yellow and stayed yellow until a few seconds after it completed the jump before they turned red. *That looks like the best I can do. I hope the simulation is accurate and has a margin for error programmed into it.*

He went to the bunk and put his hand on Liria's forehead. *She is burning up.* He got a cool, wet rag from the galley and wrapped it around her head. Her condition had gotten progressively worse over the two days since the unknown contact.

Leaving her, he drank some water before returning to his console. He reentered the coordinates into the drive computer and switched off the simulator mode. *Here goes nothing.*

The gravity drive started, and he lost focus as his vision blurred and his stomach jumped into his throat. When the jump was over, his eyes cleared. The drive alarms were going off, and the monitor displayed an overheating condition. He checked the shuttle's position and saw the jump had taken them to the edge of the Cathardi-controlled space. *Well, here we are. We made it to Cathardi space, but we are a long way out and moving farther out.*

He checked the rest of the systems. The conventional drive was now inoperable, but the thrusters were available for one brief burst. *Maybe they will give enough thrust to reverse our course and give us a little momentum toward Cathardi. Either way, we will coast until we run into something. All we can do is wait and pray.*

He fired the thrusters and checked their course. Then he activated the distress beacon and went back to Liria. He laid his hand on her chest and felt it gently rise and fall. *At least she is alive. We have a chance.* He returned to the pilot's chair and started monitoring the sensors for any signal. After sitting for several hours, fatigue overtook him, and he drifted off to sleep while the shuttle drifted to who knows where.

He awoke to bright lights over his head that let him know he was no longer on the shuttle. "Well, you woke up." It was a female Cathardi standing beside his bed. He tried to turn so he could get a better look at her, but he couldn't. Restraints held his arms, legs, and chest to the bed.

"Where am I?"

"You are in the medical facility on the Cathardi cruiser Singal."

"Where is Liria?"

"If you are referring to the Cathardi female you nearly killed, she is in another part of the medical facility. We are rehydrating her and trying to revive her so we can identify her."

"She is Liria, the Ompresti, and she has an urgent message for the council."

"We will determine her identity if she wakes. Until then, you are in the custody of the Cathardi military. After I determine your fitness, we will hold you in the brig until we take you to Melal for trial."

Josh struggled against the restraints. "You don't understand. We have to get to Cathardi before it is too late."

The nurse ignored him and left the room. A few minutes later, a squad of Cathardi soldiers came and wheeled his bed to a small cell, where they finally removed his restraints while keeping their weapons pointed at him.

"Get off of the bed and stand in the corner," one guard ordered.

He complied. They wheeled the bed out and locked the door. The cell had no windows, containing only a loo, a small sink, and a sleeping mat rolled up in one corner. There was a camera in the center of the ceiling and a small panel in the door that covered a slot.

He sat on the floor with the rolled-up mat as a back support. *Well, at least they found us, and hopefully Liria will talk to them.*

Though I haven't sensed her since I woke up. God, we need your help.

Chapter 17

Liria opened her eyes to bright overhead lights and a Cathardi's face looking down on her. *We made it! Josh, I knew you would get us back. Are you there? Where are you? Am I too weak?* "The Earthling who was with me, where is he?" Her voice was hoarse and barely audible.

The Cathardi bent closer. "What did you say?"

"Where is my companion?"

"He is on board and being held until we can determine who you are. He is in better condition than you, though we are not positive about that yet."

"Can I see him?"

"Not yet. You still need to recover from dehydration and the fever we think the bad air filtration system on your shuttle caused. You have been here, unconscious, for two days, and you must recover from the injuries your companion inflicted. There are significant bruises on your body, and you have broken ribs. Did your companion beat you?"

"No, he saved me from the Urlak." She tried to sit, but the stabbing pain in her chest prevented her. "I am Liria — Ompresti, Elder Sister of the Order, Advisor to the Council, and I need to get to Cathardi as quickly as possible. I have critical information the Council needs to hear."

"Well, you don't look like any Sister I have ever seen, and you certainly don't look like the Ompresti. When you are better, we will have someone try to verify your identity. You need to rest now." The nurse adjusted something on her monitor. "I will be back soon with some food for you."

No! I must get back to Cathardi. She tried to scream, but the dark fog of dehydration and drugs overtook her. She slept, but dreams of the Urlak caused her to struggle against it. When she moved, the pain woke her briefly. Then she would drift back into the dark fog. Once she struggled because someone touched her skin. She woke, and the nurse held her down.

"Be still," the woman said. "The doctor has not finished his examination." Liria drifted into the fog again.

The next time she woke, a younger Cathardi female stood over her. She had her hand on Liria's forehead. "How do you feel?"

"I—I think I am better."

"Good." She turned and said something to the nurse Liria had seen before. "The doctor is on his way. He has a lot of questions for you. Do you think you can sit up?"

Liria lifted herself into a sitting position. Her ribs still hurt, but not like before. "I must get to…"

"Be quiet until the doctor gets here. You can tell him," the younger woman said.

The two attendants adjusted things around her to make her more comfortable while they waited. When the doctor came into her room, he smiled. "Good, you seem to have recovered some of your strength. I am the ship's doctor, Aimol. I have several questions for you, and I need you to concentrate and answer honestly." He paused and looked at her. "Can you tell me your name?"

"I am Liria, Ompresti, Elder Sister of the Order, Advisor to the Council, and I am on a critical mission to return to Cathardi."

"Very well," the doctor said. "We will have someone verify that later. Who was your companion?"

"His name is Josh. He is a pilot from Earth. He—."

The doctor interrupted her. "How long were you his captive? When did he first abuse you?"

"You will listen to me!" She sat straight and concentrated on the doctor, staring into his eyes. She sensed his sudden unease. "He did not abuse me. He rescued me from the Urlak on Bapto and piloted us here. Back into Cathardi-controlled space. You will inform the captain that he is arranging for both of us to be sent to Cathardi as soon as possible. I have an urgent message for the council."

"I will do what I can," the doctor said. "However, your injuries are consistent with abuse. The bruises and broken ribs indicate physical abuse, as does the dehydration and starvation."

"Re-evaluate the injuries, doctor. I think you will find them consistent with tight restraints during jumps while in poor health." She sensed that he was beginning to understand.

"Possibly," he said. "There are still more questions, and I need to have your identity confirmed." He went to the door. "That will suffice for now. Keep her comfortable and provide her with something light to eat."

A short time later, the Cathardi attendant returned with a cup of meat broth and several slices of fruit. Her stomach growled audibly when she smelled the broth and saw the fresh fruit. *How many days have passed since my last meager meal?*

"I am Diorana, and I will attend to you while you are here. Please eat slowly. You don't want to shock your system. It appears to have been a while since you ate last." She handed Liria the metal tray. "They have scheduled a psychological exam since you have recovered some of your strength. Your companion badly abused you, tying you to the bed and starving you. Though we did not find any signs of sexual assault."

"He did not abuse me! You are wrong! I made him bring us here. He is the only reason I am alive."

"That is for the psychologist to determine. Now, eat. Your body needs the fuel." Diorana left the room without waiting for her to reply.

When she bit into the fruit, the juice ran down her chin, but she didn't care. She ate all of it before returning to the broth. When she finished, she pushed the tray away.

Diorana knocked and came in to retrieve her tray, followed closely by a male Cathardi officer.

"I am Chaplain Rowan. The Commander asked me to stop and see you," he said.

She recognized him. "You are here for my psychological evaluation and to confirm my identity," she said, looking into his eyes. She extended her hand. "I am Liria, Ompresti, Elder Sister of the Order, Advisor to the Council. We met at the Order's school during a convocation several years ago. We took part in a panel on the ancient prophecies."

She saw his brows knit for a few seconds after taking her hand, then they rose as his eyes widened in obvious recognition. He bowed his head. "Forgive our doubts, Ompresti, I remember, and I sense the truth of your words. Though you are almost unrecognizable in your current state. I will report your identity to the commander immediately."

"Tell him he must get me and my companion to the homeworld as soon as possible. I have urgent news for the Council. And please ask him to have my companion brought in to see me."

When the chaplain left, the attendant brought Liria clean clothes. "There is a shower through the door over there if you want to wash." She pointed to the door on Liria's left. "I will assist you into the shower, and then when you finish, I will help you to dress." She put the garments on the bed and helped Liria stand, leading her to the shower. "I will be right outside if you need help. You are still weak and need to take things slowly."

The clothes were simple uniform pants and a shirt with standard underthings. The attendant had done a good job getting the sizes right. Dressing proved more difficult than she anticipated, but with Diorana's help, she was dressed. Her ribs hurt when she raised her arms or twisted. There was no way she could reach her feet without pain. Everything fit well, except the shoes, which were too small. After dressing, Liria said, "Diorana, is there any word when I might see my companion?"

"They will bring him up later today. You need to get back on the bed, so you don't fall. You still need your rest." Diorana helped Liria back to her bed. "I am sorry about the uniform; it is all we had available."

"It will suffice, but the shoes are too small."

Diorana picked up the shoes. "I noticed. I will get you another pair that will fit."

Liria reclined in the bed. *Hopefully, they will let me see Josh soon. Though I still have not sensed him. They may have shielded him, or he has shut himself off from me. I need to find out if he is all right.* She slept without the fog of the drugs. She woke feeling rested and hungry.

Diorana returned with a tray of roasted meat and vegetables. The aroma of the hot food made her stomach growl again. The nurse set the tray beside her. "I will be back to get your tray when you have finished. Eat slowly. Your body needs to adjust to the food."

"Thank you," Liria said. Then she took a bite of the savory-smelling meat.

She chewed the meat slowly, allowing the juices to fill her mouth. Then she took a bite of the vegetables, which had caramelized edges that added a sweet crunch. She took her time, enjoying each bite.

She had just pushed the tray to the side when there was a rap on the wall outside. Diorana and a young lieutenant stood in the doorway "Ompresti, we have the prisoner as you requested". They brought Josh in, still restrained between two armed Cathardi soldiers.

"Help me stand," Liria said to the Diorana. Once she was up, she walked over to Josh threw her arms around his neck, and kissed his cheek. When she pulled back, she looked at the lieutenant. "Release him."

"I am sorry, Ompresti, only the commander can order his release. We have charged him with an unauthorized flight into Cathardi space, kidnapping you, traitorous acts against the Cathardi people, including complicity in the Urlak invasion of Bapto, and physical abuse of a Cathardi female—you."

"That is ridiculous!" *Why do they keep saying he abused me?* "He only did what I asked, and he protected me from the Urlak. He brought me safely back to Cathardi space under extreme conditions. Tell the commander that I demand his release and the dismissal of all charges."

The lieutenant turned to the guards. "Hold him here. I will check with the commander." He turned back to Liria. "I trust you will not interfere with their duty, Ompresti."

She ignored the lieutenant and focused on Josh. "Are you well?" *He is so thin.*

"I am well considering the circumstances, Ompresti."

"Please forgive the restraints. They do not understand, and they believe you harmed me." *Another reason for him to distrust us. But he seems resigned to it.* "Thank you for helping me. Eventually, they will understand."

"I hope so," he said. "But I do not trust them." He allowed her into his mind. "It's good to see you. You look better than the last time I saw you lying in the shuttle. I was afraid you would die before we were rescued."

She felt his relief at seeing her and his hopelessness. He was still hurting from Kim's death. "I will do my best to make sure they understand. The Council will hear me if we are on time."

The lieutenant returned with the Commander who said. "Ompresti, I understand you want the prisoner released." Liria nodded. "But I have orders directly from the Council to keep him in custody. They have asked me to put both of you on one of our high-speed shuttles. It will take you to the homeworld. He will remain in restraints until the Council orders differently. Your shuttle departs in four hours. Diorana will accompany you to monitor your health and the guards will remain with the prisoner." He looked at the guards. "Take him back to his cell until it is time to board." They took Josh out.

"But, Commander—" He raised his hand, stopping Liria.

"I know what you have said about him. I believe you are telling the truth. Both the doctor's latest report and the chaplain's psychological evaluation confirm your assertions. But I must obey my orders. You will have an opportunity to speak with the council soon." He left the room.

Diorana helped Liria out of the uniform and into a gown. Then she helped her back into bed. "Rest now. I will be back to take you to the shuttle."

Liria dozed a few times before they wheeled her, still in her bed, to the shuttle. When they got there, Diorana helped her to stand and walk up the ramp as they boarded for the jump and flight to the Cathardi home world. She didn't see Josh but sensed him once she was on board.

The prospect of an impending Urlak attack weighed heavily on her and increased her sense of urgency. *Creator, help us arrive in time. I am frightened and concerned we may be too late. Please forgive my lack of faith. The ordeal of the journey has taken my strength.*

***

When Liria arrived, she saw Moira waiting for her inside the shuttle terminal. "Ompresti, I hardly recognized you," the older woman said. "You look so thin and frail. Your face is drawn, and there are dark circles under your eyes. Are you well?"

"Reverend Elder." Liria's voice was still raspy. "Thank you for meeting me. I am well, considering the grueling return journey from Bapto. This was the only clothing available aboard the ship that rescued us." She pulled at the shirt that hung loosely on her thin frame.

Moira bowed her head and took the skeletal hand offered. "I understand. I received the report from the Singal's medical staff. Your message said you had something urgent to tell the Council. It is assembling and they will hear from you later this afternoon. We have time to get you dressed properly for the audience." Moira turned to lead her away, but Liria wouldn't follow.

"I have to be sure they treat Josh well," she said. "He must accompany me to the Council."

"As you wish, Ompresti, but you must explain why you need him there."

They stood together until guards brought the shackled Josh down the ramp. He looked nearly as thin and drawn as her. They stopped in front of the two sisters.

"Bring him and we will have him changed into suitable clothing to appear before the Council," Liria said.

"Our orders are—."

"You know who I am?" Moira said. "He will go with the Ompresti to the Council chamber this afternoon. You will follow us to a room where he can change."

"As you wish, Reverend Elder."

Moira led them to a private lounge in the terminal. "You may use that room." Moira pointed to the adjacent door. "I will send for the clothing and some food and beverages. Stay there until I notify you we are leaving. We will wait in here."

She and Liria entered a room where two other sisters waited. "Bring these items to the room next door." She gave her datapad to one sister and then turned to Liria. "What has happened?"

"It is a long story, and I will tell it to you after I speak to the Council. I want to save my strength for the meeting. I hope you understand." Liria plopped into a chair.

"Very well. Let's get you changed and refreshed." The remaining sister brought over the robes appropriate for her office, which Moira had provided. "I am afraid that in your current condition, they will not fit properly."

"They will do. My appearance is not important." She changed into robes, and they rested in the room until Moira received a notification that the Council was ready.

They left for the Council chamber. When they stopped at the adjacent room, Josh had changed into a clean blue tunic and washed, but his scruffy beard remained. "Captain, I apologize for the restraints, but they must remain until after the Council hears Liria's report," Moira said.

Josh nodded.

When they arrived at the entrance to the Council chamber, the Cathardi guards barred Josh from entering. But Liria stepped to Josh's side. "He will come with me. Let us pass." She grabbed Josh's arm to lead him into the chamber. She needed both his moral and physical support as she leaned against his arm.

"You will allow him to pass," Moira said to the guards. Then turning to Liria. "Wait here, while I take my seat. I will have someone open the door for you when we are ready." She entered, closing the door behind her.

My Creator, help me speak clearly and help the Council members to understand the urgency of the warning I present. Give me strength. I am weak and tired. She squeezed Josh's arm. "Thank you for bringing me here."

When the doors opened, they entered the chamber. A small audience, mostly lower-level officials, stood in the Council chamber. They murmured when Liria entered, commenting on her drawn face, pallid complexion, and loosely hanging robes. Louder voices expressed shock when they recognized an alien accompanying her. The High Council did not permit any non-Cathardi to stand before it, but Liria walked forward to stand in front of the Council, clutching Josh's arm. Once they stood directly before the Council members, she released his arm and bowed low.

"Why have you forsaken the traditions of your Order and brought this alien before the Council?" Marlon stood and stepped to the edge of the platform, staring down at Liria.

"The Council knows me," she said in a raspy voice. "And they know my respect for the traditions of our people, and my loyalty to the Order. But I believe circumstances made it necessary for me to appear in this manner." Though hoarse, her voice carried across the room. "As for the Earthling, he is my Nakir, my protector. He saved me from the Urlak, brought me safely to Cathardi, and I believe he will fulfill the ancient prophecy."

She waited for the murmurs and shouts of the audience to subside. "We came from Bapto where I was on a Council-approved mission. However, my mission failed. A party of Urlak warriors arrived before us and captured the Melal, Taibon, you sent me to retrieve. I believe he knows the location of the Cathardi home-world and the Urlak will now know it as well. We must prepare for an immediate attack."

A roar of unbelief arose in the chamber. Marlon, still standing, raised his hands to silence them. "You are certain of this?"

"I am," she said, standing straight with her shoulders back, staring up at Marlon.

"Where will they attack?" It was General Stanko, a military delegate.

"That, I do not know." She hung her head.

"May I speak?" Josh interrupted the crowd's murmur.

Marlon stomped his foot. "Silence the alien and remove him from the chamber."

Moira stood from her chair at the far left of the council table. "Mister Chairman, may I speak? The Ompresti named the captain her Nakir. Our traditions state the Nakir of an elder sister or a civilian eligible for council membership may speak before this council." She turned to Josh before Marlon could answer. "Captain, you have something to add?"

Josh stepped forward. "Thank you, Reverend Elder. One of the Urlak we encountered knew I was from Earth. This can only mean that he was familiar with my species because he was part of the force that attacked my planet. The Melal, Taibon, was a friend of Liria's father who piloted a freighter to Bapto from the Cathardi home world. Taibon would only know the coordinates from Liria's father. The most logical conclusion is the Urlak will come to those coordinates from Earth."

Marlon, his lips twisted into a scowl, raised his hands again to silence the onlookers. "Clear the chamber. The council will meet in private to discuss this information and determine what action is required."

***

After the meeting, guards escorted Josh and Liria out of the Council chamber, where another sister met them. She took Josh to a separate room. "I will have refreshments brought in while you wait for the Council's decision." She left him alone in the room with two guards posted outside the door.

A few minutes later, she returned with a tray of fruit. "The council has agreed to remove your restraints; however, the guards will remain." She turned to two additional sisters. "We have brought you clothing suitable for the Nakir of the Om-presti. Please change them before you return to the Council chamber. They are deliberating and will notify us when they have reached a decision."

After the sisters left, the guards removed his shackles. He changed clothes and paced the room. He could sense Liria praying and began praying as he paced. *Lord, you have been with me even when I did not acknowledge you. I ask you to forgive me and I ask you to forgive my anger and resentment against you and toward the Cathardi. They have only done what they believe to be the best for their people. I ask that you protect them from the Urlak. I do not want this world to suffer the same fate as my own. Open their eyes to the imminent danger and rescue them. Use me in any way you deem necessary to save this world.*

He continued to pace and pray until the guards entered to escort him back to the Council chamber. Liria was waiting for him at the door. He sensed she wanted to use him as support again to show her trust in him to the Council. They walked into the chamber together with Josh's guards following a couple of steps behind.

Marlon called the meeting to order, then said, "The Council has decided to act, though the vote was very close. Sister Sinola will present the Council's decision." Marlon scowled as he sat.

Sister Sinola stood and stepped forward. "Liria, even though some have doubts about the accuracy of your visions, prophecies, and advice, they have proven true. The Sisterhood and a majority of the military delegates believe we have no choice but to accept the possibility of the doom you have predicted. We will mobilize our forces immediately and recall as many ships as we can to prepare for this invasion." Then she addressed Josh. "Nakir, you have proven your integrity by protecting not only the life of the Ompresti but also, it seems, the secret of our location. The Council finds your logic appropriate and will position some of our forces accordingly. The rest of our forces will remain near Cathardi as a last line of defense. We once offered you a commission in our armed forces, which you declined. Now the Council believes you are a valuable advisor and need to accompany the forces preparing to meet the Urlak at the coordinates you suggested. Will you reconsider the offer and accept a commission?"

"I will, but only temporarily. After we defeat the Urlak, I must return to my planet to help them in their fight against the invaders."

He waited while the council talked amongst themselves for a few minutes. Then General Stanko stood. "We accept your terms. You will receive a commission as a captain. After the staff has had time to determine how to best use your knowledge, you will receive your assignment."

When they left the Council chamber, Liria stopped, still holding on to him. She stepped around to face him. "Captain, I can never thank you enough for getting me here. I know it has been hard for you, and I don't know if I will have another chance to thank you. I leave immediately to join the elders of my order. This, I do not believe, will be the last time I see you. She kissed his cheek and hugged him. Goodbye."

"Goodbye, Ompresti. I will see you after we defeat the Urlak." Josh winked at her.

Moira came out of the chamber. "Ompresti, are you ready?"

"Yes, Reverend Elder."

"Good, we must leave immediately." Then addressing him. "May the Creator guide you and bring you success in the trials ahead, Captain. I now know why Liria trusts you so deeply. Goodbye."

He watched them walk away. *I wonder, will I ever see her again?*

Two days later, he was again aboard the Singal, waiting for any sign of an Urlak invasion. He sat in the ship's conference room with the commanders of the six cruisers assigned to watch the area he had proposed.

Commander Delfrim of the Singal addressed the others. "Gentlemen, as you know, they stationed us here in anticipation of an attack on our home world." He pointed to Josh. "The captain has provided intelligence that he believes this is the most likely area for the initial assault. We do not know the size of the enemy force or the exact timing of their assault, so we will wait here at our post, looking for any signs. We positioned your vessels to encircle the proposed jump termination point. We plan to hit the enemy vessels as soon as they come through the singularity, not giving their crews time to recover from the jump effects. Are there questions?"

"What if there are too many enemy ships for our limited number? Shouldn't we wait for additional support?" Commander Feyd said.

"If we do not destroy the enemy here, we have stationed additional forces in defensive positions around Cathardi, and a smaller force is in reserve at the Melal station if needed. The rest of the fleet is too far away to help. It is up to us to defeat the Urlak," Delfrim said.

"How reliable is the intelligence?" another commander asked.

"I will let Captain Josh answer that question." Delfrim nodded to him.

"This is my best guess, based on the information I got while helping the Ompresti escape the Urlak on Bapto." He could see the doubt on the faces of many of the officers in the room. He was an outsider. Why would they believe him? "They got these coordinates from a Melal who came by them accidentally." He did not want to implicate Liria's father. "My estimate of the time the Urlak need to return to their base and assemble a sufficient force for the assault falls within the next three days. The Council determined the threat was credible enough to act on. Since I am the primary source of the intelligence, they assigned me to assist in any way I can."

"Thank you, Captain," Delfrim said. "You all have as much information as I have now, so return to your vessels and prepare. Maintain an alert status and communicate only when necessary. We must surprise the enemy if we are to succeed."

The commanders left the room talking quietly amongst themselves. Josh waited for the room to clear. "Commander Delfrim, what would you like me to do once the attack starts?"

"I assumed that if the attack occurs, your job would be complete. Honestly, I am not convinced there will be an attack, but I am following my orders. What would you propose?"

"I am a skilled pilot and could fly a fighter if there is a need."

"Very well. I will speak with the fighter squadron commander and have you assigned to the reserve unit."

"Thank you, sir."

CHAPTER 18

T he next day, Josh was on the hangar deck, seated in a fighter, going through its weapons array. The wing commander, Jaicen, stood behind the pilot's chair, looking over his shoulder. Jaicen pointed to the left-hand console. "Those are the laser cannon controls; forward, rear, left, and right. Above them is the forward-pointing rail gun control. It fires up to 500 rounds of one-hundred-millimeter, high-density, composite balls. They can penetrate the hull of any known adversary's vessel. It is your most effective weapon against anything larger than a fighter. The composite goes right through magnetic shielding at super-high velocity. A single accurately placed shot can disable a cruiser if you hit the propulsion or life support systems. The circle in the center of the helmet display is the targeting system. The onboard computer will compensate for the relative velocities of both the target and your ship. Do you have questions?"

"No sir, I understand everything and the flight controls are very similar to those I used on the shuttles I had flown. Though it took me several test flights earlier today to get used to the increased speed and maneuverability."

"Good. Report to the ready room and suit up. You can fly a perimeter patrol this morning to get some additional flight hours."

The wing commander left the fighter through the rear hatch, while Josh continued to go through the controls from the cockpit.

When he went to the ready room, the other pilots from the group were already changing. Four of the six stopped and looked at him, and one said, "What are you doing here?"

"I thought I could help," Josh said. "I do not want the Urlak to invade Cathardi like they did my planet."

"You say that, but you and the Sisterhood are the reason we wait here."

"Maybe, but I still want to help." He found his flight suit and began dressing, while the others made disparaging remarks until Jaicen entered.

"I see you have met our new pilot. I expect you to treat him with the same courtesy and respect that you use with each other." Jaicen came over and put his hand on Josh's shoulder. "The captain has volunteered to fly with us. He is also the only one of us with any real-world experience fighting the Urlak. Now, get to your fighters. We have a patrol to fly."

"Aye, sir." The pilots left as they finished changing.

"Thank you, commander. I understand their doubts." He grabbed his helmet. "I will try to perform well enough to dispel their doubts."

"I believe you will. But, for now, you will fly on my wing. When I am satisfied with your performance, I will move you to where I think you will fit best." They walked to the launch bay together.

Josh flew well on the patrol but had difficulty during the live fire target practice. His score was the worst out of the entire wing. When they returned to the ship, Jaicen asked him to stay in the ready room after the other pilots left.

"Your piloting skills are impressive," he said. "But you have little or no experience using the fighter's weapons. You are probably overthinking the process."

"You are probably correct, sir. But how do I improve? It might take a lot of rounds for me to get better."

"We can go to your quarters. I will show you how to practice using the training headset." They went to Josh's quarters, where Jaicen signed onto the workstation. After entering several things, he opened the drawer below the station and pulled out what looked to Josh like a pair of goggles. "Put these on."

Josh put the goggles on. "Now take the simulator sticks on the sides of the workstation. Everything operates just like the fighter controls. You can call up the practice programs using your voice. Begin firing practice one." The goggles changed to show a flight simulation. "Once you complete one exercise, the system will allow you to move on to the next level of the program."

"Just like a virtual reality game on Earth," Josh said. "I think I can do this."

"Good. The other pilots in the group use this same program to keep their skills honed. Most of them are on level eight or nine. I do not expect you to get there soon, but you should improve by the next patrol."

The wing commander left him, and Josh worked through the simulation. The first time through, he scored almost the same number of hits as he did on the patrol. After his third time through, he hit nearly seventy-five percent of the targets. Still not good enough to move onto the next level. He practiced regularly with the headset and by the time the next patrol came around he had advanced to the next level.

"Look who just walked in," Elmar, one of the more vocal pilots said when Josh entered the ready room to dress for the patrol. "It is the Ompresti's Nakir. We have a real-life hero in our midst."

"Just be careful if he has the enemy on your tail in his sights. He might miss and hit you," Dain said, causing the other pilots to laugh.

He laughed along with them. *At least they accept me enough to make fun of me. They seem only a little different from the guys at the academy. We sure gave Ray a hard time when we first started practicing soccer. He might have been a big-time football recruit, but it took a while for him to coordinate his feet.*

After the patrol and exercise, Dain came up to him. "Much better shooting today. I am sorry for what I said earlier."

"Nothing to be sorry about." Josh accepted the hand the pilot extended. "I deserved it. I am trying to get used to the weapons so I can be useful."

"We are getting together in the mess later. You can join us if you would like."

"Thank you, I would like that. But the commander has asked me to attend a briefing later. I don't think I will make it." Josh stowed his gear.

"The invitation is open if you get free." Dain left the ready room.

I might eventually fit in with these guys. Though, I sense their distrust of me. After all, I am an alien to them. Josh headed toward his quarters. He wanted to rest before going to the briefing. The wait was wearing on everyone, especially the ship commanders.

"Captain." Jaicen met him in the passageway. "Nice improvement out there today."

"Thank you, sir."

"Your forward weapons skills were excellent, but you still have issues with the lateral and rear weapons. Trust the targeting sensors there just like you do the one in front."

Josh knew exactly what the commander was talking about. When the lateral targeting sensor alerted, he would turn his head to get a visual on the target. By that time, it was often too late. "Yes, sir. I am still adjusting to the weapon system of the fighter. I will keep working on the simulator program."

Suddenly, the signal for battle stations sounded. "Get suited up," Jaicen said. "I will meet you in the tactical center.

Josh ran back to the ready room and put on his flight suit. Then he and the other pilots in his unit sat in the tactical center. They watched the large monitor on the wall and waited in case they were called.

Red circles showed where singularities formed inside the perimeter of the Cathardi cruisers. Green crosses representing Cathardi fighters spread out from the green circles of the larger Cathardi vessels. The yellow circles of the Urlak vessels appeared within the singularities. From the size of the circles, he guessed the Urlak were mostly light cruisers, though an occasional heavy cruiser also came through. As each singularity dissipated, the Cathardi fighters attacked the Urlak ships, destroying most before they could even recover from the jump. *I thought there would be more heavy cruisers and possibly a planetary assault ship or two.* Just then, three large singularities formed outside the perimeter. Alarms sounded and the orders for the reserves to launch came over the speaker.

Once inside his fighter, he did his preflight check, started the engines, and waited for his turn to launch. *I don't think we will make it to the new ships before they recover from the jump. That means they will launch their fighters. This won't be as easy as the first group.*

After the launch, he formed up with his fighter squadron and sped toward the enemy positions. His heads-up display showed the targeting in the center with the battle status on the right and a smaller version of the overall positions of all the ships and a system's status on the left. He could see the other reserve fighters, followed by two of the cruisers, approaching the new enemy targets. His squadron was closest to the Urlak. He armed his weapons.

On his first pass at the Urlak heavy cruiser, he concentrated rail gun fire on its propulsion systems, hoping to disable it. He knew the second squadron would target its life support. His targeting display showed three more heavy cruisers, and he heard the orders to proceed to the next in line, but before he could get there, the Urlak fighters swarmed out of the cruiser.

"Evasive maneuvers. Everyone, try to get through to the cruiser and target its propulsion. Help is coming. We want to keep them here if we can." Came through the helmet speaker.

He fired on two Urlak fighters directly in front of him. Destroying the first with his forward laser, then he banked left and fired his right-side lasers at the second, hitting it as he passed. The maneuver put him below the cruiser in no position to target the propulsion systems and the cruiser's laser cannons made it difficult for him to get a shot with the rail gun.

Where did you come from? Another Urlak fighter showed up on the targeting screen behind him. He fired at it and banked hard right, and down. He didn't know if he hit it, but it no longer showed on his display. *It looks like they only have forward and rear guns.*

He was now well below the cruiser on the edge of the battle. Above him, he could see the enormous belly of the cruiser. *If I head straight up toward that belly, I can put several rounds into its center where the gravity drive is probably located.* He did a quick ninety-degree turn and headed directly at the cruiser, putting ten rail gun rounds into its center before pulling away. As he dove away from the cruiser, its gravity drive exploded. The shock wave rocked his fighter.

"Good shooting, Captain." It was the wing commander. "All fighters note the weak spot on the belly of the cruisers. Add that as one of your primary targets."

The fighters surrounding the remaining two cruisers made it difficult to get any kind of clear shot. Josh got close to the last cruiser, but all he could do was fire several rounds from his rail gun into the launch bay, trying to disable it and prevent more fighters from launching.

The battle developed into a fighter-against-fighter dogfight. The superior Cathardi fighters were faster and able to fire in all directions, eventually diminishing the Urlak's numbers.

His tactical display showed the initial battle in the perimeter was over and the rest of the Cathardi forces were rapidly advancing on the two remaining Urlak cruisers. His display also showed only two of the original sixteen fighters from his squadron remained when the orders from the Singal came for him to return to the ship.

Commander Delfrim was on the hangar deck when he and Jaicen arrived. "Well done, gentlemen, that was excellent flying. I am recommending both of you for citations. And, you Captain, your intelligence has saved the Cathardi homeworld from this attack. The Council wants to see you as soon as we have finished here. Now get some rest, the mop-up will take several hours."

Josh napped for a couple of hours and then made his way to the mess hall. They gave him a bowl of hearty stew, which he took to an unoccupied table. He looked around. Groups of three to four other pilots occupied several other tables. They appeared to talk excitedly, motioning with their hands and arms. He guessed they were reliving their exploits in the battle. The hum of conversation and the occasional loud laugh helped him to feel more relaxed. *If Liria is right, and I am the chosen one from her prophecy, how am I going to save my world?*

Wing Commander Jaicen interrupted his thoughts when he came up to the table. "May I join you, Captain?"

"Yes, please do."

Jaicen sat and started on his bowl of stew. After a few bites, he looked up. "I hear it is always like this after a battle. The pilots congregate in small groups to celebrate the victory and to remember those they lost." The surrounding conversations ebbed and flowed between excitement and silence. "You are the only survivor from my squadron, and I don't even know you. Scuttlebutt is the Ompresti named you her Nakir. I don't know if it is true, but today you were a real Nakir, a mighty warrior."

"It is true, but I don't know what it entails. All I know is it allowed me to speak to the Council. Today, I just did my job with the help of all of you. Now I don't know what I will do or where I will go after we return to Cathardi."

"We would welcome you aboard the Singal if you wanted to stay. But the look in your eyes says you long for a more permanent home. I hope you find it."

Before Josh could answer, the ship's executive officer came to their table. "Gentlemen, I thought you would be interested to know the mop-up teams have found some of the Urlak alive on the last cruiser. They found them unconscious because we knocked out their life support system. Once we revive them, they could give the Council information on the plans for future attacks. They are being brought on board the Singal before we leave for Cathardi. The Commander would like you both to be in the shuttle bay when they arrive. You have ten minutes." The executive officer left them at the table, where they gulped down the rest of their food.

When they got to the shuttle bay, Commander Delfrim, the senior officers, and all the fighter wing commanders were assembled on a platform overlooking the bay. Josh watched as the first shuttle settled into position. They began carrying the restrained Urlak out on stretchers. As they watched, the Commander said. "Gentlemen, this is a momentous day. This is the first time in the history of our war with the Urlak that we have ever captured any prisoners. Today we have over one hundred alive with several senior officers. Congratulations."

CHAPTER 19

When the Singal returned to Cathardi, Josh walked off the ship into the spaceport arrival area where Moira met him. "Welcome back Captain, the Council has heard the reports of your part in the victory. They are most impressed with the accuracy of your prediction concerning the location of the invasion. The Council will meet with you tomorrow after they question one of the Urlak prisoners. We believe he was the leader of the invading forces," she said. "I will take you to a short-term living facility near the council chamber where you can rest and refresh."

"Thank you," he said.

Moira led him to a vehicle outside the facility. It looked like a stretched Volkswagen bug with only three wheels and a transparent bubble over the top. The electric motors made little noise when they pulled away.

As they started through the city, he asked her, "As a member of the Council, do you think they will be open to helping me free my home world from the Urlak invaders now?"

"I think it may be possible. The sisters will support you, but we do not know how the civilian and military delegates will vote. I have discussed the topic in private with most of them, and the only one who strongly opposes the idea is Marlon, the Council chair. He carries a lot of political weight. You will need to present at least a rough plan for proceeding during the meeting. Though knowing you as I do through Liria, I am sure you already have an idea."

They sat in silence for a few minutes with Josh looking out at the capital city. Compared to the spartan minimalism of the Cathardi military and functional spaces aboard their ships, the city architecture was ornate. The buildings were almost organic, with sweeping curves and branches resembling stout trees and shrubs. They appeared brightly colored through the expansive use of shaded translucent glass-like materials that offered color to the gray and brown building structural frames. "You know, I have been here on a couple of occasions, and this is the first chance I have had to appreciate how beautiful the city is, but there don't seem to be many people traveling around outside."

"Yes, it is a beautiful city. My people appreciate nature and like to look through the glass to see it. Unfortunately, your primary experience has been on spacecraft, which by nature cannot be open to the environment. There are few vehicles out since most Cathardi live near their jobs and those who must travel farther use the underground transport tubes."

The vehicle stopped beneath the curve of a ten-story building with blue translucent glass that swept over them like the beginning curl of an ocean wave. "This is where you will be staying. There is a transport tube in the lower level of the building that goes directly to the Council's building. Someone will meet you in the morning and escort you there. You are free to walk around the city unescorted. There are several fine dining establishments within walking distance from here. The in-room information center can recommend one to you based on your preferences. Your Cathardi is excellent, so you should have no trouble communicating. I will see you tomorrow at the Council." She smiled at him. "You are a hero to the Cathardi people."

They said goodbye, and he got out of the vehicle and entered the building. An attractive Cathardi female in a sky-blue pantsuit that matched the color of her eyes met him. "Captain, welcome." She smiled. "If you follow me, I will show you your room. My name is Mykal, and I will be your valet during your stay. If I am not available, just ask one of the other uniformed staff and they will help you."

They went to an elevator, which took them to the tenth floor. Mykal asked him a lot of questions about Earth. What did it look like? What were the people like? The only thing most Cathardi knew was that the Ompresti predicted they would find it, and a few rumors from returning soldiers and diplomats.

He answered her questions the best he could, but he was glad when they finally got to his room.

The room was on the top floor and the main living space had a curved glass wall overlooking the city. Before leaving him alone, Mykal showed him how to operate the information center, including the controls for the window shading.

He went into the bedroom, which was located just inside along the entry hall, where he found clean clothes on the shelves near the lavatory door. He was exhausted and all he wanted was a shower and to rest. The stress of waiting for the Urlak had taken a lot of his energy. He needed to unwind.

After a shower and a brief nap, he was hungry and wanted to find a place to eat. Rather than use the information center, he took the elevator down to street level. Mykal walked over to him from one of the side hallways.

"Hello, Captain, are you going out to eat?" she said.

"Yes, I thought I would find a place to eat. Do you have any suggestions?"

"I do. My shift ends in one hour. I am meeting my family for dinner. If you would like to join us, we would welcome you."

She waited for his answer while he considered her offer. "I might enjoy the company, but I wouldn't want to impose on your family time."

"You wouldn't be imposing. My mate and my children would be delighted to meet you. If you wouldn't mind, they will have even more questions than I asked. They have never met an off-worlder."

He paused again before answering. "You're sure it wouldn't impose?"

"I am sure." Her smile broadened into a toothy grin. "If you would like to wait, I can take you there after I'm off work."

"I think I would like to walk around outside. I need to stretch my legs and think. Can you tell me where to meet you?"

She took a portable data unit out of her jacket and input some information into it. "Here are the directions. The device will track your location and show you where to go and how long it should take. You can return it to me or leave it in your room when you leave." She handed it to him. "My family will be so excited when I tell them you are joining us."

"Good, but I have one condition; for every question they ask, I get to ask them a question about Cathardi." He smiled.

"That will be fun. I will see you in about ninety minutes. Enjoy your walk."

The streets of the city were clean and practically deserted except around the entrances to the transport tubes that were spaced about every half mile. At these, groups of people would gather and queue up to go down to the tubes or come out in groups and disperse once they were on the street. Only a few of the buildings that towered above him were taller than ten stories. Their curved architecture and glass reflected the setting sun in a rainbow of colors shining on the street. Most of the Cathardi people he passed gave him several feet of clearance, but occasionally, one would smile or nod as he or she passed him. He found a park with a grassy knoll where he sat on a bench and watched Cathardi children run and play on the hill, filling the air with the sounds of children's laughter. Their guardians sat on other benches scattered around the knoll and kept a close eye on them. He took a deep breath and smelled flowers, grass, and other plants around the park. It was delightful. He had smelled nothing like it since he left Bapto.

He watched a young girl roll down the hill straight into the legs of an older girl, causing her to fall on top of the rolling girl. Both cried out in pain and their guardians came running to comfort them. They appeared to argue briefly, probably about who was to blame. *Just like Earth.* He wiped tears from his eyes as he thought of his childhood and the loss of his family. The data unit interrupted his reflections, informing him it was time to head to meet Mykal.

It took fifteen minutes to walk from the park, following the directions the data unit provided him. It was nearly dark when he reached the restaurant. Lights shining through the translucent glass facade of the building lit the streets in a multitude of colors. The Cathardi words, Sea Fruit, were shown through the glass. The solid nature of the letters formed a black sign on the yellow, backlit glass.

Mykal greeted him when he entered. "I am so glad you came. My family is in the back, where there is a little more privacy." She led him around the tables that were separated by fabric-covered screens to a larger round table in the rear. "This is my family, my mate Varian, and my daughters Pria and Ces. Pria is ten and Ces is eight."

They all stood and greeted him. Mykal offered him the seat between Pria and Ces. "They both asked to sit by you," she said.

"I am honored," Josh said and nodded as he sat between the two girls.

"You are huge," Ces said, giggling. "Are all the people from your world so big?"

"No, not all. I am slightly bigger than the average. Where I come from, people come in all different sizes, shapes, and skin colors," he said, smiling at her.

"Girls, why don't we give our guest a chance to know us first before we chase him away?" Mykal said. Then turned to him. "Captain, Varian is a gravity drive engineer and is working on the latest improvements. Both my daughters attend a technical preparatory school. They hope to become scientists."

"Very impressive." Josh looked at each of the girls. "Please, my name is Josh. Captain is only a temporary title. For a while, I worked as an engine repair technician when I lived at the Melal station and then when my wife and I lived on Bapto. There I did mainly engine repairs and other repairs for the mining equipment. Your gravity drives are incredibly robust and rarely break down. You and your colleagues have done a superb job."

"Thank you. They mustn't break down in space." Varian said.

Pria was bouncing in her seat. "The people from your world have different colored skin. Is it green or blue or red?"

Josh chuckled. "Not green or blue, and not brightly colored like your buildings, but shades of brown, some almost black, others reddish, and others even a little yellow. On my world, I am considered a white man even though you find me more brown or red than the typical Cathardi. And unlike my understanding of Cathardi, the people on Earth speak many languages depending on their geographic location."

"Wow." Both girls looked wide-eyed.

"Josh, we have taken the chance and ordered a meal for all of us. I hope that does not offend you," Varian said. "This place serves large portions suitable for families or large groups and specializes in seafood."

"That sounds good to me. You know better than I do what they offer." Josh said.

"You mentioned your wife on Bapto. Was she not able to come with you.?" Varian said, changing the subject.

A few seconds passed in silence before Josh spoke with tears forming in his eyes. "She died during the incident with the Urlak on Bapto. She was carrying our first child."

"I am sorry. I didn't know." Varian looked down at the table.

"I can see you miss her," Mykal said, reaching over to put her hand on Josh's.

Just then, the server brought out a large steaming platter that took up half of the table. Josh's stomach growled at the smell of the grilled seafood. A thick chunk of fish with an oily shine occupied the center of the platter. Different shellfish surrounded it, and steaming greens surrounded the shellfish.

When the server left, Varian spoke a short blessing over the food and Mykal dished up servings for the girls while Varian and Josh dished up their own.

Josh thought the fish tasted like grilled swordfish with a tangy buttery sauce that gave it the sheen, and the greens were sweet with a vinegary sauce. Josh hadn't eaten this well in a long time. The awkwardness of the moment about his wife's death disappeared, and the conversation continued with the girls wanting to know everything about not only Earth but also Bapto. They finished the meal with tea.

"It has been a genuine pleasure to have you join us," Mykal said. "But we need to get home. We have a busy day tomorrow."

"We are going to the zoo," Pria interrupted. "Would you like to come see the animals from Cathardi?"

"Thank you Pria, I would, but I meet with the Council tomorrow and cannot." He put his hand on her shoulder. "Enjoy your visit to the zoo." He envied her innocence as he remembered going to the zoo as a child.

Mykal stood. "Can I walk you to the door?"

"Sure." He walked back through the restaurant with Mykal.

"You have been very gracious. I am sorry we did not uphold our end of the bargain. The girls were so excited to meet you and I am sure they will tell stories at school for some time."

"It was a pleasure and made me feel at home. Thank you."

"Keep the data unit to guide you back to your room. If you leave it there, I or someone else will retrieve it after you leave. I hope it goes well with the Council tomorrow."

"I hope so as well. Goodnight, you have a wonderful family. This was fun."

He returned to the short-term residence surprised at how the people of Cathardi seemed just like people on Earth. Saving Mykal's family from the Urlak was worth the hardship and helped make him more determined to help Earth.

***

After she heard the reports of the Cathardi victory over the Urlak invaders, Liria returned to the capital. She contacted Moira who would arrange for her to meet with the earthling before the council meeting. Her feelings for Josh had not waned with the separation. Though eager to see him again, she knew he would not stay with her. *How could I get so attached to an alien?* But the reunion would wait. Moira had asked her to come to the Sisterhood offices in the council building. They wanted to ask her about Urlak.

When she entered, Moira, Cili, and Sumia stood in front of a large video monitor watching an Urlak prisoner.

"You asked to see me?" Liria said, distracting them from the image,

"Yes, come tell us what you make of the prisoner." Moira waved her over.

"He is Urlak. They all look similar, with their orange skin, bald heads, muscular builds, and arrogant sneers on their faces."

Liria thought back to the confrontation at the mine on Bapto. "They have no regard for the Creator."

"Did you know they are all clones?" Cili said. "Their DNA would make them fraternal twins. But they do not have reproductive organs. I am astounded that the Creator has allowed them to exist this long."

"I did not know they were clones, but their feelings are easy to sense and very uniform," she said. "They were made for a single purpose."

"The guards are ready to enter the cell." Sumia pointed to the video showing the cell door.

"He is like a caged animal," Moira said. "Look at his eyes."

The video image wavered momentarily. "They activated his control collar," Sumia said.

They watched as the cell door opened. The Urlak tried to move, anguish twisting his face. Guards manacled his hands and feet. The control collar he wore sent an electrical pulse through his body whenever he tried to move.

When they had locked the manacles, the guards led the prisoner out into the hallway. Two on each side, armed with control rods, so they could activate the collar when needed. The Urlak's face showed stoic acceptance of the uselessness of his position.

"We should go to the council chamber now," Moira said. "Liria must go meet the earthling before the session starts. The sentries at the door already have orders to allow him inside."

She met Josh at the entrance to the council chamber. She sensed his nervousness before she saw him dressed as a Cathardi

Captain. His gray uniform displayed the medals he received for his part in the battle against the Urlak. When he got to her, he took her hands in his and looked at her. "You appear to have recovered from our ordeal," he said.

"You look recovered as well." She leaned forward and rose on her toes to kiss his cheek. "I needed the time to recover, but I missed you. Still, I don't think I have adequately thanked you for getting me here." *I miss the way he looks at me and the way I feel around him.* She felt her face redden. "Shall we go inside?"

The sentries saluted Josh when they opened the double doors. Inside, Cathardi filled the council chamber. She led him to a less crowded area at the back of the room, near another set of double doors. "Everyone is here to see the prisoner. Once the council finishes with him, most will leave." She held onto his arm, remembering their last audience with the council.

The doors near them opened and soldiers brought the Urlak prisoner into the chamber. They led him to a spot in the middle of the room and cleared the onlookers from between him and the platform where the council sat. After they chained his restraints to the floor, the guards stepped back.

Marlon stood and walked to the edge of the platform. "I am Marlon, chair of the Cathardi Council. We believe you to be the commander of the forces that invaded our system. Is that correct?"

Another Cathardi standing near the prisoner translated the chair's words into Urlak. The Urlak stood tall with his shoulders back and a defiant stare as the interpreter finished. But when he tried to speak, he could not.

"Answer me!" Marlon made a hand signal to the guards.

"I can speak your filthy language," the Urlak said in Cathardi. "You may address me as Commander Garond. I led the small expeditionary force to test your defenses."

Liria whispered to Josh, "He is lying about it being an expeditionary force. They are easy to read. The sisters on the council will know he is lying."

"A force that was defeated," Marlon said, pacing along the front of the platform. "Now this Council wants to know what other plans the Urlak have concerning Cathardi."

"You are weak fools. You think because you have defeated me, you have won." Garond jerked at his chains. "Hah! We will destroy you. My people know where you are. We will not stop until you are all destroyed."

The council members behind Marlon whispered amongst themselves, and a murmur arose from the crowd until Moira stood up behind Marlon. "Mister Chairman, let us remove this unbelieving enemy from our presence. God has prophesied our victory, and I along with my sisters know he is lying. Though I am sure the generals will plan for future attacks."

"My people will destroy not only you, but this god that you worship," Garond laughed. "Where is he? Can you see him? Can he help you? No! You are doomed!"

Liria felt the Creator's presence welling up inside her. "You mock God?" she said. Her voice carried above the roar of the crowd. "This is what the Creator of the Heavens says to you. 'Your people are an abomination to me. You are a disease of corruption. I can no longer endure your cruelty and violence. You are the last generation of Urlak. Neither I nor my people will mourn your passing. You have said in your hearts we are gods. We have created ourselves. Our science has exceeded God. But I say your science has failed." Her voice echoed through the now silent chamber.

"Who are you, witch?" Garond said.

"I am Liria, and I am no witch, but a prophetess of the Creator. Look at your hands!"

He looked at his hands. Ulcers were forming on his skin.

"Before you die, all the rest of your people will be dead. You will be the last Urlak."

Garond struggled against his restraints. He tried in vain to break free while staring at Liria. The ulcers on his hands grew and new ones appeared on his face. He howled in pain and anger until the shock from the collar cut off his screams. The guards surrounded him again and took him from the Chamber.

The crowd in the chamber was silent. They stared at her. She held onto Josh.

Marlon's voice echoed through the quiet chamber. "The council will take a recess. Everyone, clear the chamber."

The crowd moved toward the door, but a sister came up to Liria. "Ompresti, please come with me. The elders want to have a word." She led them through the same doors where they had taken Garond and down the hall to the room where Liria had met the sisters before the meeting.

The three women stared at the video monitors. Even with the volume lowered, she could hear the screams of the captive Urlak. Moira turned to her. "That was incredible. Every Urlak has developed sores. We have sent doctors to look at them. But if it is the Creator's judgment, I am not sure we can help them."

Liria still held tightly to Josh's arm. "What would you have me do?"

"Nothing for now. It may take some time before we know anymore." She turned back to the video. "Marlon will recall the council in an hour. Captain, you will need to be prepared to present your request. I think it is important that Liria remains by your side. It will help influence some of the council members to help you. You can rest in there." She pointed to a door to their left.

***

When Josh and Liria returned to the council chamber, they passed through the crowd from the morning session that packed the halls outside the chamber, clamoring about what they saw.

"You certainly caused a stir among the people this morning." He leaned close so as not to have to speak too loudly in the noisy passage.

"Like all things with the people, it will pass rather quickly." She still held his arm.

Inside, the council chamber was nearly empty, with only three other requests on the docket, and twenty or thirty interested parties. He and Liria waited at the rear since they would hear his request last.

After an hour, they called Josh forward. "Captain, we are in your debt. Your intuition and actions have saved the Cathardi people from the Urlak. How can we repay you?"

"Mister Chairman and esteemed council members, if the ancient prophecy is correct, I have only completed half of my task. I have fulfilled the initial portion with the saving of Cathardi, but I still need to save my world from the Urlak. Earth is still in their control, and it is in danger of being destroyed before all the Urlak succumbed to the plague. I would like to lead a small force of Cathardi ships against the Urlak on Earth."

Marlon returned to his seat, and the Council discussed his request amongst themselves.

Liria came to stand at his side. "I believe you will receive your approval. The sisters and military support you and Marlon wants to be rid of you. You are a reminder of the Sisterhood's power," she whispered.

After several minutes, Marlon called the council to order, and General Stanko stood. "The Council has agreed to help if it does not further endanger Cathardi. How large of a force do you think you require?"

"Sir, I need one of the captured Urlak cruisers repaired and enough soldiers to crew it, along with two Cathardi light cruisers for reinforcements. I hope to surprise their orbiting forces.

If we can destroy the orbiting forces, especially the planetary assault ships, my people will have the chance to defeat the stranded Urlak forces on the surface. We are a stubborn and resourceful race when pressed."

Again, the Council talked often getting quite animated. Then Marlon said, "We will grant your request, including the two additional cruisers. You are free to begin preparations. General Stanko will contact you to make the arrangements. May the Creator speed your hand."

Josh turned to Liria, gazing into her blue eyes. *Is she controlling my mind? Why do I always feel so helpless when I am close to her?* "I must do this." He shook his head to clear his mind.

"I know you must. But promise me I will see you again," she said as Josh watched a tear run down her cheek.

"I cannot promise that." He gently wiped the tear away with his thumb. "Neither of us knows God's will for my life. But if I am successful in defeating the Urlak, we may see each other again. After all, I am your Nakir."

"You have been more than that." She looked away from him. He sensed her closing off. Trying to keep him from knowing her feelings for him, though he could see them. "I wish circumstances were different and we had time to know each other more deeply." She took his hand. "You will be successful in your mission, but I fear it may be difficult for you. You need to recover from Kim's death and the other losses, which are greater than even I can comprehend. Cathardi is changing and I am not sure what the future holds for me either. May the blessing of the Creator go with you, Joshua Albertson." She kissed his cheek and walked away, but Josh could still sense her sadness and longing.

Two weeks later, He was at a fleet repair base where the Cathardi worked day and night on the Urlak command cruiser. They replaced the life support systems and bridge with Cathardi systems. They repaired the significant structural damage to the ship using sections recovered from the other Urlak vessels destroyed in the battle.

The key to Josh's plan depended on convincing the Urlak forces around Earth of the return of the Urlak command ship. While the physical repairs were underway, He worked with Cathardi technicians on a communications system to translate and broadcast audio and visual, mimicking the Urlak Commander's voice and appearance. When activated, the deep fake would allow him to sound and look just like Garond. Though not perfect, it should fool the Urlak long enough for them to get within range to destroy at least one of the orbiting ships.

After a long day of trying to imitate the Urlak Commander, he sat in the temporary office assigned to him in the hangar. There was a rap on his door. "Enter," he said, without looking up.

He heard a familiar voice. "Captain, I would like to accompany you on this mission, if possible?"

He looked up and there in a Cathardi fighter pilot's uniform was Steve. He rose to his feet and hugged his old friend. "Permission granted. It is so good to see you. What have you been doing?"

"Mostly flying recon missions, but I fought the Urlak with you at the jump point, though I was on the other side of the perimeter. It felt good to get some payback after what they did to Carla and the others."

"Where is Jason?"

"Assigned to a cruiser in another sector. It was too far away for him to be a part of the battle. What about Kim? Is she still on Melal?"

Josh looked down at the floor as tears welled up in his eyes. *Will it ever stop hurting when someone mentions Kim? It is just so hard to talk about.* "The Urlak killed her." He stopped and closed his eyes, still trying to quell the emotions. "We married there, and she was pregnant with our first child when it happened."

He watched Steve stare at the floor. "I am so sorry. Even at the Academy, I thought the two of you might get together, but I never thought she would be killed after we avoided the Urlak on that first trip."

"It's all too fresh in my mind right now to talk about. Maybe we can catch up after the mission." Josh stood straighter and forced a smile. "It is great to have you here. We have a briefing early tomorrow morning. I would like you to be there since we will cover the latest reconnaissance of the Urlak positions orbiting Earth."

"I will be there. Now I'll let you get back to work." He saluted and left.

Josh sat back down, but he couldn't concentrate. Seeing Steve brought back a lot of painful memories and all the painful feelings he had repressed. He needed to be alone, so he put his work aside and left the hangar. After taking a transport tube into the city, he walked, remembering his days at the Academy and their close-knit pod. Of the eight of them, only three remained with more fighting on the horizon. He was just approaching the transport tube that would take him back to the repair terminal and his quarters when he heard.

"Captain?"

He looked up and saw Mykal and her family. The two girls ran to him for hugs. His mood lifted. "How are you guys?"

"Great. We are on our way for an after-dinner treat. Would you like to join us?"

"Please do. The girls would love it." Varian added.

Both girls chimed in. "Please, please."

"Sure, I could use the diversion."

They went to a place that served a frozen fruit treat like sorbet. The girls talked the whole time, telling him about the zoo, and about how jealous their friends at school were that they had got to meet an off-worlder. When it was time to leave, they both hugged his neck, smiling at him.

"Thank you, Josh, for joining us. You can see how much the girls enjoyed it. I know this is probably the last time we will see you. Word is you will leave on your mission soon. It has been a privilege for us." Varian reached out his right hand. "I understand from some old reports, that this is the proper method of greeting and farewell."

"It is." Josh shook his hand.

Mykal hugged him. "If you ever make it back to Cathardi, please come see us. We are praying for the success of your mission."

"I will. You make me feel at home here. Because of you, I realized how much alike we are. Good night."

He walked back to the transport tube refreshed, and his mind went to the mission. *We must make this work. Surprise is our biggest advantage if we don't destroy the orbiting Urlak forces. Earth doesn't stand a chance even with the plague.*

CHAPTER 20

Josh and the Cathardi crew aboard the Urlak command cruiser entered Earth space, where the two planetary assault vehicles orbited. The closest PAV was two hours away, but already its fighters were advancing on the jump point.

"Unidentified Urlak cruiser, identify yourself." The demand came from the PAV, which was broadcast over the ship-wide communications system and to the other Cathardi vessels over a secure channel.

"This is Garond, you fool. Give me the status on the surface. Have you eliminated the resistance?" Josh used the translation unit, which transmitted Garond's voice.

"Commander Garond, we are making progress on the surface, but the resistance is persistent, and they are in difficult terrain scattered across the planet."

"Incompetent fools! I will be aboard your ship shortly for a briefing. I need a PAV to finish the Cathardi after our victory.

Have your commander prepare so we can leave once the briefing is complete. You must return to Cathardi with me so I can claim the victory before any other units arrive."

"Yes, Commander. I will return with the message immediately."

Josh turned to the communications officer and signaled for the communications to be ended, then turned to the navigation officer. "How long until we are close enough to fire on the PAV?"

"Seventy-five minutes, Captain."

"Very well. Inform Commander Delfrim to jump seventy-five minutes from now. How long will it take the second PAV to threaten our position?"

"That is unknown, sir. We do not know its capabilities, but my best guess is one hundred- minutes."

"It will be close. Let's hope the Singal and Antomay arrive in time." He sat at the command station, waiting.

He heard the transmission from the approaching fighters. "Commander Garond, this is fighter group leader Drex. We will escort you to the Carinus."

"Should I reply?" the communications officer asked.

"Just confirm receipt of the transmission and tell them we will follow." He watched the main viewscreen as the PAV grew from a small dot to an enormous circle that nearly covered the screen. *That thing is huge. We need to get as close as we can before we open fire.*

The bridge crew grew quiet. Josh glanced around. They appeared nervous. "Have the fighter crews prepare to launch, but keep the bay doors closed until we fire. Inform me when we reach weapons range."

The bridge crew looked at their monitors without speaking while they waited. Many fiddled with small objects. Some drummed their fingers on the panels in front of them. All seemed tense.

"Sir, we are at optimum weapons range now," the navigator said.

"Fire everything and launch the fighters." Josh watched the explosions on the surface of the enemy ship. "Navigator, evasive maneuvers, but keep us within weapons range. Have our fighters form a defensive perimeter."

"Captain, the first volley disabled their propulsion, but damage to the rest of the vessel appears minimal." He heard over the com.

"Continue firing. We need to put them out of commission as quickly as possible," he ordered.

Enemy fighters swarmed out of the gigantic ship, attacking his captured cruiser. With only a few fighters of their own for support, the Urlak fighters were causing heavy damage. Even with the Cathardi enhancements, Josh's ship could not withstand the fighter attack for long.

"Captain, our engines are down, and we have lost most of our fighters," the navigation officer reported.

"How long until we can get support from the Singal and Antomay?" *I may have underestimated the strength of the PAV.* He felt an explosion rock his ship when an Urlak fighter crashed into the deck below the bridge.

"The Singal fighters will be here in less than fifteen minutes."

"Do we have thrusters?"

"Yes, sir."

"Then put us into a spin. Maybe we can make it hard for them to hit us in a critical area."

"Yes, sir."

As the thrusters fired, the ship spun fast enough to overcome the artificial gravity. Everything and everyone on board not restrained flew toward the outer bulkheads. Still, he could feel the effects of the Urlak weapons as they hit the ship. He didn't know how long the cruiser could withstand the assault. When the Urlak weapons disabled one thruster, the ship went into an erratic wobble, throwing him against the restraints that held him at his station.

"Captain, the Singal fighters have arrived and the Urlak are moving away to face the oncoming cruiser."

He gripped the arms of the command station chair. "Good. Can we stabilize our attitude?"

"I think so, sir."

"Have all sections report their status once the ship is stable."

He watched the tactical display which showed the battle between the Singal fighters and the Urlak around his ship. He could also see the fighters from the Antomay, as they battled the Urlak fighters defending the second PAV.

"Captain," the comm interrupted him. "All sections have reported. The main engines are down. There are hull breaches on three decks that are venting atmosphere faster than the life support systems can replace it. We will lose life support in less than three hours."

Josh looked back at the tactical display. The Antomay and its fighters were still in a pitched battle with the second PAV. "How long before the Singal can send shuttles to help us abandon ship?"

"Ninety minutes, Captain," the navigator answered. "Only two of our launch bays, four and six, are usable. Shall I let the Singal know?"

"Yes. And open the ship intercom."

"Your channel is open, sir."

"Attention, this is the captain. Our ship has sustained significant damage and we are losing life support. I am ordering you to abandon ship. The Singal is sending shuttles to take you to safety aboard the cruiser. Make your way in an orderly fashion to launch bays four and six to await the shuttles. We will maintain necessary ship functions as long as possible to ensure they transport everyone to the Singal." Josh glanced at the tactical screen and saw the Singal shuttles moving toward his ship. "Lieutenant, inform section leaders to stay on post until their personnel have made it to the shuttles. All personnel need to have their emergency breathing units in case of delays."

He dismissed the bridge crew and told them to make their way to the launch bays. He put on his breathing unit and turned back to watch the progress of the shuttles. *Well, that didn't go as planned, but it worked out in the end. I wonder how many of my crew we lost. Battles are easier in a fighter where all you need to worry about is yourself and the next target.*

"Captain, all the surviving crew have boarded the shuttles and we are waiting for you in bay four." He heard over the com.

"I am on my way," he answered. Walking through the empty ship to the launch bay reminded him of the first time he was on board before the modifications began. The damage then was more severe than now, but the eerie emptiness was the same. She had been a good ship and maybe they could refit her someday.

When he disembarked from the shuttle on the Singal, Commander Delfrim met him. "Captain Albertson, our sensors show the life support systems on the PAV that you fought have failed. We are moving to assist the Antomay with the second PAV."

"Thank you, Commander. May I join you on the bridge to monitor the battle?"

He walked to the bridge with Commander Delfrim. There he stood and watched the tactical display. The Antomay had inflicted considerable damage to the PAV, but their enormous number of fighters prevented them from completing its destruction. When the Singal arrived, it neutralized the enemy's advantage. The Singal's fighters and shipboard weapons quickly put a hole in the Urlak defensive shell, enabling both cruisers to concentrate heavy weapons fire on the PAV. Thirty minutes later the PAV exploded.

"Commander," Lieutenant Sala said after entering the bridge. "I request permission to take a squad to the other PAV. I would like to board it and look for any intelligence we can find."

"Permission granted," Delfrim said.

"Commander, I would like to accompany the boarding party to look for anything that might show the locations of the Earth's resistance forces," Josh said.

"Very well. I must oversee our forces as they continue to mop up the Urlak, who are still flying," he said. "Lieutenant Sala will help you find a suit and he will report on your status."

"Thank you, Commander."

When they disembarked from the shuttle in a launch bay on the PAV, the dark, still ship appeared deserted. The only sound he heard came from his breathing, and their headlamps provided a limited field of view.

Lieutenant Sala split the forty-man team into two groups to search. "Captain, we landed near the equator of the sphere. Our suits will provide three hours of life support. Do you want to search the decks above or below this point?"

The limited visibility had him disoriented. He didn't know what was best. Finally, he said, "Above. Let's start with the decks above."

The lieutenant acknowledged his request and sent the other team to check the decks below them. Both teams walked toward the center of the massive ship until they came to an opening on their right that led to what appeared to be a large transport tube that ran vertically.

"Without the transport tubes, how are we going to search this ship?" Josh stared into the darkness above and below in the tube.

"We will use the suit thrusters, but we must control our speed," the lieutenant said. "Link up." He pulled a line from his suit and showed Josh where to connect it to his suit. Josh took his line and handed it to a soldier next to him.

They flew up for several minutes until the lieutenant said, "This is as far as we can go. The transport car stopped here."

When he lifted his head, Josh saw the metal plate and supports of the car. "What do we do now?"

"I think we should cut through the car floor and see if the door is open." The lieutenant had them move toward the walls of the tube while one soldier used a laser to cut through the car floor. Josh expected it to drop, but without gravity, the soldier had to push it out of the way once he cut through it.

The lieutenant led them into the car. He stepped through the open door into another chamber. "Cobesti!"

There, beyond the lieutenant, Josh saw the distorted orange face of an Urlak warrior staring at him. The warrior's wide eyes and gaping mouth appeared to have died mid-scream. "Are you okay, lieutenant?"

"Yes. It startled me. The face hit my mask as I entered." Muffled laughs came over the com from a few soldiers.

"I could tell," Josh said. "Never have I heard a Cathardi officer swear like that. If I remember, I have only ever heard that word twice, and I have only a vague idea of what it means."

The rest of the squad entered what appeared to be the bridge. Dead Urlak sat restrained at their stations or floated around the room. The Cathardi soldiers detached their tethers. They seemed to enjoy pushing the floaters, sending them caroming into each other. Josh and the lieutenant concentrated on the workstations. Without power, they wouldn't learn anything. Josh moved to a room on the left of the transport tube. Inside, he saw a sphere in the center of the room. When he got closer, he saw it was a globe. He recognized the continents. There were markings on the globe that he thought represented troop positions.

"Lieutenant, I think you should see this."

"I am on my way." When Sala got there, Josh explained what he thought the markings meant. The lieutenant agreed. "Do you think we can take it back to the Singal?"

"Possibly. It depends on how they mounted it." Josh put his arms around the sphere and tried to dislodge it. To his surprise, he could wiggle it. "I think, if we cut along the base, there and there." He pointed to two fasteners. "It will come off."

The lieutenant took his laser pistol and cut through the fasteners. Josh took the weightless sphere into his arms. "We should get this to the shuttle."

Once they got back aboard the shuttle, the lieutenant called the other team to find out their status. "You need to come and see this," the voice over the com said. "We have found their cloning lab. We are four levels down. You will see the open passage on the opposite wall of the tube."

The lieutenant asked, "Do you want to join me, Captain?"

The two of them went back to the transport tube, leaving the others in the shuttle with the sphere. When they reached the opening, a dull green light emanated from down the passage. They made their way to a large open chamber, nearly six levels tall, filled with tanks containing a luminescent liquid that produced the green light. Inside each tank, an Urlak in various stages of development floated. The other search team stood at the railing overlooking the chamber.

"There are thousands of them, Lieutenant." The soldier waved his hand around the chamber. "No wonder they destroy planets. It is like they have an inexhaustible supply of warriors. I hope the Ompresti is right, and the Creator destroys them all."

***

Back aboard the Singal, Josh went to his berth and had an orderly bring him a cup of tea. He missed coffee. Maybe one day soon he could get some.

He logged onto the ship's data terminal and pulled up the casualty report. All of the fighter pilots and nearly half of his volunteer crew, sixty had died in the initial battle. His eyes grew moist as he read the list of names. Though none of them were friends, he knew all of them, and they all served gallantly. He took a swig of the strong, bitter tea. He closed his eyes and slouched in the chair. *Now I understand how Loral could leave the service and settle on an out-of-the-way planet like Bapto. It hurts too much to lose people, even if they consider you a hero. I hope we are not too late for the people of Earth. I wonder if anyone I know is still alive down there.*

After the evening mess, Josh went to the main briefing room with Commander Delfrim. The globe that the boarding party had brought back from the PAV sat on the table in the center of the room. He displayed the Singal's map of Earth on the large monitor in front of the room.

"You asked to see me, Captain?" Steve who, as tactical commander of the fighters survived the battle, entered the room.

"Yes, Steve. I need a pilot for a mission, and I would like you to volunteer." He looked up at Steve.

"Okay. What's the mission?"

"I'm taking a shuttle down to the surface to do some reconnaissance. I want to determine if any significant resistance units still exist." He pointed to the globe. "The information we retrieved from the Urlak PAV shows several pockets that might contain resistance units. I want to check them out. And, if possible, make contact. Can I count you in?"

"Yes, sir," Steve answered. "I wouldn't miss it."

"Good, I thought so. How is your Morse Code?"

"Pretty rusty, but I think it is passable. I haven't used it since the Academy. Why not just use voice communication?"

"Just a hunch." Josh paced the front of the room. "I think it might provide some assurance that we are not Urlak."

"That should work if anyone there still remembers it. When do we leave?"

Josh walked over and put his hand on Steve's shoulder. "Thank you. I will meet you in the shuttle bay at 0630."

The next morning, Josh arrived at the shuttle, where he saw Steve wearing a Cathadi fighter pilot's uniform. "I should have told you to wear civvies, but that will have to do. Let's get on board."

They boarded the shuttle, where the rest of the small Cathardi crew were doing their pre-flight checks. When they got to the bridge, Josh pointed to the pilot's chair. "You have probably been doing more flying than me lately, and the first thing we want to do is get a quick assessment of the surface conditions, looking for air defenses and Urlak troop concentrations and any significant human populations."

"Aye-aye Captain, any place you want to start?"

"Let's try Washington D.C. first, then the other major U.S. population centers."

Steve flew the shuttle out of the shuttle bay and made a slow descent into Earth's atmosphere. They flew over the major East Coast cities, starting with Washington D.C. He couldn't believe the destruction he saw. They circled the city and when they flew over to where the Academy had been, Josh looked away, fighting back tears.

"That's enough. Let's head up the East Coast to see the cities between here and Boston."

"Yes, sir," Steve said.

They flew over Baltimore, Philadelphia, New York, and Boston. Josh began to lose hope that, with all the destruction, they would find any survivors.

"I can't believe we are even looking at major cities," he said. "They have destroyed all the landmark buildings, along with the other larger structures, and there are Urlak troop concentrations everywhere."

"But no air defenses," Steve said. "They didn't think they needed them."

"Let's head South and check the rest of the Eastern seaboard, then head inland."

They flew over the rest of the country and saw the same thing with all the major cities: Miami, New Orleans, Houston, St. Louis, Chicago, and even Denver destroyed.

"The Urlak intelligence showed some remaining human resistance forces concentrated in pockets, in remote, rugged terrain," Josh said. "Some of the largest concentrations in the U.S. appeared to be in the Rockies. It looked like the Urlak forces had massed along the front range, from Albuquerque to Casper. But around Durango, Crested Butte, and other mountain communities, they didn't show any significant Urlak troop presence. Maybe we can find the resistance there. Let's circle low over the Durango area. If we don't see any Urlak, we'll send a message to see if we get any response." Josh peered at the chart on his display.

They flew increasingly wider circles over the mountains, transmitting their message.

"I can see why this is an excellent area for the resistance." Steve banked them into a turn. "Since I'm from the Midwest, I never realized this area's inaccessibility."

Finally, after several unsuccessful passes, they received a Morse Code response near Vallecito Reservoir. The commander there agreed to meet them in the valley south of the lake. Steve sat the shuttle down in the clearing on the valley floor. He and Josh walked away from the shuttle and into the open, where they waited. The smell of pine trees, the crisp, dry mountain air, and the sound of birds flooded Josh's senses, bringing back memories. He dropped to one knee. *Father, thank you for allowing me to return to my home planet. I pray we are not too late, and that Liria's prophecy is accurate. That we can save my world.*

Thirty minutes later, a solitary figure appeared from the tree line. He walked towards them slowly. When he finally reached them, he extended his hand. "I'm Commander Tolifson. We weren't expecting humans." He stared at Josh. "I know you. You're Josh Albertson. I remember you when you were big news around here before the Urlak arrived. We thought you were dead."

"We are alive. And with the help of the Cathardi forces, we have defeated the Urlak vessels orbiting Earth." Josh saw the commander smile. "Unfortunately, we don't have sufficient forces to help you fight a ground war, but we should be able to keep your airspace clear and prevent them from re-supplying. That should help you defeat them."

"How do I know you are telling the truth?"

"It won't take long for you to notice the Urlak are less effective, and their numbers are decreasing. We can resupply you with some weapons and provide aerial reconnaissance and some close air support. Do you have any prisoners?"

"No! Why would we do that?" Tolifson said. "We can't communicate with them, so they are worthless as prisoners. We kill them just like they kill us."

"Here is the frequency you can use to communicate with us." He handed the commander a slip of paper. "You probably won't need to use morse code. You can arrange for airdrops and reconnaissance missions from the Cathardi forces."

"Where are the others, the others that flew away with you that day?"

"Only three of us remain." Josh fought to keep his voice steady. "Jason is a pilot for the Cathardi in another sector, while Steve and I are coordinating this mission. The Urlak killed the others."

"I'm sorry to hear that," the commander said. "They killed most of us here, too."

"After we leave, remember, the Urlak won't be able to attack from the air and they won't have any satellite images. The Cathardi will have fighter patrols flying over regularly. You should be able to communicate with them. Good luck." They shook hands with Commander Tolifson before they walked back to the shuttle, leaving him standing in the clearing. He was still there when they flew out of sight.

"That was an odd meeting," Steve said, once they were airborne.

"It was. I don't think he trusts the Cathardi or us. We must be patient. If we can help them, they will understand. When we get back to the cruiser, we can plan how we contact other resistance pockets."

CHAPTER 21

On Cathardi, Marlon greeted Bakar at the door to the dining area of the Council building. "How did the meeting with General Stanko go?"

"It went well. He shows signs of resentment against the sisterhood and seemed open to my implications that their actions brought on the invasion."

"Good." Marlon stepped into the dining room. "Let's find a table away from the crowds where we can talk quietly."

They walked across the room, stopping occasionally to talk with people at tables they passed. They found a table in the far corner, where only one of the adjacent tables was occupied. It had junior officers who appeared to be discussing their recent training mission. Marlon and Bakar sat and talked about the upcoming agenda for the council until their food arrived and the adjacent officers left.

"Do you think the General will support a move against the sisterhood when the time comes?" Marlon asked between bites of the baked fish he was having.

"With enough of the right information, I think we can persuade him. He will be a big help in persuading the other generals once he sees our side of the issue." Bakar smiled. "What about the Ompresti? She still has a considerable following among the populace."

"The Sisterhood has isolated her by sending her to a convent to rest and recover from her ordeal. I am working on a plan to have her sent back to Bapto. There are reports that the child of the alien is alive and living with my old friend Loral."

"Will he help us?"

"No. He is old-fashioned and supports the sisterhood. But we can use the child's existence to get the meddlesome prophetess off Cathardi. Rumors are that Loral has taken the child away from the settlement to a smaller community further from the coast. If we can get her there, we can keep her isolated." Marlon pushed his plate to the side and sat back. "If we time our move correctly, she will not be a problem until we already have control."

"What about her Nakir? He could cause trouble," Bakar asked.

"The reports from our forces there say they were victorious over the orbiting Urlak forces and they are currently supporting the surface war. We can call one cruiser back to Cathardi. This will reduce the support and allow us more time while the Nakir finishes his task there. We will also slow the delivery of materials for the construction of the orbiting station. Again, we could have firm control of the Council before they complete it. If he wants to cause trouble, he will be too late."

"It almost feels too easy, but I will be glad when we can get those mind-reading sisters off the council. I will continue my conversations with General Stanko and with General Ao." Bakar took another bite of pui fruit. "We only need to persuade those two to have a majority."

"Good. But we must keep everything discreet. The Sisterhood must not know the full extent of our plans for them until we take control." Marlon leaned closer to Bakar. "Are you aware of the latest reports from Melal?"

"No."

"A new alien race has arrived aboard the station. They call themselves the Yaki, and apparently, they want to talk about opening trade with us. One of our cruisers discovered their vessel while on patrol. They have gravity drive technology and some weapons, but they allowed the cruiser's troops to inspect the vessel before it could proceed to Melal."

"We have not encountered another technologically advanced race since the Urlak. What do you think we should do?"

"I don't think we need another enemy," Bakar pushed his plate away and signaled for the server. "So, I think we will open negotiations with them. They seem peaceful and reports show we could benefit from some of their sensor technology. I will bring it up in the next council meeting." Marlon stood up. "Keep working on the generals."

He walked back to his office. It would take months before they could convince the generals to support their move against the Sisterhood. But with the Ompresti away, their influence in the capital will weaken. The time she had spent on Earth had allowed him to build his support. Once she hears of the child, she will go to find it. The older sisters appear to have lost their touch.

***

Liria flew to the convent shortly after the Council meeting where she pronounced the plague on the Urlak. She had not seen or spoken to Josh since that day. He seemed to have become immersed in the plans to rescue his home world. Though she could still reach out to him mentally, she didn't always get through his mental blocks. Things were changing.

"Ompresti," she heard the familiar voice of Lenara. "It is good to see you again, though you look awful."

"It is good to be here. I am planning a long rest." She hugged the older woman.

"I will arrange that. We prepared your quarters and instructed the other sisters not to disturb you. But when you are ready, you will need to tell me about your ordeal."

"Thank you." Lenara's understanding eyes reassured her. "Perhaps we can talk tomorrow. Today, I need to rest."

Lenara walked with her through the passages to her room. "I will have someone bring your evening meal up to you tonight. Tomorrow, we can talk over tea after morning prayers."

"I would like that. I have fond memories of our morning talks."

After Lenara left her, Liria looked around her room. Nothing had changed since her last visit except they had left extra blankets folded on the bed and added two large fur rugs, one on the floor near the bed and the other out on the balcony. She laid down on the bed and before she realized it, the sounds of the novice, Bashi, setting down the tray with the evening meal awakened her.

Liria sat up. "Thank you," she said.

"My pleasure, Ompresti. I did not intend to wake you." Bashi bowed her head.

"And I did not intend to sleep the afternoon away either." Liria walked to the table and sat. "Would you like to join me? I could use some light conversation."

"Yes, Ompresti." The novice sat and told her of all that had transpired at the convent since her last visit, while Liria ate.

The next morning, Liria went to pray with the other sisters before joining Lenara for tea in the kitchen. They talked about her mission to Bapto and her return to Cathardi. She did most of the talking, with Lenara listening attentively. The pattern went on for several weeks. When she did not attend the communal meals, Bashi brought her meals to her room. Between talking with Bashi, praying, and talking with Lenara in the kitchen, she felt her strength of mind and will return. Her face filled out, and her color returned. She felt herself again.

Sitting in Lenara's room one morning, holding the cup of hot tea that warmed her hands, she said, "You have been such a good friend to me. I feel almost normal."

"It has been my pleasure. You are more than a friend. You are my sister." Lenara took a sip of hot tea. "You have talked a lot about the events of your trial. But you have not told me anything about your feelings. Especially your feelings for the alien who rescued you. Are you still connected to him?"

Liria stared into the steaming cup for a few seconds. "I still have the connection with him. But he must fulfill his destiny and save his world. He guards his feelings closely because he still suffers from the loss of his companion. I fear I will never see him again." She wiped a tear from her cheek.

"You have deep feelings for him." Lenara reached over and put her hand on Liria's. "Do you love him?"

Shocked by the question, she did not know if she should answer. She pulled her hand away and sat with her eyes shut and her hands pressed together in front of her mouth. Lenara sat quietly, waiting for Liria to respond. Finally, she said, "I love him. I have loved him since the first time we made the connection on the shuttle. It is embarrassing, but I would like nothing better than to spend the rest of my life as his wife if he would have me. Even if it meant I would have to leave the Sisterhood and become a farmer's wife on some frontier planet."

The older woman smiled and pulled Liria's hands away from her face. Holding them, she said, "Your heart is finally healing. I suspected you had deeper feelings for him than you admitted. But now that you have admitted them, you can act accordingly. Even if it means you let him go to pursue his destiny."

"I am trying. But it is hard to leave him alone when I know that if I try, I can reach out to him with my mind." She looked into the caring eyes of her friend.

"You will find it easier with practice. And you cannot know what the Creator has planned for either of you. I sense in my spirit that you may see him again. After you have both healed."

Liria felt as if the Creator had removed a weight from her chest. Lenara was right. Now she could heal. He held both her life and Josh's life in his hands. She wanted to sing.

***

"Captain, may I enter?" Josh saw Steve standing at the open door. "I have a message from the surface."

Josh put down the report he was reading and pointed to the chair. "Sure, come in." He waited for Steve to sit. "What does the surface want? The reports show everything is going better than planned. They have isolated the Urlak to only about a dozen pockets."

"It is a personal request, sir."

"You don't have to be so formal. We are friends."

"I know, it is just habit. Captain Kel and Wayne Anderson have requested you perform their wedding ceremony."

Josh sat silently thinking about Kim, blinking to keep the tears back. "Why me?" he finally asked.

"As the Captain of a ship, according to Earth custom, you may perform the ceremony and you are familiar with Cathardi customs. They think you would be perfect to perform Earth's first interspecies wedding."

"When do they want an answer?" Memories of his wedding day on Bapto flooded his mind.

"As soon as possible, they feel like the war is winding down and they have a real chance at a life together."

"Tell them I will be honored. But I need at least a week before the ceremony to prepare."

On the day of the wedding, Josh, Steve, and the recently arrived Jason landed in the shuttle at the old Durango airport. They held the ceremony at what Josh remembered was the city park along the river. Several times during the ceremony, Josh had to stop. Unable to speak as grief welled up in his throat. He had tried to compose himself as he prepared, pushing back memories of Kim's bloody body, but the memories would not stay buried.

After the ceremony, Josh sat at the table with Wayne and Kel. "At least we didn't have to fight off a trio of dinosaurs before our vows." Wayne laughed.

"Who told you that story?" Steve sat across the table, grinning. "No, and you don't have to worry about being deported, either," Josh said.

"We are lucky," Kel said. "Though I know we will deal with some prejudice. Living out here in this beautiful country amongst people we fought with will help."

"A toast," Jason said as he stood. "To Wayne and Kel, long life, peace, and happiness."

"Here. Here," came the response from the others seated at the table.

Shortly after the toast, Josh wandered down to the river and sat on a rock overlooking a rapid listening to the water run. Alone, away from the people who reminded him so much of Kim, he sobbed. *Why did she have to die? Why couldn't we have found happiness? Was it my fault? Am I being punished for my connection to Liria? God, I don't understand any of this.*

After he sat there and let out the emotions he had held in since that day on Bapto, he remembered other things. He remembered playing soccer at the Academy, watching the mandili, and holding Kim's hand in the clearing above Loral's, the gleam in Kim's eyes when she saw his reaction to her pregnancy. Then he remembered summers as a boy, fishing this river with his dad. *Thank you, God. I have had a good life, and I hope Wayne and Kel can find their happiness.*

The sounds from the reception had died when Commander Tolifson came to him. "May I have a word with you in private?" he asked.

"What can I do for you, Commander?"

"Some of the other leaders wanted me to ask you to stay down here and lead our people into this new age. Everyone knows you and what you did here and on Cathardi."

"I am flattered, Commander. But I can't. I don't know where I am going or if I will settle down. You won the victory against the Urlak. The Cathardi are building the new orbital station which is nearly complete. You have talented people here, including Kel, Wayne, Jason, and Steve, to help establish your orbital defenses. I don't see a place for me here, and I have always dreamed of being in space. Someday I will fly again."

"I am sorry to hear that, but it doesn't surprise me. Hopefully, the Cathardi will be more forthcoming with information about potential threats, even though I know we cannot rely on their help to protect us."

"They may be more forthcoming, but I wouldn't completely trust them. They have a lot of politicians just like those we have on Earth. Their policies are changing. You have enough captured Urlak and leftover Cathardi Technology to develop your defenses. Trust your instincts."

Six months later, Josh boarded the Phoenix. The freighter that originally belonged to the Melal Faili was now the first Earth-flagged merchant ship. Josh had resurrected it using technology from the captured Urlak vessels and new Cathardi engines. He also had an Urlak weapons system adapted and installed, despite the objections of the Cathardi. The crew comprised various species, including three former Academy cadets.

Their maiden voyage would take them to Eir, where they would deliver a load of asteroid-harvested iron ore and pick up advanced medical technology.

"Mister Lurneq, are we ready for departure?" he asked his first officer as he took his seat at the command station.

"Aye, sir. All systems are ready at your command."

"Very well. Take us out." Josh smiled.

The End

EPILOGUE

After being revived by the medics and seeing the carnage in the parlor, Loral sat on a sofa near the door to the hallway while the Cathardi medic examined him. "You have a concussion, but you have survived the encounter." Then, before the medic moved on to a soldier with a wounded arm, he said, "You will need to take it easy for a few days."

The medic's words sounded like he was in a cave echoing through his brain. His head ached. Trying to make sense of the surrounding chaos, he focused on Josh holding Kim's lifeless body. He overheard as the commander told the Ompresti she needed to leave. But she didn't know where to go. Loral stood but had to grab the arm of the sofa.

A soldier came over. "Are you all right, old man?" he asked.

"Yes, just dizzy," Loral said. "Can you tell the commander something for me? I'm not sure I can walk over there just yet."

"What would you like to say to him?"

"Tell him that Josh can lead the Ompresti to safety," Loral said.

The soldier paused. "Who is Josh?"

"He is the alien holding the young woman. The Ompresti will know that I am right. She must convince him to go with her." Loral let go of the arm and tried to balance.

He watched as the soldier went to the commander. But he could not hear the conversations between them nor between Liria and the commander, or between Liria and Josh. But he saw Josh get up and leave with the Ompresti along with a platoon of soldiers.

As he finally became less dizzy, the soldier who delivered his message to the commander came over to him. "You look a little steadier on your feet."

"I am, thank you." Loral pointed to Kim's body. "Take me to her, please."

The soldier helped him to where Kim lay. He kneeled beside her put his hand on her and prayed. Then he addressed the escort commander, "Sir, I insist you have your medic help me remove the child from the dead woman. I believe it is still alive, but we must act, or it will also die."

"Very well, but it may be futile. There is a larger Urlak force coming." He called to the medic, "How are the wounded?"

"I have done all I can. They should all be able for the coming fight."

"Good. Help the old man," the commander ordered. "Do as he asks while we still have the time."

"Thank you, Commander," Loral said. "I can hide with the child in the cellar. The Urlak may not find us there."

"You do what you think is best. My men and I must get ready to fight and give the Ompresti as much time as possible."

The medic bent over Kim's body and cut her top, exposing her swollen belly. He cut into her uterus and removed a male child from her body. "He is barely alive." The medic handed the boy to Loral. "You need to keep him warm and get him to a hospital as soon as possible if he is to survive."

Loral took the child to the kitchen, where he wrapped him in towels and found a bottle of bonogo milk before going down the stairs. The cellar was dark, but he didn't want to turn on any lights that might alert the Urlak. So, he waited until his eyes adjusted to the dark. Though cluttered, the cellar did not appear dirty. There was a little dust and a few cobwebs. On his left, he saw shelves stacked with foodstuffs. Randomly arranged pieces of furniture blocked the walls on his right and in front of him. He might find a hiding place there.

As he scanned the room, he felt a slight draft. It seemed to come from under the stairs. There, he saw an enormous wardrobe. The draft was coming from the wardrobe, but it was too heavy to move. He opened the doors, but it was too dark to see, though the draft came from inside. He needed to see, so he laid the infant on a chair and turned on the light. The back wall inside the wardrobe had a small gap on one side.

Did Taibon have an escape tunnel? Loral climbed into the wardrobe and slid the back open. Beyond it was a dark tunnel.

When he stepped into the tunnel, small motion sensor lights activated. *Brilliant, this will do.*

He went back into the cellar and retrieved the infant and a basket full of rags. He laid the baby in the basket and set it in the tunnel while he turned off the cellar light and closed the wardrobe door completely. Then he hung rags around the back of the wardrobe to help seal the draft. He picked up the baby and moved to the far end of the fifty-meter-long tunnel, where a ladder went up into another shaft. At the top of the ladder, he pushed open a trapdoor and found himself inside a feed trough. Looking out, he could see the Urlak moving toward the house. After closing the trapdoor, he went down the ladder. He waited and listened to the battle above while he held the baby, who seemed too weak to cry.

He prayed silently. *Creator, please guard this child. Give him the strength to endure the wait. Protect us from the enemies outside and help us get to safety.*

GLOSSARY

Bapto — A frontier planet on the edge of Cathardi's influence. Controlled by the Cathardi military, it has a diverse population of miners and those who provide for the needs of the miners. The major settlement is on the southern continent at the edge of the jungle below the mountains where the mines are located.

Bonogo — A mammal native to Bapto. They resemble a cross between a horse and a llama with a long neck, smallish head, and slanted back. Partially domesticated, they have been used primarily for pack animals.

Bytor — A hand weapon carried by the Urlak. It resembles a short sword with an axe head on the back side of the blade near the point. The Urlak use it to finish off wounded enemies and to chop off trophy parts.

Carrollian — A race of humanoids from the planet Carrolla. They are a large, heavy-boned race.

Cathardi — A race of humanoids originating on the planet of Cathardi. In appearance, they resemble the Ocampo from Star Trek Voyager.

Gwenna — A raptor-like animal standing nearly six feet tall. It is bipedal, able to move quickly with four long limbs that end in taloned hands. The lone hunters will band together to attack larger prey or groups.

Huldo — A rodent native to Bapto that is notorious for nesting in electrical boxes and gnawing through insulation on wires.

Kavi Vines — A vine native to Bapto. It resembles a pumpkin or squash plant with large green leaves that spread across clearings in the jungle. The vines have tendrils that react to anything that disturbs the vines, wrapping around the legs of creatures moving through, causing them to fall.

Mandili — A small carnivorous mammal that lives among the Kava vines. They resemble elongated Canada geese with brown and white bodies, four short legs, and long black necks ending in a thin pointed head. With mouths filled with razor-sharp, pointed teeth used to tear the flesh from any creature entangled in the Kava vine. Their short, narrow bodies allow them to move freely in the vines with which they have a symbiotic relationship. The blood from the fallen creature soaks into the ground, feeding the vines, while the flesh feeds the mandili.

Melal — A race of humanoids originating from the planet Mela. Allied to the Cathardi, they jointly operate a large space station that orbits their planet. Physically, they are shorter than the average human from Earth and roundly built.

Nakir — A Cathardi word meaning warrior. Also used as a title for a personal protector.

Ompresti — A Cathardi word meaning God's voice. Given to one considered a prophet. It is the title used for Liria.

Urlak — A warrior race of humanoid clones. Genetically engineered to fight, they are orange-skinned and powerfully built with hairless bodies. They are the mortal enemies of the Cathardi.

About the Author

C. Buck Jones writes science fiction and fantasy novels with a Christian perspective. When he retired as an engineer, he took up writing to occupy his time and keep out of his wife's hair. When not at his computer writing or editing, he fishes with his grandkids or his dog in the Colorado streams and lakes near his home. He enjoys soccer, walks with his wife, and spending time in God's infinitely beautiful creation.

If you enjoyed reading this debut novel, please leave a review on either Amazon or Goodreads.

For more about C. Buck Jones visit his website: https://www.cbuckjones.com

Acknowledgements

When I started this novel, I thought it would be easy. I had a story in my head, so I needed to just put it down on paper. Ha! Coming to the end of the journey with the publication of this first book, I realized the important contributions made by so many others. I thank God for the vision he gave me for the story, and my wife Carol for the patience to put up with the hours of writing, the endless videos on publishing, marketing, and creating a following, and the money spent on editors, software, and a cover design. She may not realize how important her constant support and encouragement were to the completion of the book.

One thing I learned during the process is that I don't write as well as I might think. Fortunately, several editors helped me hone the book into a final product. Savannah Gilbo provided an editorial assessment to help me bring the meat of the story into focus. Nicole Neuman provided the final developmental edit and some much-needed encouragement. Belle Manuel did the final proofreading to polish the text. Both Nicole and Belle are providers at Fiverr. Being retired and having a limited budget, they were perfect for me.

As a new writer, having other people read your work is frightening. What if they don't like it? Thankfully, I found support and help at the Colorado Springs ACFW chapter. The critique group provided early insights and support, offering suggestions for improvement, and encouraging me to keep working.

I also received a lot of encouragement from my Beta readers, Mikayla Steiger, Elle R. (@elletay on Fiverr), Kaitlyn G. (@pol_slattery on Fiverr), and my wife Carol. They let me know the story was something people would read. I also owe thanks to many friends and co-workers who supported me. Also, Randy Ingermanson, whose Snowflake Method helped me get unstuck halfway through the book.